# The Opinion Page

RAIN and
BREEZE
BOOKS

# The Opinion Page

David Ackley

Rain and Breeze Books

MOSCOW, IDAHO

**David Ackley/Rain and Breeze Books, LLC**
**P.O. Box 9874**
**Moscow, ID 83843**
**www.rainandbreeze.com**

Publisher's Note: This is a work of fiction. Any references to historical events, real people, or real places are used fictitiously. Other names, characters, places, and incidents are a product of the author's imagination and any resemblance of these to actual people, living or dead, businesses, companies, events, institutions or locales is purely coincidental. Locales and public names are sometimes used for atmospheric purposes.

Book Layout © 2014 BookDesignTemplates.com
Cover photo: by author

**The Opinion Page/ David Ackley.** -- 1st ed.
Library of Congress Control Number: 2020909958
ISBN 978-1-950631-10-0 (Paperback)
ISBN 978-1-950631-11-7 (Ebook)

*You give your hand to me
And then you say hello
And I can hardly speak
My heart is beating so
And anyone can tell
You think you know me well
But you don't know me (no you don't know me)*

— Ray Charles

# Chapter 1.

His TWO grandsons sat between him and his wife, but there was no need to corral them—they both stared listlessly ahead in silent prayer for an end to the sermon. Galen reached over and tousled his youngest's hair in a secret attempt to tame the unruly mess. His eldest's jeans and baggy shirt were a sight better than the faded sweats he'd been wearing at home and had argued vehemently but unsuccessfully to remain in. Galen let his hands settle into his lap and stared at the back of the balding head before him and then down at the polished amber-colored pew with the hymnal books ready for the hint of a song to spring them open. The minister was speaking passionately about family values and the need for diligence in an election year, subtly suggesting which side of the ballot he wanted the congregation to vote for—very much in line with the wishes of most of those in attendance, based on the nodding of heads in response.

Galen's earliest memories of his own Sunday morning routine were of donning a stiff white shirt and struggling one-handed at the cuff buttons, pulling on pressed pants, and then squeezing into his shiny black wing-tip shoes, newly polished the night before. He could still smell the Brylcreem that he plastered into his hair and feel the comb as it sought a part in, and then slid through, the sleek greasy mass easily forming tiny aligned rows. Once every strand was laying smoothly in one direction or the other, he'd comb upward from his forehead to make the required surf wave that led the remainder of the calm, parted sea of hair behind it. Sitting rigidly between his mother and his father, the only things that stuck out from any sermon on any Sunday were Satan and the hell that awaited those unfortunate souls who strayed from the path. There was never a peep about social issues back then.

Today, the church was only a third as full as it had been in his childhood, but the upcoming Easter holiday would bring in a few more worshippers. He sometimes wondered why they continued to drag the boys here, but Jan insisted that she wanted them to have the same Christian upbringing that she'd had. The pastor was reading from an article in the newspaper about a correlation between social media and immorality when Galen's cell phone quietly vibrated in his pocket. He surreptitiously slid it out and glanced at the display, discretely angling it so that Jan could see he had a call he needed to take. She nodded and then he quietly rose and made his way down the aisle to the entrance hall.

"Hey, Tom, what's up?" he asked as the doors whispered closed behind him.

"Hope I didn't catch you at a bad time, Galen," said Tom, not sounding like he really meant it, "but we have a reported sighting of that missing girl, Melissa Davidson, and need extra help at the scene. The address is near you if you're at church, and our boys and the Special Emergency Response Team are going to converge there in ten minutes. Think you can make it?"

"What's the address?" asked Galen.

"1921 NE Thompson."

"That's nearby—I can almost walk and make it in time... In fact, I think I will," he said. "See you there," ending the conversation as he immediately strode off to the north and through the parking lot while texting Jan that he was leaving her the car but hoping to make it back by the end of the service.

He appreciated this time of year—neater, cleaner, and more orderly. Most of the fruit trees were near or in bloom, lawns were in need of mowing, and the bulbs were already flowering in profusion, all leaving the wet, matted mess of winter behind them. He tried to enjoy the sights and smells of the welcome spring despite the sharp pain he was feeling in his knee as he pushed for a ragged near-trot, but had to settle for a fast walk instead. Turning right on Thompson, the length of another block brought him up behind two police cruisers where a small squad of uniforms gathered awaiting the go-ahead signal. Galen recognized a few of the officers and nodded as he watched them in final preparations for the raid. Up the street he could see a similar group had formed behind a pair of unmarked cars. There was no sign of SERT so he reasoned that they must already be inside.

At a squelchy command over the portable radios, everyone surged forward at once. Rounding the corner of the yard, they could now see the front of the house situated well back from the street where the SERT team leader, Hoagland, stood at the head of the walkway and signaled with a closed fist for everyone to wait behind him. A few of the uniforms spread out and crouched on the lawn with pistols drawn but pointing down at the ground. Within a minute, black-clad members of SERT were leading two young men down the steps, forcing them onto to the wet lawn and into a prostrate position, while an elderly woman was being escorted out onto the veranda by a female officer. Then the search began.

Galen joined detectives and forensics officers in a thorough sweep of the house, and unless forensics turned up something they hadn't noticed, there was absolutely no sign of the missing girl to be found. The two college-aged young men were escorted into separate squad cars for questioning, and Tom and another detective grilled the agitated old woman on the front porch. His own help no longer required, Galen waved to Tom as he headed back to the church, half-expecting an empty parking lot, but finding instead a lone car where Jan and the boys awaited his return.

"Sorry, it took a little longer than I expected," said Galen.

"Oh, that's OK," said Jan, standing beside their sedan, obviously enjoying the rare sunshine for this time of year. "I thought I might as well wait, and I don't think these two even noticed that we haven't left the parking lot." She pointed to their grandsons sitting in the back seat of the car, oblivious to all around them except some irresistibly engrossing phone apps.

"What was the call?" asked Jan.

"We had a tip that that missing girl, Melissa Davidson, was seen in a house not far from here, and Tom said he needed backup. To me it looked like half the force had shown up, meaning he didn't really need me in the first place, but as it turns out she wasn't there after all, and we found absolutely nothing."

"That's too bad," said Jan, "Such a sad thing to happen. I expect the girl's parents are worried sick by now."

"I'm sure she'll turn up soon," said Galen, although he knew that if her missing status stretched into a week with no clues or leads as to her whereabouts, the odds were increasingly unlikely.

# Chapter 2.

AS HE expected, there was an unscheduled meeting in the conference room the first thing on Monday morning, and not everyone in the gathering was happy. Especially their captain, Tom Weston.

"...have checked it out first!" Tom yelled as Galen opened the door and chose an empty seat to the side of the entrance.

"We did research it," said Pembrook defensively, "and one of those two students showed up on the do-not-fly list—Youseff Kouri."

"The do-not-fly list?" asked Tom in a quieter but more aggressive tone. He was silent to the count of five and then burst out, "We're not looking for a goddamn terrorist, for Christ's sakes! We're looking for a fucking kidnapper, aren't we, Michael? And that's never going to be what a terrorist does in Portland—is it? No—he's going to blow something up! The nabber has got to be somebody who knew the girl. Ninety-five percent of the time!" as he crashed into a seat near the podium.

The door cracked open, and a hand tapped Galen on the shoulder. He looked up and nodded that he'd received the message. He stood to leave, but part of him wanted to hear the rest.

Abstractly shuffling the papers in his hands and visibly trying to calm down, Tom craned his neck to stare at a point in the ceiling. "OK. We're OK. But we," and he stood again glaring pointedly at Pembrook, and then over at Hoagland, head of the SERT team, "just added significantly to the paperwork that's already flooding us surrounding the girl." Tom held up two fingers. "We made two mistakes yesterday. Rushing to action on an iffy tip wasn't bad enough. Mr. Hoagland compounded things inside." Now his hand had become a fist poised in the air. "Did you know," as Hoagland began to shift in his seat, "that the landlady is already threatening to sue us for improper search and seizure? We didn't even seize anything, except for her two tenants..." Tom raised his fist even higher as they saw the pressure build. "Two tenants who are also thinking of suing us for improper procedure—SERT dragged them out of their apartment without a word of caution, and they had a webcam running in the living room at the time to prove it!" The fist came crashing down on the podium. "Jesus Christ!"

*So that's why the sudden meeting,* thought Galen as he slipped through the door and headed for the elevator bank and the courtroom downstairs. He was due to present his statement in a kidnapping case that had come to an unfortunate end. As he waited for the elevator, he thought about the lack of progress in the Davidson case. There'd been a report of Melissa being seen at a Yellow Line MAX station on the northside—the girl was reported to be with an elderly woman, and they were seen entering a nearby Fred Meyer's. Jenkins and a uniform had responded and found the pair inside shopping for a puzzle—the girl was obviously not Melissa. Another sighting near The Grotto failed to pan out either. After yesterday's raid, they were back to nowhere.

Melissa and her mother had been shopping in the Washington Square mall on the previous Friday afternoon when she disappeared. She was a towheaded four-year old with blue eyes, last seen wearing a pink sweater and green pants. Her mother had stopped at one of the candy counters along the main hall, turned to ask Melissa what she wanted, and the girl was gone. There were no traceable witnesses and no video footage near the spot to give a clue to what happened to her, and it was a busy time of day so none of the nearby shopkeepers noticed anything unusual. The man at the candy counter didn't remember a little girl, but then he wasn't sure that he remembered Mrs. Davidson either. There had been no ransom demands, the parents and close family all checked out, and so they had no choice but to wait for a lead, and it was obviously frustrating Tom. Their captain had come from New York and had risen to the top of the Detective Division in the twenty years he'd been in Portland. He still had a faint Brooklyn accent and had never shaken off the air of someone from a much bigger, much harder city. Galen knew that he was always back to his normal self after he'd let off steam and so did the others, but he pitied poor Pembrook and Hoagland all the same.

He was ushered into the court's waiting dock and was told that he would be up next. Galen felt well-prepared to give his testimony. He'd been on this missing person's case for two months when they'd discovered the body, and eventually, he was on the team that tracked down the girl's killer. He knew that homicide was a rarity in missing persons cases, but he found himself praying for Melissa Davidson just the same.

# Chapter 3.

An HOUR later, the normal Monday morning staff meeting was held in the same room, and many of the same players were in attendance. Tom was in no better mood. "What is it with this city? We go for seven months with a routine number of crimes, and suddenly in the past two weeks we have four homicides, a rash of burglaries, and five, no, six substantive missing persons cases? Did Mars go retrograde or what?" No one answered because everyone knew that Tom's wife was into astrology and, even though he wasn't a believer, such interjections were common. A frequent topic of conversation was how hard-nosed Tom Weston came to be married to perpetual-hippie Carol, who for a time had operated a tarot parlor downtown and now offered psychic readings in a tent at the Saturday Market. "OK," he continued, "we know we have the Melissa Davidson case to fret about, but there are several other pressing matters as well," and he went down the list.

The Detective Division, led by Tom Weston, was divided into sex crimes, property crimes, and person crimes, and this was a meeting of the person crimes unit which included robbery, homicide, and missing persons. Galen normally found himself the lead in missing persons cases, but when one came up that was heavily in the public eye, such as the Melissa Davidson disappearance, he was happy to defer to Tom and Pembrook, or anyone else who was interested in the attention—usually Tom.

"And Galen, we have a new missing person that I'd like you to look into," said Tom, breaking Galen out of his thoughts.

"Who's that, Tom?" asked Galen.

"Emma Armlin called this morning and said that her husband Robert didn't come home Saturday night—she hasn't seen him since that afternoon." There was a pregnant pause, and all eyes turned to Galen.

Sensing something significant about the name, Galen asked, "Robert Armlin?"

With an exaggerated raising of his eyebrows, Tom prompted, "Bob Armlin? Opinion Editor of The Oregon Sentinel? Writes weekly in the same newspaper you probably read every day?"

"Oh, him," said Galen. He and Jan read The Oregon Sentinel over breakfast each morning, but the Armlin editorials were ones that Galen usually skipped. Armlin tended to represent the more liberal side of the slightly conservative paper, and Galen rarely agreed with his views—so he had stopped reading them. "What do we know?"

"Just what I said," replied Tom. "His wife says that this has never happened in all of the years of their marriage, and she's very worried. She's expecting us to stop by her house this morning."

There were other items on the agenda, but the grisly murder of a drug dealer named Cordoba and the disappearance of Davidson took up the remainder of the hour. Pembrook was dragged over the carpet again, but this time he had a recording of the phoned-in tip which detailed Kouri's roommate, Dennis Hoskins, being seen leading a little blond girl up the steps to the house. Tom reacted to the news with contrition, and he politely asked Pembrook to follow-up on the details.

That concluded the meeting and Galen left the conference room somewhat surprised. Armlin seemed to be a well-known and high-profile community figure, and his disappearance was likely to be well publicized. Since Galen wasn't normally assigned to cases rising to this level of public attention, it made him wonder, *Is it because of my seniority? Because of my temperament? It must be temperament*, he decided. *An old man looking into the disappearance of another old man.*

Galen Young had grown up in Enterprise, Oregon, attended college with a major in criminal justice at Western Oregon University in Monmouth, and had been one of only two detectives in Pendleton, Oregon for twenty-five years before retiring. His wife, Jan, had been a stay-at-home mom and had raised their two daughters until they'd graduated from high school, at which point she'd enrolled with an online university and taken courses towards a degree in religious counseling. It was Jan who'd dragged him to Portland so she could pursue her new vocation, and in order to make ends meet in the much more expensive city, Galen had renewed his own career in law enforcement. The need for his employment had been exacerbated by the arrest and conviction of their eldest daughter, Beth, for drug trafficking, and Galen and Jan had taken over the responsibility of raising her two middle school-aged sons. Reaching sixty, Galen sometimes felt that he was running on his reserve tank, with a long way to go and far from any gas station.

# Chapter 4.

THE ARMLINS lived on Myrtle St. in the Goose Hollow neighborhood, a well-to-do, older section of town situated at the base of the hills that rise to the west of Portland, below the famous Rose Garden. Galen parked his car and walked through the professionally landscaped yard to the porch of the Craftsman-style house where Emma greeted him and invited him inside. They sat down in the small sunroom off the main living area, as he said, "Beautiful yard and home you have, Mrs. Armlin."

"Thank you, Detective," she replied. "You can call me Emma—and your name again?"

"Galen, Galen Young." He could now tell that she had been crying recently but was determined to put on a brave face.

"Well, pleased to meet you, Galen, and thank you again for coming."

"Certainly," he replied, taking out a pad and pencil, never having taken to the newer computer tablets everyone else was using. "I understand your husband didn't return home Saturday night?"

"No, he didn't," said Emma, "and I'm terribly anxious about him now." Her arms shook slightly as she lowered herself into her chair, and the strain on her face became even more apparent. "This is absolutely not like Bob at all. I called your station several times on Sunday, but the police said I needed to wait until today to officially report it."

Galen nodded. "We can't initiate any actions until a person has been missing for at least 24 hours. Can you tell me a little about that night and any reasons he might have had for not returning?"

"I have no idea why he didn't come home," she said. "His normal routine on Saturday afternoons is to go to the Multnomah Athletic Club for some exercise and then maybe have a beer afterwards at the Goose. I talked to him before he left home, and he said he'd met a new friend and that he was going to have a drink with him after the Club workout but before dinner. He called from the Athletic Club and said he expected to be home in an hour or two, and that was the last I heard from him. I tried his cell several times before I went to bed, but there was no answer then or all day yesterday."

"Who was the friend he met?" asked Galen.

"He never said, and I didn't think to ask," she replied.

"Did he say where he was going for the drink?" he asked.

"No, but I assumed it was the Goose Hollow Inn. It's a favorite of his and is only a few blocks from the Athletic Club. It's the neighborhood spot we usually go to when we eat out."

"I'll check there and the Athletic Club and interview anyone who remembers talking to him in either of those places," said Galen.

"Oh, I called the Goose last night, and they said no one had seen him."

"You're sure they would recognize him there?" asked Galen.

"Of course!" she said. "Bob's known Bud Clark since he started the place in the '60's, and everyone who works there knows Bob."

"OK," said Galen, "and what car was he driving?"

"Our black Toyota Prius," said Emma. "Do you need the license plate number?"

"No, thanks, we'll have that in our records," said Galen writing down the information about his movements on Saturday evening. "Now, can you tell me a little about your husband, Emma? Especially anything that might explain him not coming back home this weekend?"

"I don't know where he's gone, or why," she worried, suddenly more agitated and determinedly pushing herself up from the chair to retrieve a picture of him from another room, moving somewhat more spryly than Galen expected for someone of her age. "This is a picture we took last year on vacation in Vietnam. He looks just like this, only not quite as tan."

Galen took the proffered photograph and studied the lean, white-haired gentleman posed beside a grinning street vendor while Emma continued. "Bob's going to turn 73 in two weeks, and he's worked for The Oregon Sentinel for at least forty of those years—first as a reporter and now as an editor."

"Does he have any enemies that you know of?"

"Goodness, no!" replied Emma. "He's the sweetest man anyone could meet, and well-liked by the entire community," she paused. "Of course, he does get some negative feedback from his columns, but everyone is entitled to their opinion."

Galen nodded. "I have to ask this," said Galen gently, "but there haven't been any problems at home or with extended family?"

Emma stared at him for a moment and then said, "We've been married for fifty years and hardly had an argument in that entire time. We have no children, and he gets along fine with three of his four brothers."

"And the fourth brother?" asked Galen.

"Happened long ago, and it's water under the bridge," said Emma. "There was a disagreement over politics that escalated, and those two haven't been in touch for twenty years."

Galen finished writing these details on a page in his pocket notebook and rose to leave. "Thank you for this information, Emma. We'll put all our effort into locating your husband. Please call me if you hear from him or anything about him," he said, handing her his card. "I'll let you know how things progress."

"Thank you, Galen," she said, suddenly near tears as they stepped out onto the front steps. She fought for a smile, and said, "Please find him soon," as she turned quickly and retreated inside.

Galen spent the remainder of the afternoon interviewing the staff at the Multnomah Athletic Club and The Goose Hollow Inn. He found that Bob was at the Club on Saturday afternoon and had been through his normal routine consisting of a workout on the treadmill and rowing machines followed by a sauna. No one had thought that he seemed out of sorts, and he reportedly had no interactions with any members at the Club who were unknown to him. Galen obtained a list of members present that afternoon for later interviews. Bob wasn't seen in or around the Goose Hollow Inn that day, and so Galen made a mental note to check out any other pubs or restaurants in the nearby area that he might have chosen instead of the Goose.

# Chapter 5.

THE NEXT day, Galen set out to pay a visit to Mr. Armlin's place of work at The Oregon Sentinel, the Portland-based newspaper with one of the largest circulations in the state. The offices were a short four-block walk from the Bureau, and he stopped off in the first block for a take-out coffee from a corner Starbucks along the way. An impressive display of scones, muffins, and croissants beckoned from behind the glass counter as he waited for his cup of regular drip to be poured and he gave an inward groan at the sight. Stereotypes about policemen and his lowering metabolism meant that he'd never be able to eat a doughnut in either public or in private again. But he still cherished the memories of biting into them, warm and glazed, in the old diners while chatting with the locals in the Pendleton area. Somehow, he still saw doughnuts as being part and parcel of being a cop, so he definitely couldn't picture himself walking out of this café with a scone. Sipping on the cup of regular coffee with one shot of cream he thought wistfully, *Even breathing the air of those pastries has probably made me gain an extra pound at my age anyway. Jan has me on some sort of celery granola or something, so that breakfast ought to hold me for the morning. I hope.*

He was stepping out of the café, when he suddenly thought *Ah, screw it!* and headed in the opposite direction—straight for Voodoo Doughnut, a ten-minute walk out of his way in each direction. As he approached the old building with a re-modeled interior, he remembered Tom lamenting the passing of Berbati's Pan when the doughnut shop had expanded into its former space. He and Tom had discovered the unexpected co-incidence that Galen's older grandson, Ryan, and Tom's wife, Carol, both loved The Decemberists, whom Ryan had played constantly on his stereo over the past year. There were days when Galen couldn't get a song of theirs out of his head. Tom had said that Carol had dragged him to see a show in Berbati's before the joint closed for good, and it ended up being the first time the group had played under that name. Tom had surpris-ingly found himself liking the music.

Galen waited outside in an overly-long line under a light drizzle thinking about the Armlin case. With a warrant, they'd obtained a trace of his cell phone, and it was apparently now turned off. The last recorded location from that Saturday was roughly in the vicinity of the Hillsdale Shopping Center in Southwest Portland, leaving Galen pondering what the man had been doing so far away from his neighborhood that afternoon.

He finally gained access to the doughnut shop, and nearly squinting his eyes at the Voodoo's bright yellow ceiling and vibrant lime green wall in front of him, he ignored all of the fancy icings and ordered two old-fashioned cake doughnuts to go—insisting that they not be placed in one of the garish pink cartons normally used for that purpose. He was tempted to order another cup of coffee to accompany them, having drunk his first on the way there, but decided he'd had enough caffeine for the time being. He ate the first doughnut as he walked and had wrapped the second in a napkin and tucked it into his coat pocket with the intent of finishing it, too, by the time he reached the newspaper building. Midway to his destination, however, he passed yet another homeless man, this one with a poor excuse for a lower leg prosthetic and lying tucked under a bicycle rack. He was two steps past when he suddenly backtracked and asked the man if he'd like a doughnut—the answer being a cracked-lip smile and acceptance of the pink napkin package. This helped assuage most of Galen's lingering feelings of guilt for downing the first doughnut, and he wiped his mouth and brushed his coat to sweep the remainders away.

Stepping up to the security area in The Oregon Sentinel lobby, he informed the person on duty that he wished to speak with Mr. Armlin's supervisor, and after a quick conversation over the phone by the guard, he was given access to the elevator which took him to the second floor and the office of the Managing Editor. Ed Comstock was immediately engaging and struck Galen as being very sincere. "I'm glad you're here detective. I'd learned from Bob's coworker, Monica, that he hadn't shown up for work yesterday and so I called his wife, and she said she'd already spoken to the police. Like most of us here, Bob works remotely a few days a week and now I've learned that he isn't at home this morning either, so we're all becoming more than a little concerned about him. Monica talked with Emma and they're both terribly upset about his disappearance, as am I. You've met Emma? Bob's wife?"

Galen nodded back to him, "Yes, I was the interviewing officer yesterday morning."

"Good. Have a seat," he said, gesturing. "I'm happy to see that you're looking into this, and I hope it's nothing serious. We want to help out all we can."

"We hope this isn't serious, too," said Galen. "You mentioned a Monica?" pulling out his notebook.

"Monica Stevens, the associate Opinion Page editor," said Comstock. "She and Bob have worked hand in glove for years and are very close friends. Actually, she came into my office this morning and said that she had a funny feeling about Bob. And from her expression, I'd guess it wasn't a good feeling, either."

"A funny feeling, huh?" Galen asked and made a quick note. "I hope to talk to her this morning, too. So then, just to bring me up to speed," he prompted, "what can you tell me about Mr. Armlin, and have you noticed anything different about him lately? Anything that you might flag as unusual behavior?"

"No, nothing unusual," replied Comstock. "I've worked with Bob for probably ten years, and he's always been witty, sharp as a tack, and yet as steady as a rock. He never misses a thing on the editorial pages, and he's like clockwork on his column deadlines. In fact, we just published his latest opinion piece yesterday. Perhaps you read it?"

"Nope," replied Galen. "I guess I'll have to make sure that I do."

"Well, here's one hot off the press and a couple from the last few weeks," said Ed and chose some newspapers from among more than a dozen short stacks of recent editions arranged in a line on a sideboard near his desk.

"Thanks, Mr. Comstock," said Galen. "Is it at all unusual for him not to show up for work or not to make contact with you if he doesn't?"

"Please, call me Ed," said the editor and paused for a moment. "I'd say it's totally unlike him. Bob's what I'd call a straight arrow, if you know what I mean. He's one of the most intelligent and well-read friends that I have, and we can get lost in political or philosophical discussions for hours on end. Most of my staff want to talk about sports, movies, music, or some local politics—and, of course, about their families or life issues. Bob's been around long enough that he's been through all of the mundane stuff, and only seems to want to talk about the things that really matter. I don't know about your own political bent, but Bob's a flaming liberal, and proud of it."

Galen didn't reveal his own political leanings. "Do you know anyone close to him besides his co-workers here at The Oregon Sentinel or his wife who might know anything about his whereabouts?"

"Well, he's currently a member of the Multnomah Athletic Club, and has pals at the Goose Hollow Inn," replied Ed. "Not to mention, he's been on many commissions and boards in the past. Oh, and for some reason he often likes to go to the Kells Irish Pub, that place just down near the Burnside bridge, for an after-work drink with a buddy. It's such an old and rowdy spot, or so I hear, that I can't imagine why they chose it. I've only been in there a few times, myself, but the whole place seems rather dark. Something seems to draw them there though."

"Do you know the name of his buddy?"

"Sure, John Doherty, an editor for The Messenger—our... our polar opposite," replied Ed.

"Irish name in an Irish pub, that's easy to remember. I think I'll ask around there, too. Thanks very much, Ed," said Galen, "you've been most helpful."

"This can't be a real thing, can it?" asked Ed suddenly. "I mean, an established member of our community—and a senior member of my staff—just wandering off into oblivion? He must be somewhere. What if he had a stroke or amnesia or something? Have you followed any other leads, checked the hospitals?"

"No, well, of course we've called the hospitals," replied Galen. Then in a voice he hoped would help add an element of calm authority to his reply, "We only received the report yesterday and he might have just dropped off of the radar for a while, you know, needed a break as some do to recharge his batteries. In these preliminary stages we're laying the groundwork—we're looking at possible explanations for this change in his normal routine and we're visiting the places he might frequent and talking to the people he might hang out with. No reason for great concern yet." He then stood. "Thanks again, Ed. Any chance I can talk to..." paging back to a previous note, "Monica?"

"Yes, definitely," said Ed, rising and shaking hands with Galen, "if she hasn't taken an early lunch." He led the way and opened the door. "Follow me, Detective Young."

They both left Ed's office and walked to the elevator bank where Ed pushed the 'up' button. As they waited, he asked seriously, "So what's your take on how this is affecting Emma? Over the phone she seemed fine, but she must be worried out of her mind." The elevator opened and they both stepped in, Ed holding the door for a FedEx man with parcels and pushing the button for the next floor up.

"She seems anxious, of course, but in control, and I assured her that we're doing all we can to try and locate her husband," said Galen.

"This is not like him," said Ed, slowly shaking his head, "at all."

"Well, I'm sure there's a simple explanation that we're just not aware of yet," assured Galen. "That's usually how these things turn out."

They stepped into a noisy, bustling scene of people in motion and walked through the maze of desks dotted with the occasional high-walled cubicle to the entry of one such cubicle with a small placard that announced, "Associate Opinion Editor" where they found Monica sitting at her desk, crying discretely. She started and quickly dabbed at her eyes with a hastily grabbed Kleenex when Ed tapped lightly on the frame.

"Are you OK, Monica?" he asked as he approached.

"Oh, sure Ed, given, you know..." said Monica, stashing the Kleenex. "Come on in."

"Monica, this is Detective Young," said Ed, introducing Galen. "He's trying to find out what's happened to Bob and wanted to speak with you."

Monica rose quickly from her chair, tossed her blond hair back from around her eyes, and offered her hand to Galen. Some strands of hair remained attached to her damp cheeks, so she used the other hand to pull them back into place. "Hello, Detective," said Monica somewhat anxiously. "Have you heard anything about Bob? Where he might be?"

Galen shook her hand and said, "No, we're just now trying to gather information from those who know him to give us a little background. So far nothing's turned up on its own."

"I'll leave you two to talk," said Ed. Galen nodded as Ed left the office and headed further into the busy, congested newsroom.

Turning back to Monica, Galen asked, "So, would you have any information that might help us find Mr. Armlin?"

Monica began to reply when she suddenly choked back a sob and tears welled up in her eyes again. Galen reached over, gently patted her shoulder, and said, "Perhaps you should sit down and tell me what you know."

Monica made her way back to her chair, took another tissue to dab her eyes and then said, "That's just it—I have no idea where he could be." There was a long pause while Monica seemed to gather herself. "I just woke up this morning with the feeling that something horrible has happened to Bob."

"Is there anything that might have prompted this feeling? A dream? Some memory? Some little detail?"

Monica shook her head. "No, nothing, not even a dream. Just this very bad feeling—and then he hasn't shown up for work again today," she choked.

"Do you often get feelings like this?" asked Galen.

"No, never," and Monica began to sob again.

"Ms. Stevens—Monica, I'm sure that he's perfectly fine and that he'll turn up soon," comforted Galen.

She stared at him for a long moment with glistening eyes. "I sure hope you're right, but that's not what I feel."

"So, tell me a little about him," said Galen.

Monica took a deep breath and said, "Well, we enjoy working together, and I think we make the perfect team for the Opinion Page. He's funny and kind, but he'll never back down from an issue if he thinks he's right, either. We balance each other out, and nearly always agree on what should be published."

"Do you know him casually as well?" asked Galen. A look crossed Monica's eyes, and he clarified, "You know, socially—afterhours drinks, dinner parties, outings?"

"We eat lunch together a couple of times a week—Bob always likes the Park Avenue Cafe, and once in a blue moon we might have a beer after work, but no, for some reason we've never mixed our work and social lives, unless it's like at the company picnic," said Monica. "But we talk about our personal issues with each other all the time, so he's one of my best friends."

"And has anything changed in his personal life over the past few weeks? Has he been showing signs of depression?"

"Bob? Are you kidding? No, he's stayed the same old Bob for years," said Monica, again blinking rapidly and visibly trying to contain her emotions.

Galen had the feeling that the cause of the tears was more than the normal worry about a missing colleague, but decided to end the line of inquiry for now. "Well, thank you for your help," said Galen, rising and again taking her hand. "I'll let you know as soon as we find him, or I may be back with some more questions if it takes longer than we think."

Monica was nodding and reaching for another tissue as Galen turned and picked his way back to the elevators through the maze of desks.

# Chapter 6.

MARILYN AND Ralph Grant had insisted on meeting over lunch for their interview. The steady drizzle earlier in the morning had changed to a downpour, so Galen drove to one of the underground parking garages in the vicinity and dashed the three exposed blocks to Jake's Famous Crawfish on Southwest Twelfth. Jan and he had eaten there a few times when they first moved to the city, enticed and excited by the seafood offerings, but this was the first time Galen had visited the place in at least three years. It had been established in the late 1800s and still had much of the original woodwork, including the long bar that ran along the front, now topped with copper to protect the old surface. As he was led to the table Marilyn had reserved, he was happy to see the original painted murals of Northwest scenes that still graced the walls. He especially loved the one that pictured what he guessed was of the Willamette Falls.

"Hello, I'm Detective Young," said Galen, lightly shaking Marilyn's hand and receiving a hearty pump from Ralph as he sat. "Thank you for agreeing to meet with me."

"No, Detective, we're happy to tell you anything we can to help find Bob. It's absolutely our pleasure," said Marilyn. "Whatever has happened to him?"

Marilyn was the current chair of the Portland Rose Festival Board of Directors on which Armlin had served for many years, and she and her husband Ralph were some of the Armlins' closest friends. Ralph had served on another community board with Armlin, so the pair knew him intimately. The waiter approached and took their orders, Galen requesting the seafood gumbo.

"We're still searching for any reasons to explain Mr. Armlin's disappearance, and Mrs. Armlin, Emma, said that you would be the perfect couple to ask about him and his background."

"Well, I think that nothing less than 'pillar of the community' springs to mind when anyone asks about Bob," said Ralph, and the pair spent the better part of the meal describing the man in glowing terms.

"Yes, thanks," said Galen. "I can see how valuable Mr. Armlin has been to the community and how close the two of you are to him." He took one of his last bites of the gumbo and folded his napkin beside the bowl. "I guess another thing I was curious about was his current frame of mind. When was the last time you saw him?"

"Oh, the four of us were together only a week ago," said Marilyn. "We ate out together downtown, and then played a game of rummy at our house which is only a few blocks from the Armlins'."

"And how did Mr. Armlin strike you? Nervous, out of sorts? Anything out of the ordinary?"

"Goodness no!" said Marilyn. "That man is as constant as the Northern Star, and funny?" Ralph nodded in agreement and added, "Bob has always been the same old Bob—S.O.B., get it? That's why we love him and Emma so much."

Galen thanked them profusely for the lunch and ducked out into the rain, heading for Powell's Books. The huge store was located nearby the parking garage, and Jan had asked him to pick up two books she'd ordered in the past week for her business. He stopped at a crosswalk and watched a bearded man across the street in a long, wet trench coat open the mailbox he was standing next to and start yelling into it. The traffic noise was such that Galen couldn't make out what he was saying. The man finished, took a few steps away from the box, and then had a second epiphany, turning back and opening the deposit slot to begin yelling additional ideas into the empty space. *Just like lunch with the Grants,* thought Galen. *I have no more information to help me than that poor mailbox.*

§

Curious to learn more about his new missing person, Galen opened the top copy of The Oregon Sentinel from the three editions Ed Comstock had given him. He flipped to the Opinion Page and found an editorial that had been written by Bob Armlin, Opinion Editor.

*After the Hunt*

*I've owned rifles in the past, I did some hunting as a youth, and I've always loved to fish, so you might consider me an outdoorsman. In my own humble (as all who read my col-*

umn know) opinion, it was a different world back when I was young—a mere five decades in the past, when there were half as many people on the planet as there are now. The changes since then have led me to maintain that gun ownership in this currently over-populated, urban-centric world we share with declining or heavily managed other species is becoming unconscionable.

If you're a hunter, please think about what I have to say. If you're not a hunter, you might still be interested in what I've learned. We humans now number around 7.6 billion individuals—that's 7,600,000,000—and this figure increases with each passing year. I'm not aware of any other mammal that even comes close to this total—possibly only the brown rat outnumbers us. Among the invertebrates, there are more ants, termites, and krill than us, and among vertebrates, it is estimated that there are around 19 billion chickens on the planet. Otherwise, among mammals, the numbers drop off significantly with the top contenders being 1.5 billion cattle, about 1 billion sheep, and 1 billion pigs. I have read recently that the biomass of humans and their livestock make up 96% of the biomass of all mammals on the planet. The world also has around a half-billion dogs and over a billion cats.

Compared to the 362,000,000 people living in the U.S. and Canada, there are roughly 100,000 mountain goats, 110,000 Dall sheep, around 500,000 bison, 700,000 pronghorn antelope, 900,000 black-tailed deer, 1.2 million caribou, 1.5 million moose, 3.5 million mule deer, and 11.5 million white-tailed deer for a total of 20 million mammals typically hunted for food on our continent. As a rough estimate, there are around 13 million hunters in the U.S. and Canada. That amounts to 1.54 prey for each hunter, and if they were all taken in a single year, there would be precious few prey left. Almost all the prey species listed above, except for the white-tailed deer, are heavily to severely restricted in hunting opportunities due to the high hunting pressures exerted on them. All of these populations are in a steep decline compared to pre-settler numbers—we would be astonished at the number and variety of animals if we could walk through pre-Columbian America. So, I must ask, given the multiplication of our own species, how many of the other species can thrive or even maintain their current levels while being hunted? At what point does this sport become outmoded, and the tools it employs outdated along with it?

I was at a fishing lodge up in Bristol Bay, Alaska sitting around a campfire one evening talking to some out-of-state caribou hunters who'd paid vast amounts in travel, supply, lodging, guiding, and permit expenses for the experience. The conversation drifted over into the realm of conservation. When I asked what they thought about the declining numbers of large mammals, and the sometimes-severe restrictions enacted to protect them, several of those around the fire scoffed at the idea. "God put them here for our use, and he will make more," was the argument. This is what they truly believed, and I had no response that could have dissuaded them. There is no such thing as spontaneous generation. How will the lord possibly be able to provide unless we give him a lot of help? Large mammals are running out of many of the things needed for survival, *especially given the changes in climate and human presence—space, contiguous habitat, access to food and water, and a safe place to rear their young. A glance at the situation in Africa illustrates the pressures of hunting, human sprawl, and unpredictable climate on all species and should give each of us pause back here in North America as we watch African elephants, giraffe, even lions all plummet in number. At some point we will need to give other species a break if we want to continue to share the planet with them. Things are tough enough without being hunted, and when do we come to the point where we accept that? When do we pass a tipping point?*

Galen sat back in his chair and, as he expected from an Armlin editorial, was completely put-off by what he read. He totally disagreed with the hunting statistics. There were after all, millions of those registered hunters who sat at a desk for months on end and then went out into the woods during hunting season and missed everything they shot at. It wasn't like everyone with a rifle was a crack shot. And then there were those in the northern states, Canada, and Alaska who actually subsisted off of game. They had no options to run down to the local meat market and pick up a pound of beef. They had nothing unless they shot it themselves. And as far as he knew the animal populations were doing just fine, in fact what he read lately seemed to say that if we didn't hunt many of the deer, their numbers would plummet from disease and overpopulation.

Taking umbrage at being preached to, he found himself wondering how others had reacted to Armlin's editorial. He looked up a phone number and dialed.

"Hello, Ms. Stevens, this is Detective Young; we met this morning," he said when Monica Stevens answered.

"Have you found Bob?" she asked immediately.

"Not yet," said Galen, "but I have a question for you. Have you received any replies to Mr. Armlin's editorial of..." and he flipped to the front page of the newspaper, "March 27th? I just want to get a feeling for the kind of responses he gets to his articles."

"Yes, we almost always have several. Some are the usual, and not worth printing—they're hardly written in English. Let me see." Stevens was back on the phone in a few moments. "There is one that we printed a few days later on the 29th."

"Do you mind reading it to me?" asked Galen.

"Sure," said Monica, "just a sec." A moment later she read to him over the phone.

*Dear Editor*

*It is my right and privilege to be able to make use of this great nation's resources. Who are you to tell me that I can't have my share of game? Isn't that why I pay taxes, and dish out money for permits and sometimes guides? You probably know nothing about wildlife, but our hunting helps keep the animal populations at healthy levels. Deer are suffering from Chronic Wasting Disease and luckily are being culled out by healthy numbers of their natural predators—bears, wolves, and pumas. Without responsible hunting to keep the populations at manageable levels, who knows what epidemic would hit the herds? Rather than being a conservation issue, we are dealing with cases of extreme overpopulation, and it is up to mankind to help control it.*

*I can also see that this is another back-door attempt to restrict our use of firearms which you cleverly cloak as 'tools' in your article. You can call them anything you like, but we have a God-given right to bear arms in this country, and it is easy to see that you are part of the propaganda machine that is trying to take away that right.*

*James Madison*
*Portland, Oregon*

"Wow, thanks, Ms. Stevens," said Galen when she'd finished. "Is this the normal sort of reaction to his articles?"

"I guess so," said Monica. "The responses are usually across the board on the rational scale."

"Any positive reactions to this editorial?" asked Galen.

"None that we printed," said Monica. "But we usually don't get many when people agree with Bob."

"I suppose we would need a warrant to obtain copies of all of those responses?"

"Not necessarily, but I suppose you would if you wanted information about the senders, too," replied Monica. "You'll need to go through Ed and our legal team, but gathering the information shouldn't be much of a problem from our end."

"OK, thanks very much," said Galen and was about to ring off. "Oh, before I go, do you happen to know about what time Mr. Armlin usually takes off from work?"

"He almost always leaves at 5:00," said Monica.

"Thanks, Monica, I'll be talking to you soon."

# Chapter 7.

AT 5:00, Galen left his office and put on his cap, tucking up his collar as he walked the several blocks in the late-afternoon drizzle to the Kells Irish Pub. He pulled on the tall door and entered the long, narrow room, pleasantly warm with wooden floor and ceiling, small tables down the center, and narrow booths along the brick wall to the right. He wondered about Ed Comstock's taste in taverns because he instantly felt that he could spend time here. He walked up to the tall bar counter that ran along the wall to the left and selected a Harp Lager after perusing the choices.

When the woman who'd taken his order arrived with his glass, Galen asked, "Do you happen to know Bob Armlin? Apparently, he's a regular here?"

She thought for a moment and said, "No, but I only work here two days a week. Maybe Seth, the bartender will know. Just a sec."

When he'd finished placing the last mug on a tray, the bartender walked down the bar to where Galen stood and asked, "Grace told me that you were asking about one of our regulars?"

"Yeah, I'm Galen Young with the Portland Police Bureau, and I was wondering if you know Bob Armlin, an editor with

The Oregon Sentinel?" asked Galen without showing his identification.

"Sure, I know Bob," said Seth. "Why are you asking?"

"Mr. Armlin hasn't shown up for work lately, and we're trying to track him down. I'm asking for any information that might help us locate him. Have you seen him recently?"

"He comes in here two, maybe three afternoons a week, but I haven't seen him lately," said Seth, shaking his head. "I don't really know him that well to tell you the truth, but John over there sure does."

"John?" asked Galen. "John Doherty? Can you point him out?"

"Yeah, he's the one about your age sitting by himself in the booth near the window wearing a brown jacket," said Seth, pointing over to the corner of the room. "You obviously know his name."

"John Doherty," said Galen, "kind of sticks with you—especially here. Thanks, Seth."

Galen grabbed his beer and walked down the room to Mr. Doherty who appeared lost in thought and was nursing a Guinness Stout.

"Mr. Doherty?" asked Galen, breaking the man's reverie.

John looked up questioningly with a lined face, white hair pulled back in a ponytail, and a yellowish drooping mustache. *Obviously, a smoker*, thought Galen.

"Yes?" John asked.

"My name is Galen Young and I'm a detective with the Portland Police Bureau. I understand that you know Bob

Armlin, and I was wondering if I could ask you some questions about him."

John was momentarily flustered, but then said, "By all means, have a seat." And as Galen plopped his coat on the bench opposite, set down his beer glass, and arranged himself across from the man, John asked, "Why are you interested in Bob? Has something happened?"

"Mr. Armlin never returned home this weekend, and he hasn't been there or at his workplace yesterday or today. We're now treating him as a missing person, and I'm trying to discover what may have happened to him."

"Well, that explains him not being on time, I guess," said John, glancing at his watch and nodding to himself. "Now you've got me worried. We always meet here on Tuesdays and Thursdays at 5:00 for a beer or two, and he's never more than a few minutes late."

"So, he's a friend of yours?"

"Yeah man, as it happens, we're very good friends," John paused. "What's happened to him? Do you think he's all right?"

"We sure hope so," said Galen. "We just don't know where he is at the moment."

"Well, let me give him another call," said John, pulling out his cellphone.

"We've tried that several times, but please do try and see if you can reach him."

John dialed, waited, and then shook his head. "No answer. It goes straight to his messages."

"How long have you known him?"

"Wow, well, let's see," said John. "We met right out of college in the 60's. We were both journalism majors and both started off as reporters for The Oregon Sentinel. Then I got a job with the Berkeley Barb and lived there for maybe 15 years, while Bob stayed here. He continued to rise up the ranks to become an editor, and I moved back here to Portland twenty years ago. I hacked away at The Portland Mail for a few years at first but am now extremely happy at The Messenger."

"And you still see him regularly?"

"Two or three times a week, right here," said John pointing at the table.

"When was the last time you saw him?"

"Four—no, five days ago, and he was fine. Just his normal funny self."

"So, nothing stood out as unusual? He wasn't distracted, nervous, forgetful?" asked Galen.

"Nope," replied John. "We had one of our rambling, free-wheelin' conversations, and he left in a good mood."

"What was the rambling conversation about?" asked Galen. Then, seeing from the look on John's face that he was taking this question as excessive prying, the detective added, "I'm only asking to get a feel for his mental state."

John nodded. "Well, let's see," and he began ticking things off on his fingers. "Last time, we talked about logging and the spotted owl, Mount Saint Helens, vaping, air pollution in China, the Free Trade Agreement, the economy, the tech sector, identity theft, and then anonymity, probably because that was on Bob's mind lately—he'd just written an editorial on the topic in fact."

Galen raised his eyebrows and said, "I'll have to read it."

"Oh, then as I recall, the conversation ended with us discussing personal identity in particular. Yeah, that's right—Bob went off about how we never really know anyone—about how just because someone tells you their name, or even shows you an identity card, you can never really be sure who they are. It's easy to lie, and to fake ID's. With all the identity theft going on today, you never can tell who's who anymore."

Galen leaned back in the booth to pull out his wallet and display his badge, but John waved him off. "No, it's, OK, I believe you—it was Bob who was going on about the subject. You know, I wouldn't be surprised to find an opinion piece about identity theft in the next issue of The Oregon Sentinel." He took a sip of his stout and then set it down, continuing to stare at the brown foam that slid down the side of the glass. "If he ever shows up to write the damn thing, that is."

"I'm sure we'll find him soon," said Galen. "Thanks so much for letting me join you."

"No problem, detective..." said John, not remembering the name to go with it. Then reaching into his wallet, "Here's my card if you think I can be of any more help."

"I was just going to say the same thing," said Galen as they exchanged business cards. Galen swallowed the last of his lager and then headed back to the Bureau to fetch his car.

# Chapter 8.

WEDNESDAY WAS one of Galen's normal days off, however, as always, he showed up for the daily morning briefing. He'd checked all of the information that had come in overnight, and nothing new had emerged regarding either Melissa Davidson or Robert Armlin, but there had been an arrest made for one of the recent homicides. Tom opened the meeting with that report, and then they discussed the missing Opinion Page editor.

Galen stood to address the group and went down his list. "I spoke with Armlin's wife, Emma, at their home up in Goose Hollow. Armlin had a normal weekend routine of working out at the Multnomah Athletic Club, and then possibly going to the Goose Hollow Inn for a beer afterwards. On this particular Saturday, he said that he was going to have a drink with a new friend, but Emma doesn't know who that would be. He said goodbye to her that afternoon and showed up at the Club, and no one noticed anything unusual in his behavior. He didn't go to the Inn afterwards and a check on his cell phone location data had him last recorded in the vicinity of the Hillsdale Shopping Center, of all places. I checked his office at The Oregon Sentinel and talked to his boss Ed Comstock and his close co-worker Monica Stevens. Same lack of info there; they noticed nothing out of the ordinary and have heard nothing of him since last Friday prior to him going missing. I interviewed the Grants who are close friends, but they had nothing to add about Armlin's state of mind. Comstock mentioned that Armlin has a friend he meets with on a regular basis at the Kells, and Mr. John Doherty knew nothing about his disappearance either, expecting to meet him yesterday after work. There's an APB out on the car and, of course, for Mr. Armlin. I've asked patrols to keep an eye peeled in the Southwest Portland area. So, for now we're still waiting at the starting gate."

"Do you think we should issue a public appeal?" asked Tom.

"Once the APB went out, the press got ahold of it. The Portland Mail has run a short article titled 'Missing Newspaper Editor?' on the second page, but the others are holding off on any big stories since we have zero information so far. The Oregon Sentinel has also printed what amounts to a formal appeal in the hope of drawing out tips to help locate him. I'd say the insistence for detailed information by all newspapers will happen in another day or so as it becomes evident that he really is missing, and his disappearance passes from speculation to safe news. We'll have to hold a press conference or give interviews soon, so the public appeal will happen at the right time—when we're sure this is a solid case and that he didn't just decide that he needed a long weekend," replied Galen.

After the meeting, he spent another hour or two searching for whatever he could find about Bob Armlin on the internet. He discovered several historical references detailing Armlin's significant involvements in the Portland community. The man was active in the Democratic Party, had been on the board of directors for both the Portland Symphony and the Portland Rose Festival, and, until recently, had been involved in several local and national writer's groups and workshops.

Galen drove home for lunch and checked off several household chores before 2:15. Since Jan was absolutely in love with Portland and the spot they'd chosen in it, she was a fanatic about keeping the house and lawn in tip-top shape so that the family wouldn't embarrass itself in the neighborhood. Galen had always thought of her as a small-town girl, but he'd never seen her take to any of the places in Eastern Oregon the way she'd taken to Portland. He, on the other hand, wasn't so enthralled with the city. He missed having his nearest neighbor way out of earshot, viewing wide sky-filled unpopulated expanses, and having stores where the choices might be fewer, but everything was affordable. But, given all of that, he was happy that Jan was happy.

At 2:30 sharp he was in front of Mt. Tabor Middle School to pick up Ryan and Monty early from classes and take them on the half-hour drive south to visit their mother at the Coffee Creek Correctional Facility in Wilsonville. The weekends were the popular, and crowded, visiting days at the facility, however, those two days were usually very busy for the boys. Instead, both of them had arranged with the school to skip the seventh period every Wednesday so that they could have a visit with their mother in a calmer setting. Jan had vowed to never visit Beth while she was in prison and she still refused to take the kids there, so the task had fallen to Galen.

The boys hopped into the car and immediately turned on their cell phones—instantly messaging.

"How was your day, guys?" asked Galen as he pulled out of the parking lot and headed for Wilsonville.

"Fine," both replied in unison and in perfect harmony, glued to their smartphone screens.

"Well, tell me a little bit about it."

Both boys knew the drill with their grandfather—that he wouldn't put up with pat answers and would pull the car over and stop it by the side of the road if they didn't communicate with him in a meaningful manner. Even if it had been a bad day, or they were in a lousy mood, they couldn't avoid genuine contact with the old man. The boys glanced at each other and Monty, the youngest and in sixth grade, could see he'd been elected to go first. He chatted with Galen in depth about his school day for fifteen minutes and then the two boys traded turns as Galen threaded his way down I-205 while catching up with the events in Ryan's classes. The eighth grader was just describing a botched frog dissection when they were admitted through the security gate and into the correctional facility parking lot.

Galen and the boys spent a minute removing everything from their pockets except for their ID's and stashing the rest in the car before they headed to the walkway and the main entrance. They recognized the guards, and the guards knew them, but they still had to endure security checks and be admitted through several locked doors before they could meet with Beth. Unfortunately there was no outdoor meeting area, so in spite of the beautiful day they'd just left behind them, the boys were happy to join her in the large institutional room lit by fluorescent lights and lined with utilitarian chairs and tables. Both boys ran up and gave their mother a huge, but brief, hug as this was all the contact allowed them, and then they began chatting with her excitedly across the table they'd chosen for the visit. Galen said hello, but received no reply. During a lull in the conversation, he tried again. "Hi Beth, how are you doing this week?"

"Fine," said Beth, and then glaring at him defiantly, "What did you expect? 'Great!'?"

"No, I was just wondering how you were doing."

"Like I said, I'm fine," she said in a clipped, monotone. Galen knew that this was all he'd get out of her today, and let the boys retake charge of the conversation. Some weeks were like this, as he was well aware. And he sympathized that it was tough to be cooped up with no rights, few privileges, and few friends in a sterile, secure facility. He also knew that she blamed him for her being there. In fact, he had had nothing to do with her arrest or conviction, but he realized that he was at fault for being in law enforcement in the first place. She'd been arrested twice for misdemeanor drugs in high school, had finally graduated, and had seemed to be living a clean but tumultuous life with two young sons and iffy friends. However, she'd then been arrested for cooking and dealing meth as well as for identity theft to support her habit. She now had two years left out of seven at Coffee Creek, pending good behavior.

"Guess what?" she asked the boys after they'd told her about school and Monty had squealed that Ryan had a girl-friend. "I just got accepted as one of the gardeners in the green-house, so I'll get to spend hours in there watering and tending the plants!"

"Mom! That's sick!" said Ryan enthusiastically. "You've always liked plants, so that's perfect for you."

"I'll say," said Beth. "Plus, it's in the native plants section, which means that everything we grow goes from here to wher-ever they're needed in Oregon for habitat restoration."

"That's great, Beth," Galen chimed in, but he wasn't sure if she noticed. She'd always been head-strong and had had more than her share of heated arguments with her parents over what, in their view, were very trivial issues. After she'd been admitted to the facility, he and Jan had learned that she'd been diag-nosed by the state medical staff as having oppositional defiant disorder, or ODD. He knew from past experience that if she wasn't in the right mood, anything he said or did would only escalate things into a shouting match. He'd learned to lay low at strategic moments even before they knew of the diagnosis, just to help keep things with her on an even keel.

There were still 15 minutes of visiting time left when a guard approached them, with Beth eyeing him warily. "Detective Young?" the guard asked as he drew near. At Galen's nod, he continued, "You have a phone call from a Detective Jenkins. It's this way." Galen followed him out the visiting room door.

"Hey, Stan, what's up?" asked Galen as he took the wall phone handset offered by the guard.

"Hi, Galen, I tried your cell but got no answer. Then I remembered it was your day to visit Beth. We just found Armlin's car."

"Great! Where is it?" asked Galen. "Any sign of Armlin?"

"Nope, just the car so far. It was at the end of Lee St., one of those lanes that terminates in a cul-de-sac near Fanno Creek, just off the Beaverton-Hillsdale Highway, so that coincides roughly with his last known cell phone location. Luckily, the car hasn't been broken into, and we're securing the scene."

"Thanks, Stan. I still have some time with Beth, and then I need to get the boys back home, so it might be an hour or so before I can get there. Are you going to hang around?"

"Yeah, I think it will take a while to get into the car, do a search, and canvas the area. You have plenty of time."

"OK, see you there," said Galen and hung up.

# Chapter 9.

GALEN PICKED out a black-and-white squad car and a tall forensics van the moment he turned onto Lee St., and he pulled up behind Jenkins's unmarked car which was parked the closest to Armlin's. Jenkins was tapping on a tablet while standing beside the black Toyota and greeted Galen as he walked up.

"How was the visit with Beth?" asked Jenkins.

"Better for the boys than for me, but that's how it's supposed to be," replied Galen, realizing that he was becoming resigned to the low status he'd been relegated to by his daughter. "What have you got?"

"The neighbors didn't consider the car being parked here for so long to be unusual, and each thought it belonged to a visiting friend of the other. One older lady thought she heard what she described as a crunch and then some doors slamming in the middle of the night, but she thought it must be the neighbor kids. She thinks it was one of the weekend nights, but she isn't sure. The Toyota looks like it was struck from behind by another vehicle at some point, and there's a scrape along the driver's side front panel. Some white paint was found along the scratch, so it could've come from a white car or a white-painted structure or barrier. We opened her up and have taken photos. Nothing jumped out as unusual, except forensics has found some light-colored hairs on the passenger seat. They're just setting things up to dust for prints."

"Good, thanks," said Galen as he donned a pair of nitrile gloves. "Anything in the back?"

"Nope, it looks clean."

Galen ran his fingers lightly over the front-panel scrape and could see the flecks of white that Jenkins had mentioned. To him the paint appeared to be metallic, so he was guessing it would be from another vehicle, but they'd have to wait on the lab analysis to verify that hunch. The rear bumper looked like it had either been backed into something stationary or had been lightly hit from behind—one of the rear backup lights was cracked and the fender showed that there'd been enough of an impact to cause a dent. The hatchback appeared to have been rarely used for hauling anything and was still in pristine condition. The usual sales receipts and coins were scattered about the Prius, but otherwise it appeared to have been kept in fairly tidy shape by Armlin. Galen went around to the passenger side and watched Rigby, their main forensics officer, use tweezers to place another blond hair into her collection bag. "I'd say it's from a woman with medium length blond hair," she said to his inquiring look. "Natural—not dyed, based on the roots. And I'm not seeing many opportunities for fingerprints on the available surfaces, but we'll give it our best shot."

"Thanks, Brenda. We'll be anxious to see what you find," he replied.

Walking back over to Jenkins, Galen said, "I think I have an idea about those blond hairs—they're about the same length as Armlin's co-editor, Monica Stevens.

Jenkins nodded. "Perhaps more than just a co-worker?"

"Maybe so," said Galen. "I think I'll have another chat with her. Have we searched around the area, like down by the creek?"

"We've done a visual, but haven't conducted a thorough sweep or used any dogs. Do you think we should?"

"You know, since the car might not reveal much, maybe we should bring in some help, just to make sure we're not missing anything."

"Overtime?" asked Jenkins.

"We should use the dogs now, but with dusk coming on, tomorrow morning should be fine for a thorough search, don't you think? If there's anything out there that the dogs don't find, it's not going anywhere overnight anyway. Let's cordon off the area after they've done their sweep to keep it secure. Let me know what turns up, Stan. I think my next step is to pay Ms. Stevens a visit." Jenkins was already on the phone calling in the canine unit as Galen left.

Half an hour later, Galen was knocking at a door in one of the high-rise condos overlooking the Willamette River in downtown Portland. Lights were coming on all over town as the sun was setting and the darkening orange glow was now reflecting off only the tallest buildings. It was dinner time, and he could smell something resembling a Thai meal wafting in the air of the spacious corridor when the elevator let him out on the tenth floor. Monica Stevens opened the polished wooden door a crack, and her one visible eye widened in surprise when she saw Galen. "Hello, detective," she said as she unclasped the security chain and swung the door wide to let him enter. "Have you found him? Is he OK?"

"No, I'm sorry to say that we still have no substantive information concerning Mr. Armlin's whereabouts," said Galen, "but I do have a couple more questions I'd like to ask you, if that's all right. Is this a good time?"

"Sure," said Monica. "I'm just glad that you didn't come bearing horrible news."

"No, nothing like that. We do have some leads now, and that's one of the reasons I stopped by."

"Anything I can do to help," she replied. "Would you like to take a seat?"

"No, thanks, this should just take a minute," said Galen. "For starters, how often does Mr. Armlin give you a ride home?"

"Bob? Why... never. I always walk or take the bus if it's too rainy—but you know Portland—I mainly take the bus."

"Have you been in his car recently for any particular reason?"

"No, certainly not," said Monica. "I don't have any cause for him to give me a ride, and he lives in a different part of town than I do anyway. Why are you asking?"

"Well, we know that someone with blond hair was a recent passenger in his car, and you were the person that immediately came to my mind. I know it's embarrassing and unpleasant, but if you were seeing Mr. Armlin outside of work, that would certainly explain the hairs."

"Are you kidding? Me and Bob? Are you suggesting that we were having an affair?"

"I honestly don't know, Ms. Stevens. Were you?"

Monica's eyes suddenly misted over, and she momentarily caught her breath. "No, absolutely not!" she said adamantly.

But Galen had naturally seen the easily detectible change in her. "As I said, these matters can be delicate, but they will come out as we pursue this investigation. I have to ask again. Were you having an affair?"

Unexpectedly, Monica completely melted down. She was wracked with sobs, and Galen led her over to the couch where she collapsed and buried her face in her arms. Galen went into the kitchen and found a tumbler and filled it with water from the tap. It took a few minutes before he could offer it to her, but she waved it off and wiped tears from her face. "I think wine would be better," she said in a thin voice, and got up to pour herself a glass. "Do you want some?" she asked.

Galen shrugged, "Sure, why not?" and she brought over two glasses, sinking again into the couch while he took a stuffed chair to the side.

He was about to say something when she weakly held up her hand. "I can explain," she said. "I can explain my reaction." She looked at him for a long moment. "But, you're right—it is embarrassing." Galen waited and she eventually proceeded. "Bob will never hear about this, will he? Hear what I tell you?"

"I won't say anything to him, but we'll see what comes out in the process of this investigation."

She sighed. "You see, we did have an affair," while Galen began to nod his head in a knowing manner, "but it was all in my head." Galen's eyebrows shot up and he now gave her a questioning look. She hesitated and then continued, "I've loved Bob since we first met, and for a while we were getting pretty chummy. I wanted like anything for us to take it further than a close friendship, but then I realized that I'd be destroying his marriage, and I didn't want to do that to Emma. Who am I to ruin someone's life like that? So, I cooled things down. Bob is so nice that I don't really know if he saw things going the way I'd hoped they would or not, but we've been great friends ever since. Nothing truly romantic has ever happened between us."

"Ms. Stevens, we have blond hairs that match yours in the car..." began Galen in another attempt to gauge her story.

"And I have no idea where they could have come from. They aren't mine, and I don't know any other blond ladies he might have given a ride to."

"I hate to sound harsh, Ms. Stevens, but could I ask you to stop by the police bureau tomorrow morning and volunteer for fingerprinting and a DNA swab? It's not that I don't believe you, but we have to check out every angle in a case like this," Galen said, abandoning his full wine glass on the table and standing. "Thank you for your time."

Monica rose as well and walked him to the door. "OK, I can do that," she said determinedly. "I've done nothing wrong, but I can do that. Is it just like a mouth swab?"

"Yep," said Galen, "and it only takes a minute. If you have any questions or any more information for us, please stop by my office or give me a call," handing her a business card.

"Goodnight, detective," she said a little coldly as she closed the door behind him.

# Chapter 10.

THE FIRST thing Galen did the next morning was to read the article Armlin had written about anonymity which Doherty had mentioned in Kells Irish Pub. He found the piece in one of the newspapers that Ed Comstock had given him a few days before.

*Anonymity*

*An actress was recently body-shamed on social media and felt the need to respond to the remarks made by the anonymous jerks, or 'trolls,' who thrive on disrupting and clogging the internet. She had been stung and rightly outraged by the hurtful, mean-spirited comments about her physical appearance, but in defending herself, I'm sure that she felt like she was swinging at smoke.*

*Here is my take on anonymity. When we meet someone new or even an old friend, we entertain scores of instantaneous thoughts about them, including,* Wow, he's gained weight, *or* She's looking older lately. *These and countless other thoughts flit through our minds, and to some measure, we don't really own any of them until we give them proper consideration and screening. In the end, the worthwhile thoughts that constitute what we would actually do or say define us, and they are the thoughts worth keeping:* She has such a beautiful smile; *or*

What a great idea; I'm glad I talked to her. *Everything else is just the common noise of a busy mind.*

*Many of the anonymous voices that we encounter on the internet are those bubbling, ultimately meaningless thoughts, and definitely not the ones we would have define us. The trolls are working without filters and realize that the words they utter can never be traced back to them. In any decent society, it is almost certain that, given a chance to personally encounter the object of their derision, especially with an audience within earshot, they would never, ever utter the things that they, ghost-like, type in their computers. Not only would they lack the courage to do so, but they also know that there is a code of behavior to live by and when they can't hide behind anonymity, there are consequences to their actions. Mocking or providing empty criticism opens yourself up for criticism as well, so you'd better have a damn good reason and support for what you say or do.*

*What's the best path forward in this age of anonymity? We need to do to the trolls exactly what we do in our own minds when those bubbling random thoughts pop up—ignore them. We shouldn't react to them, we shouldn't give them any consideration, and we certainly shouldn't offer them public recognition. This amounts to giving our unbidden thoughts voice and would totally embarrass us if we should ever utter their bitter words ourselves. If there was a means to identify the trolls, or a way to block their words, I would be totally behind the effort. Everyone has the right to voice their opinion, and I stand by that, but not without identity, not without consequences. Stand* up for your beliefs, and state who you are when you do. We're a long way from being able to require a valid identification for every voice out there, and the internet has created a garden of aliases, so this may be nearly impossible. But until then, we should do what we can, and that is to give the 'trolls' absolutely no credence at all.

As a last word, the poor actress is certainly not immune from those who impugn her and are openly willing to identify themselves when they do. One who is not afraid to sling mud and let everyone know that he has done so is our own president. The name-calling and insults that issue from him are the result of an unfiltered, antisocial mind, but at least he is brave or misguided enough to sign his own name to the missives. With each tweet, he is telling us all about himself, and really nothing about the person he is attempting to debase. The Troll in Chief?

Yep, Armlin is obviously very opinionated, thought Galen, shaking his head. I can see where he might ruffle some feathers in the course of his business. He himself had supported the president in the last election, but was, defensively, wondering lately if his decision had been the right one; still, he took some umbrage with the final paragraph. Wondering whether others had as well, he flipped through the copy of The Oregon Sentinel he still had on his desk from the day before and found a reply.

*Dear Editor,*

*Isn't it ironic that a person with a guaranteed mouthpiece spouts his drivel on a weekly basis, and at the same time denies us the right to express ourselves? This country was built on the foundation of free speech, and that means that each person should be able to state their opinion whenever they see fit. Mr. Armlin would gladly muzzle the rest of us so that he can continue to preach from his tiny soapbox.*

*Back in the days when 'decorum' and 'good manners' kept the rabble in check, the aristocracy was happy to crush dissent in any manner they saw fit. Now we're able to pull back the curtain and see the wizard for who he truly is. What you call 'trolls' are the very citizens who are keeping a watch on this great nation of ours and calling bullshit when they see it. There is no need any more to hide behind the mask of 'political correctness' when a true and honest assessment of conditions is called for.*

*I'm thankful for people who are willing to call it like they see it and speak up when they think some overrated actress or overblown politician has overstepped their bounds. The cult of celebrity and the new royalty of the ruling class in our government are degrading this great country of ours, and I think it refreshing when we can honestly and diligently take these pompous hypocrites down a notch or two.*

*Continue to write your column. You have the right. But I for one am going to continue to ignore the 'bubbling apparitions' of your articles. Bask in the light of your elite pulpit, but realize that you are preaching to an empty choir.*

*Oliver Leavy*
*Portland, Oregon*

*Yes, people have taken offence,* thought Galen, *but I wonder if any of them were wishing Mr. Armlin harm?*

§

During his lunch break, Galen had driven over the Willamette to the southern end of Mississippi Avenue. Apple Music, which had been located right downtown and much closer to work for him, had closed but he'd heard good things about Black Book, a small guitar store on the east side of the river. Jan had asked him to scope out a possible vintage guitar for Ryan's still distant, but upcoming birthday. "Just check them out, but don't buy anything until we talk about the price," she'd said.

Galen had just pulled up near the shop when his cell phone rang. "Hi, Deb, what's up?"

"Hi, Galen," said fellow Detective Deb Cushing. "We just had a report that your Robert Armlin may have been witnessed crossing the street near where Mississippi and Graham meet. A patrol car is checking it out, but Tom thought you might be in the area and want to look into it too."

"Really? Who called it in?"

"A technician who works at Emanuel Hospital. He said he sees Armlin's picture in the paper every week and is certain it was him. Patrol is interviewing him now."

"OK, thanks Deb. I'll take a swing around the area and see if he turns up."

"Good luck, Galen," and Cushing ended the call.

Galen spent a half-hour cruising the area beneath the snarl where several freeways wound and merged overhead. Once the home to a small town of tents and temporary shelters, the city had herded all of its occupants to other parts and thrown up chain link fencing to keep them from coming back. Galen saw no sign of Armlin and couldn't imagine why he would be hanging out in the now uninhabited grounds, but thought he might have been near the hospital for a reason. He met with the beat officers, the man who phoned in the report, the ER staff, and general admissions, but there was no hint other than the alleged sighting that Armlin had ever been in the area. *Well, there went another lunch hour,* thought Galen with a grumbling stomach as he headed back to the Bureau offices and straight for the little cafeteria there.

§

Weston, Pembrook, Jenkins, and Galen had a small meeting about the Armlin case that afternoon.

Jenkins started things off and described the discovery and processing of the black Toyota Prius. "The white paint chips definitely came from a late-model white Ford or GM—that's as close as they could get. Forensics is unable to tell how recent the scrape is, but Brenda had one of her crew check with Armlin's wife and she is sure that if Armlin had been in an accident, he would have told her about it. Anyway, there's no rust or corrosion showing in the scrape site, so the accident has been within the last month or two. Forensics is also running DNA tests on the blond hairs found in the car, but it will be a few days before we know anything. Brenda was able to lift some partial fingerprints from the passenger side, but so far they've been unable to find a match. She said that it appeared that sections of the car had been hastily wiped down to destroy any prints." He picked up his mug of coffee and sipped at it while Galen took over.

"The dogs in the K9 unit did come up with something last night. They homed in on a used roll of duct tape in the bushes down near Fanno Creek just off the walking path, and spent quite a while sniffing the immediate area. Then when the handlers expanded the search radius, the dogs found some torn bits of tape with small dark hairs imbedded in the stickum. The vegetation there appears to have been disturbed and laid flat in one particular spot by the creek, but that's all we've got so far. There don't appear to be any prints on the duct tape roll, and it'll take some time to run those dark hairs through analysis."

"Did they take the dogs further up or down the creek?" asked Tom.

"Yeah, as soon as the tape fragments were discovered they broadened the search area even more, but the dogs didn't get excited about anything else that might have been in contact with Armlin," answered Galen. "I spoke with Emma again this morning and dropped by Armlin's office. There's no trace of either his briefcase or his cellphone—both of which Emma said he kept with him constantly. Pinging the phone still yields nothing, meaning either the batteries died, or it's been switched off."

"I don't know what to make of the duct tape," said Tom, "or if it's even connected to the case at this point. But not finding his phone or briefcase in the car or surrounding area makes it look to me like he ditched the Prius and did a runner for some reason. Anyone check flights or his credit card account?"

"Yep," said Galen. "No activity on the card, and no flights lately listing an 'Armlin' leaving from PDX. Of course, he could fake a name and ID or hop another means of transport, but that would be tough for us to know. I did check and no 'Armlin' has flown from any airport in the Pacific Northwest since his disappearance. And another thing—I suspect that those blond hairs found on the passenger seat came from his coworker, Monica Stevens. I stopped by her place last night and had a chat with her, and she claims she's never been in the car, but her body language said something different. She intimated that she'd desired an affair with Mr. Armlin some while back, but claims they never carried through with it. I don't know whether or not to believe her about that, but she promised to stop by the station this morning and submit to a DNA swab. Just a sec, let me check if she did." The others carried on the discussion, commiserating on the lack of evidence while Galen dialed the lab downstairs. "Yep, she submitted a sample this morning on her way to work," he reported as he hung up the phone. "And I agree that we are absolutely stuck until we get some lab results back. I helped check out a possible sighting of Armlin just this noon-hour, but it came to nothing."

"Any recommended next steps until we have something solid?" asked Tom.

"We already have a warrant request in for the responses to Armlin's editorials received by The Oregon Sentinel, but we can't physically search his office or work computer without a new warrant," said Galen. "Otherwise, I plan on digging into his life as much as possible. I'll see what additional information The Oregon Sentinel or Ms. Armlin might offer up, but I've pretty much exhausted his close friends and social contacts, so I'll keep searching the internet for any historical info or any presence he may have had on it."

"OK," said Tom. "I'll see if I can't get them to speed things up at the lab," which brought a chuckle from the others since they knew this was a near impossibility.

# Chapter 11.

GALEN WAS feeling agitated, and his jitters weren't solely due to the caffeine jolt his second cup of coffee provided the next morning. He always felt this way when he was making zero progress on a case and left awaiting the results from forensics or other sources. Rather than focusing on the Armlin disappearance, he sought diversion and spent the first half of the day going over all of the information gathered so far about Melissa Davidson and bringing himself up to speed on her case. There had been no progress in this investigation either, but at least he wasn't directly involved in it, so it didn't engender that feeling of inadequacy he'd experienced when he'd first come into work that morning. He was about to jump into the remaining three homicide files to see if he could be of any help there when he received a message that Ms. Stevens had been able to fulfill part of the warrant request, and she had a stack of Armlin's old editorials along with the letters that had been published in response to each one waiting on her desk when he arrived after the lunch hour. The unpublished responses and articles on microfiche were still being compiled by staff.

"Hello, Detective Young," said Monica a little anxiously as he entered her office space.

"Hi, Ms. Stevens," replied Galen. "I appreciate your getting these files together for me."

"No problem," said Monica, "and they're yours to keep. I had one of our interns xerox available copies of Bob's printed articles this morning." She looked suddenly sheepish and her voice lowered. "Um," she began, "have you had any results from my mouth swab?"

"No, not yet," said Galen. "DNA samples sometimes take a few days to process and we're awaiting the results of yours along with those from several other tests to come back. We'll let you know as soon as we learn anything. And we do appreciate your volunteering the sample."

"Well, like I said, I have nothing to hide, so I was happy to do it."

*I certainly hope you weren't involved*, thought Galen, nodding at the same time. "We expect to have more information soon. And thanks again for these files."

Back at the office, Galen sifted through the pile of articles, and much of it contained what he'd expected, especially after talking to Ed Comstock and Armlin's friend, John Doherty. There were numerous political opinion pieces, most written during the high points of election cycles, especially surrounding this most recent one including both the leadup and the aftermath in the following year—all, shockingly to Armlin, reflecting the losing side of the campaign. Many recent columns were directed at the perceived shortcomings of the current president. Ed Comstock was right; Armlin was a flaming liberal. However, many of the opinion pieces were along the lines of the editorial Galen had read about anonymity—they were written in a more thoughtful or philosophical vein. Galen picked out some of the less political editorials written during the past year and began to read from among these. One titled *Homeless* caught his attention.

*It's nearing spring, but winter isn't finished with us yet, so even on our recent warmer days, the wind still cuts like ice. Yesterday, I was thinking I should have worn my thicker coat and was walking past a pile of trash next to the street when it moved. There was a person under there—huddled under cast-off clothes and blankets trying to stay warm—on the cold hard pavement in a bitter wind. And here I was wondering whether I'd survive the walk back to the office.*

*I am so accustomed to the increasing number of homeless around our city that I must admit that I sometimes don't even notice them anymore. But when I do pay attention, it's obvious that their numbers are increasing by the year. Why is that? Now, I know that our fair city has turned on the gigantic leaf-blower that has blown them out from under the snarl of freeways across the river on the east side, and that they have to alight somewhere, but I also know that the total number is growing regardless of this recent purge.*

*Again, why are there are so many homeless now? Is there a huge calamity afflicting our nation? Do we have another Dust Bowl going on? A potato famine? A depression? A major war? The plague? No? Things seem to be humming along well for many of us—but not for a growing number who had been able to survive in the past.*

*And I blame corporate America. The new kid in town. The new citizen. The new bully on the block. I'm picturing it like this: We all live off each other, with each of us at work or in business to make a reasonable profit—a livelihood. We used to pay local businesses for insurance, food, entertainment, healthcare, other services, and they in turn bought our labor, goods, and services. Things were working well until the arrival of the bullies who beat up and ate up most of our local friends and started taking more than their fair share, all with the excuse that they needed to pay for research, infrastructure, and development. Which really translates into an obscene profit, since these expenses must have been accounted for—otherwise there would be no profit. You don't believe me that the profits are obscene? Read any major corporation's balance sheet.*

*So, the average Joe is now shaken down once a month by a small handful of communications, insurance, entertainment, and health provider behemoths at rates that are nonnegotiable and inexcusable. Meanwhile our neighbor's income (many of whom work for these very corporations) has not increased at near the level that the rates have. Those who can no longer make ends meet have become thin wraiths. So that we can barely see them. So that they have become ghosts.*

*And there is currently no remedy for this. The corporations are never going to pat their corpulent bellies and say, "OK, I'm full now." After all, they have the rest of us to feed on.*

*The fault of the corporations?* wondered Galen with a hefty measure of skepticism. *But Armlin does have a heart, that's for sure. Maybe I do agree with some of what he has to say.* A reply showed that not everyone was of the same mind as Armlin.

*Dear Editor,*

*OMG are you ever holier than thou! Your latest article is the perfect example of the left trying to portray us all as help-less victims. All so that we will roll over and play dead while you bring in sweeping governmental reforms to protect us—at a crushing cost to us through higher taxes, and at the price of our freedom. And then you'll tell us that it's for our own good—all because you invented the problem in the first place!*

*Those people you see on the street have made their own bad choices. They choose drugs, alcohol, sloth, and sexually trans-mitted diseases over hard work and a stable homelife. Any of them can get a job any time they like, but they prefer to live on governmental handouts and mooching off others instead. And who is paying for their laziness? Us, the poor working slobs.*

*Please quit your job. You are no good at it and are sim-ply the mouthpiece of the liberal propaganda machine. In fact, maybe you don't exist—maybe you are the machine. If you really do exist, it would be better for all of us if you didn't. Or, better yet, join the mooches on the street—you probably wouldn't notice the difference.*

*Peter Harkness*

*Beaverton, Oregon*

Galen shook his head. Not only did this verge on threaten-ing, but he found himself wondering whether the newspaper staff took the fringe responses and printed these to make themselves seem more edgy and to increase sales. Mentally storing the name Peter Harkness, he picked another article out at random and read through it both to learn Armlin's viewpoint and to see what sort of responses it received.

*Truth in Advertising*

*OK, I received some feedback from my recent editorial on advertising, and most, but not everyone, agreed with me, but do you know what? I have more to say. That's my job. This time about truth in advertising.*

*Advertisers are clever. They want us to relate to or empathize with the ad they've created, otherwise they've failed at their job if we turn away from the screen without watching. So, the emphasis is on making the actors in them seem as real as possible—and it works. At some level we know they're actors, but we forget that these are talented individuals and that they've been through hundreds of takes to make sure they come off as believable. We think that Joe next door would act the same way and say some of the same things under the same circumstances as portrayed in the ad. We think that these are real reactions to real situations and real endorsements of the products. Of course, they throw in humor, irony, slapstick, or pathos, but even in the funniest ads, we still take the actors as sincere. Just as, once we're immersed in a TV show or movie, we accept the actor as genuine and, usually, believable. So, in a one-minute commercial for a new ulcer medication, we ignore the forty seconds of disclaimers and side effects, while the hap-*

*py, trim, handsome grandfather cavorts with his grandson. By the way, have you ever seen an advertisement portray a single one of the multiple side effects? The person doubled up with cramps or stumbling with blurred vision? And the commercials that claim these are real people, not actors? Oops, now they are actors. Every single person you see in a commercial is a paid actor, and they are paid for one reason only—to sell the product. Please remember this.*

*Why is it that we see advertisements of pickup trucks towing semis out of the ditch, having hay bales tossed in the bed by manly cowboys, hauling a swimming pool's worth of bricks in the back, splashing through pristine wilderness, and yet nearly every truck I see on the road is polished, and the beds are brand new and always empty? In the ads, why don't we see shots of trucks taking up more than their lane of space? Using their size to bully the car in front of them? Trying to park downtown or daring to enter a parking garage? And why do ads for sports cars depict them racing around sharp turns, the wind whistling through the driver's hair while speeding down a completely empty road, or zipping through deserted city streets? Where are the shots of traffic jams, speed-limit signs, and traffic tickets being issued? Unfortunately, advertising must work. What else explains millions of trucks that are never used as intended and millions of sports cars constrained by nation-wide laws and speed limits? Sure, you can justify your purchase of the utilitarian or overpowered thing, but do you use it as it is designed? Well, you know better than I do.*

*I wonder if there is some level of panic currently being experienced by advertisers as television is turning to streaming episodes and moving fully into the digital age. How many people realistically view their ads anymore? If watching commercial television, don't people TIVO the ads off? Tape over or fast-forward through them? In the end the advertisers need us to be engaged, so they will find us somehow, or convince the manufacturers that they have found us. When they do so, I'm just trying to remind us all that the ads, the people you see in the ads, the person at the car showroom, the loan officer to help you buy the car, the banker or financial adviser who works with your money—they're all sales specialists. Every one of them. They are in it for the money—your money, and for no other reason. Nothing is free anymore—oh, and my boss has just reminded me that this column is paid for by a generous gift from Winfield Motors, Beaverton.*

Galen found himself agreeing with the premise, but feeling that the tone of the article was a little strident and at the same time nigglingly condescending. There were several responses to this opinion piece, and he read one of the more animated of these.

*Dear Editor,*

*I was insulted by your latest editorial. You depict us consumers as a flock of mindless sheep who see an ad on television and immediately run out to buy a new car without another thought. Maybe you just write your articles so that you stay in business and are trying to dupe us yourself.*

*We work hard for our money and put a lot of time and effort into deciding how and where to spend our paychecks—if there is any left after all our other expenses. I find advertisements to be very informative in showing me options or newer products that I wouldn't otherwise have considered. You basically said don't shoot the messenger, but these are messengers you are blasting away at who are trying to reach us and survive in a cutthroat business world.*

*You can sit on your high horse and try and make us think that you're the only one with a brain in your head, but every one of us is very capable of making the choices that are right for us. And the companies that make their products for us are doing their best for us, too. Try and live in Russia where you have only one option for the toilet paper you buy. Maybe you should find a job that suits you better than filling this type of paper with your mindless ideas.*

*Amos Billings*
*Portland, Oregon*

*Wow,* thought Galen, *some of these guys are over the top. I still wonder—would they get personal? Turn to crime to make a point or get back at him? I think it's time I found out.*

§

Galen pulled up in front of the long, low brick house off NW 6th in Gresham. A fine mist had settled over the neighborhood—and then his hair and coat by the time he reached the front door. A middle-aged man with a huge belly constrained by a tight tee shirt opened the door on the second knock, and eyed the detective up and down, inviting him inside only after Galen had introduced himself and displayed his badge.

The home was dark shag carpet, stuffed leather loungers, big screen TV, and mounted trophies of a dozen animals, leading Galen to presume that Peter Harkness was a dedicated bachelor.

"Mr. Harkness, I understand that you've submitted several letters to The Oregon Sentinel, and that they were... harsh towards the editor."

"Yeah, so what?" asked Harkness. "That ain't a crime that I know about."

"No, you're right. That's no crime," said Galen. "But I'm investigating a case which involves Mr. Armlin, the editor of the paper, and wondered about your feelings towards him, personally."

"Personally, I hate his guts," said Harkness in an easy manner. "And, I see in the papers that the guy's gone missing, so maybe that's a good thing."

"It's statements like that that have made me drop by."

"So, you think that I had something to do with him being missing?" Harkness asked with a derisive laugh.

"I don't know. Did you?"

"Well, I don't see how I could since I was fishing up the Columbia with my buddies this weekend and didn't get home until yesterday."

Galen sat in his car with his cell phone and verified the contact information Harkness had given him, confirming with two "buddies" that the group had been in Arlington during the entire period in question. *So much for that idea,* he thought as he swung the car out and headed north for I-84.

# Chapter 12.

A PREDICTED warm and sunny Saturday afternoon was an excuse for holding the first precinct picnic of the year and it provided a welcome prelude to summer. The boys had eaten two hotdogs each, potato salad, and downed how many Cokes Galen wasn't sure, to the point that they needed to burn off some energy. Both of them were glad that they'd brought their baseball mitts, because as usual, the picnic was held in Irving Park near the northern ballfield, and a pickup game of softball was *de rigueur.*

Ryan was old enough that he was chosen on a team right away and was happily playing third base, while Monty was content to act as the batboy for both teams. Tom Weston was pitching for Ryan's team during the first inning when his wife, Carol, came up to join Galen and Jan who were watching from the sidelines. They greeted each other and Carol said, "Wow, Beth's two boys have really shot up lately, haven't they? They look so grown-up now."

"Yeah," said Galen. "Even we can tell that they've put on some height over the winter, and they eat like they want to put on more."

Within the span of this short exchange, Jan had politely sidled off to join some of the officer's wives with whom she was better acquainted. She'd never been a fan of Carol and her esotericism and had once likened her interest in astrology and the occult to witchcraft. For her part, Carol, for some reason, never seemed to notice the subtle digs Jan gave her when she was in her company, nor his wife's studied avoidance of her.

"It must be a trip watching them change as they enter puberty," said Carol conversationally. Galen was unsure how to respond and merely nodded. Tom and Carol had never had children, and Tom had never mentioned their desire to have any. "By the way, how's Beth doing?"

"She seems to be fine, Carol," said Galen. "Of course, she doesn't deal well with being locked up, but then who would?"

"Loss of freedom is probably the biggest loss one can have," said Carol. "Luckily, we're always free in our own minds and can go wherever we want in here." She gazed up at Galen. "I could meet with her and talk to her about lucid dreaming and astral projection if you thought she'd be interested."

"I'll ask her the next time I'm out there," Galen replied, doubting that he'd remember or be inclined to do so. The top of the inning was over, and the other team invited Monty to play fourth man in the outfield. The ecstatic boy grabbed his glove and ran out to stand between the center and right outfielders. As the other team sent up their first batter, Monty waved to Galen from the field and Galen waved back.

"Say, Carol," said Galen in a contemplative tone. "I have a question that you might be able to answer."

"Oh? What's that?"

"I have a case that involves a missing person, and one of his coworkers said that she woke up one morning soon after his disappearance with a horrible feeling about what might have happened to him. I know that we cops have our own kind of nose for something fishy, but in your experience, how often do those kinds of premonitions turn out to be true for regular folks?"

"More often than you might think, Galen," said Carol. "We're all much more in tune with what's happening on a psychic level than most people realize. If you have good or bad thoughts about a person, they have real impacts on the spiritual plane. In fact, we all interact with one another on that plane, and know about it intuitively, if not consciously."

"But even if it just registers as a funny feeling?" asked Galen.

"Those are the ones that you should pay the most attention to," said Carol. "Something is really happening on several levels. Were the two close?"

"She says that she was in love with him," said Galen.

"All the more reason to pay heed to the feeling," replied Carol.

Galen nodded and they turned to watch the game. A fly ball came to Monty and he fumbled it, but grabbed it on the grass and quickly flipped it to the right fielder who pegged a throw to second base, saving a possible double by the other team. The small crowd watching went wild and a grinning Monty waved both hands in the air in excitement.

§

Dragging himself into the Bureau on Monday, Galen was bushed. He'd worked all Saturday morning helping with one of the homicide cases that had shown promise, but ultimately no arrests were forthcoming on that front. The picnic had been that afternoon, then on Sunday, Jan had decided it was time to prepare the house for summer which meant most of the day was spent cleaning the deck and garage. He'd also promised to take the boys to one of the final Trail Blazers' basketball games of the season, and they hadn't arrived back home until 10:45 that evening, a school night. The boys were pumped up, especially Monty, and the tired grandparents hadn't been able to get them settled down and into bed until near midnight. How those two had both managed to bound out of bed the next morning was beyond Galen, and he wished he could bottle whatever they had. *Oh, yeah,* he thought. *Youth and testosterone, and I seem to be running out of both lately.* What made matters worse was that they'd tossed around a basketball before the game which had left Galen with persistent pain in his right shoulder, making it difficult to sleep on that side.

There was the normal briefing at 8:00 am, and Galen felt as though he'd slept through it. In fact, Pembrook later remarked that Galen had. After several cups of coffee, he was beginning to feel like the cobwebs were clearing and he mentally vowed to find someone else to take the boys to those late-night games. He was just alert enough to start going through the Armlin editorials again when Tom Weston unexpectedly summoned the entire unit together for a briefing just before lunch.

The conference room was packed—Tom appeared to have invited heads of other units and some of his superiors to the meeting as well. "Ladies," said Tom, addressing the few female officers present, the Bureau Chief, Karen Osborne, detective Deb Cushing, and Brenda Rigby, the forensic lead, "and gentlemen." This quieted the general hubbub of separate conversations sprinkled about the room. "We have some interesting findings to present that might change the course of several ongoing investigations. And towards that end, I turn the floor over to Brenda Rigby from Forensics."

Brenda flushed red, which she did anytime she was in the presence of more than two people and approached the small podium. "I don't have any fancy PowerPoint presentations this time," she began, and the entire room laughed, some clapped, and the shade of red on her face verged on crimson. Brenda was known for preparing elaborate, and at the same time riveting, presentations to accompany nearly every talk she gave. Some in the building suspected that this was a crutch due to her fear of public speaking and anyone who asked her would have received an answer in the affirmative. "But I've made handouts that you can pick up on your way out," she said perkily, pointing to a stack of papers near the door. "I basically didn't have time for anything else since the results just came back a few minutes ago." She had everyone's attention.

"First, and most importantly, we now have the identity of the owner of the blond hair found in the car belonging to the prominent missing person—Robert Armlin, opinion page editor of The Oregon Sentinel." She looked quickly at her notes as if to confirm what she already knew and then looked up. "And she is Melissa Davidson."

"What?" shouted Galen at the same time that the entire room erupted. "You mean he's a kidnapper?"

No distinct words reached either Brenda or Tom, who was standing a little to her side. When the clamor subsided, Tom gave Brenda an encouraging nod and she continued.

"Yes," she said to a suddenly hushed crowd. "The blond hair belongs to Melissa Davidson, our missing girl, based on the DNA extracted from the hair samples in the car, and from samples taken from Melissa's belongings a week ago."

Galen found that his right arm had shot up, bringing immediate pain to his right shoulder, and that he was asking, "How is this possible? What link could there possibly be between a very elderly pillar of the Goose Hollow community and a 4-year old missing girl abducted from across town in Washington Square? Just how definitive are these results?"

Brenda directed her attention towards Galen and answered, "I can't say anything about the possibility of any links, but I am 99.8 percent positive that the hairs in the car belong to Melissa."

Another clamor of voices erupted, and she paused for them to fade into murmurs before she continued. "And the hair samples taken from the duct tape found along Fanno Creek near Mr. Armlin's recently discovered Toyota Prius belong to Mr. Armlin himself."

Galen nearly shouted "What?" again, but checked himself amid the more subdued reactions to this news.

"This is corroborated by DNA extracted from personal items taken from Mr. Armlin's residence with the permission of his wife. And the third bit of data we now have is informative but inconclusive. We were able to gather a good set of unidentified fingerprints from the exterior of the Prius' driver door handle, and from along the upper portion of that door. Another group of fingerprints within the car were only partials, and we have not found a match for these either, but they are not the same as those we lifted from the exterior driver's door, and they are not Mr. Armlin's."

As soon as the floor was opened for questions, Galen was again the first to raise his hand and speak. "Let me get this straight. It looks like it's possible that Armlin has kidnapped Davidson, that they both have disappeared from the car, that Armlin somehow duct-taped himself down by Fanno Creek, and that his are not the last prints on the driver's door handle? This makes no sense."

Galen was aware that he'd obviously asked questions that Brenda couldn't answer, but Tom quickly rescued her by taking the podium and addressing the question while glancing at Chief Osborne. "Well, there is in fact a certain logic to the whole thing. Picture this: Armlin, for reasons yet unknown, kidnaps Davidson and has her in the car; he wants to elude us in Portland so he ditches the car and takes Melissa to the trail near the creek; she resists so he uses duct tape to restrain her, but in wrestling with her, he leaves a patch that had stuck to his arm. The prints on the car's door handle are from one of probably many persons trying to gain entry to an abandoned vehicle."

Galen nodded at his reasoning. "That makes sense, but I still want to know why on earth the prominent editor of a local newspaper would kidnap a four-year-old girl? This doesn't sound anything like the man I've been investigating."

"What if a third party came upon the pair down by the creek?" asked Cushing. "Or rendezvoused with Armlin," ventured Jenkins. The remainder of the meeting was filled with speculations about these questions, and the possible scenarios that explained the results they'd just been presented. In the end, Tom's version seemed the simplest and most rational, and they all agreed that this was the most likely sequence of events.

Tom then took control of the meeting again. "So, this obviously changes the focus of several investigations. We're moving from Melissa's disappearance being due to a possible kidnapping, to her definite abduction, and from Robert Armlin being a missing person to him being the likely kidnapper. This ramps up the criminality on both fronts, and I believe we now have ample reason to issue some search warrants. Galen, I want you to head up the searches of both the Armlin home, and of his office at The Oregon Sentinel. Don't forget to include a warrant request for his cell phone voicemails and messages. I believe that Ms. Stevens is now off the hook for involvement in the disappearance of Armlin, so we can end that line of inquiry. Pembrook and those involved in the search for Melissa can now focus on sightings of the pair, any signs of contact for ransom,

Armlin's bank and email accounts, and so on." Officers began to rise from their seats. "Before we go," he waved his hands to settle everyone down for a moment, "we'll need to have a press conference and boost publicity to help in the search for both victim and perp. I hope we can count on Chief Osborne and…" he scanned the crowd, glancing for a moment at Galen, "and Jenkins to help me out in this media event." Galen was glad that Tom remembered that he hated news conferences.

The meeting broke up quickly, and Galen was on the phone as soon as he was back in his office to request the necessary search warrants.

# Chapter 13.

THE NEXT two days were busy, but they only seemed to compound Galen's frustration that the Bureau was making no tangible progress on the now combined cases. Emma had, of course, been utterly shocked by the news that her husband of fifty years was a possible kidnapper, and it had bothered him to upset her so. However, his assurances that these were the early stages of the investigation and that they were still trying to uncover the underlying facts left her stoically accepting the purported version of events. She had also reluctantly allowed them into her house, and after a thorough search and easy access to the Armlin's shared home computer, not a single indication was found of any interest shown by Armlin in children, porn, Melissa, the Davidsons, or kidnapping. Her husband appeared to be, as Ed Comstock had described him, a straight arrow.

Searches of Armlin's work computer yielded the same negative results, and so if any information existed linking him to Melissa or young girls in general, it would have to be stored on his missing phone or the laptop computer Armlin used when he worked from home. Stevens helped in the organization of Armlin's digital work files, and she provided Galen with several draft editorials Armlin had composed but not yet published, as well as additional personal-interest pieces and their responses the editor had garnered on The Oregon Sentinel's Facebook page.

The call records obtained from his cell phone provider were cross-checked and verified by either his wife or The Oregon Sentinel, and there were no unknown or unusual listings among them. In the end, the investigators found nothing on Bob Armlin that made him seem anything other than how he presented himself to the world.

The first day after the news of the kidnapping broke, Armlin's face was on every newspaper in the city. Galen read one of the articles written by The Portland Mail.

*It is now confirmed by police that Melissa Davidson has been kidnapped. In a bizarre twist, two separate missing persons cases were linked by police yesterday, as hair matching that of Davidson was found in an abandoned car owned by Robert Armlin, an editor for The Oregon Sentinel. Four-year-old Davidson was reported missing a week ago after disappearing during a shopping trip with her mother in the Washington Square mall. Armlin was reported missing five days ago and his whereabouts remain unknown. Police recently found Armlin's car abandoned on Lee St. and after processing hair samples from the scene, they have now confirmed through DNA tests that the hair belongs to Melissa Davidson. It is assumed that Armlin has abducted Davidson and a statewide search is on for the missing pair. Anyone with any information on either person is urged to contact the Portland Police Bureau.*

*Police are also searching for the site where Armlin harbored Davidson in the days following her kidnapping and before he himself fled with her. Possible motives for the abduction are also being pondered by police. Rumors of a cache of children's pornography found on Armlin's computer have yet to be confirmed.*

Galen folded the paper in disgust. *I bet they have,* he thought.

He gathered together several of the day's newspapers and a few photographs of Armlin and brought them with him when he visited the Davidson's residence in the late afternoon. He hadn't yet met her parents, and he was interested to see if Melissa's mother recognized Armlin. Stepping around several news cameras and bored-looking reporters on the walkway, Galen climbed the steps to the porch and knocked on the Davidson front door. A small woman with mousy brown hair peeked out through the curtains and, seeing his badge, hustled him in. A few of the more curious reporters had followed him up the steps and they voiced some disapproval when the door was slammed in their faces.

"Thank you for meeting with me, Mrs. Davidson. I'm Detective Galen Young with the Portland Police Bureau. I believe that my colleague Detective Pembrook was over yesterday afternoon with the news that it's now possible your daughter has been kidnapped? And of course, the story is now spread all over today's papers."

The shock of this news had evidently worn off because Mrs. Davidson accepted his introduction with a sad indifference. "Yes, we heard," she said as she offered him a chair in the clean but sparsely decorated living room. "At least it's news," she reflected philosophically, "and strangely better than not knowing anything at all."

"Yes, the more information we can gather the better, even if the news isn't always good."

She nodded and seemed lost in thought. Pembrook had described her as hysterical when he'd spoken to her earlier, and Galen wondered if she'd perhaps sought medication to help with the anxiety.

"Mrs. Davidson," he began again.

"Joni," she said flatly.

"Joni," he echoed, "I believe you've seen the pictures in the newspaper, and I have some clearer photographs of Mr. Armlin, who we believe may have been involved in the kidnapping. I was wondering if you could give these a look and see if you recognize the man in them. Maybe he was in the background at the Washington Square mall? Perhaps you interacted with him?"

"I've stared at the picture on the cover of The Oregon Sentinel..." Joni hesitated, but she still took her time with the photographs he offered her. She gazed at each picture and closed her eyes at several intervals, obviously trying to think back to that day. She returned to the first picture and stared at it again.

"No, I don't recognize him from the mall—I'm certain of it, but of course I know the face of Robert Armlin. You know in this photo he looks a little like Melissa's granddad, Peter. I like his columns..." she tapered off as she held Galen's eyes. "You believe that that thoughtful, educated man, has taken my daughter? What reason could he possibly have for doing that?" She hesitated a moment and then blurted, "Oh, my god! Not that reason—he wouldn't, would he?"

"We honestly don't know for certain that he has kidnapped her," Galen calmed her, "and from what I know about the man, any kind of sexual motive would be extremely unlikely."

"The world's gone crazy..." The hand holding the picture was trembling, and Galen gently took the photographs from her. Joni Davidson finally broke down into quiet sobs.

"We'll do our best to find your daughter, Joni," said Galen after she had dried her eyes and he rose to leave. "And don't read too much into this Armlin connection. It seems to us implausible," he lied somewhat, "but we have to follow the leads."

§

On the afternoon of the second day after they'd learned that Armlin was the kidnapper, Galen received a phone call from Detective Lockhart in Spokane. Galen had worked on several cases with Lockhart when they were stationed together in Pendleton and knew him to be thorough and unlikely to jump to conclusions. After pleasantries, Lockhart said, "So, Galen, I hear that you're working on the Melissa Davidson case."

"Yeah, Tony, that's right," said Galen. "And it appears that that case might be linked to one we have here of a missing newspaper editor, Bob Armlin. We have indications that he may be the kidnapper."

"OK, that's what I heard, and that's why I'm calling," said Lockhart. "We don't have a clear description of the driver, but we have a very credible report of a girl that matches Melissa Davidson to a tee."

"How credible?" asked Galen, sitting forward at his desk.

"An off-duty patrolman was driving into Spokane on I-90 when he matched speed with a silver car in the next lane. He looked over and noticed a girl in the back seat who seemed to be familiar, but he couldn't quite place her. The car had just pulled into a short exit lane and started to slow when the girl, who seemed to be playing with something, lifted her hands and he could swear they were duct taped. That's when it hit him that she might be Melissa Davidson, but by then the car had veered off on the exit heading north on Division. He immediately called it in, but we've been unable to locate the car."

"Jeez, Tony, that just might be our girl," said Galen. "Did he get a look at the driver?"

"No, not a good look. Because window glare blocked his vision, he wasn't willing to hazard a guess at all."

"Have you put out an APB?" asked Galen.

"Yep, let me read it to you," said Lockhart. "Be on the lookout for a blond, four-year-old female, possibly the missing Melissa Davidson from Portland, Oregon. Last seen wearing an olive-green tee-shirt. Possible tape, or tape burn-marks on her wrists. The driver of the silver sedan of unknown make and model is believed to be a gray-haired gentleman in his seventies. Approach with caution, but the driver is not believed to be armed."

"That should do it," said Galen. "Do you want me there to help out?"

"I'd love to see you again, Galen, but I'm not sure what you could do even if you were here right now. Our APB is as specific as we can make it and it's out to all the units and hotels in the area. If anything comes back, we should have them."

"OK, Thanks, Tony. We'll standby here and see what develops."

Galen alerted the others in the office about his conversation with Lockhart, and there was some anticipation for a breakthrough in the case, but none came that day. Tony called Galen the next afternoon to say that they were losing hope that anything would come of the sighting. Two traffic cams had picked up images of what they thought was the same car, but there was no child visible in the back seat. The Portland Police Bureau was not surprised—tips were streaming in on a daily basis, and there had been excitement earlier that day about a possible spotting of her in Olympia, Washington which had also yielded no results.

# Chapter 14.

GALEN HAD read through several of Armlin's editorials when he thought that the newspaperman was a missing person or someone who wanted to disappear for a while, but since they were now of the mind that the editor could be a kidnapper, he wanted to discover anything that might shed light on this possibility. Sifting through some of files Armlin left on his work computer, Galen found a series of unfinished or unpublished articles that Armlin had been composing and most were riddled with strikeouts and edits. He skimmed them for anything relevant and came upon one that he sat and read all the way through.

*Knowing your neighbor*

*Are our eyes the windows to the soul or are they the mirrors of the soul? Do we truly perceive a person when we look into someone's eyes, or do we simply see a reflection of ourselves and who we want them to be? How well do we know our fellow beings? The extent to which we can really gauge a stranger has been a common subject in fiction, with books toying with the fact that much lies hidden behind our presentation of ourselves, including a very dark side. Deep down, I believe that we should go through life trusting that our fellow human beings are fathomable. I'd like to believe that we see our friend, relative, colleague, or a stranger and can trust that we truly do know who they are. That we are all essentially good and making our best of this existence.*

*I was struck by a recent news story about a baker who refused to bake a cake for a gay couple based on religious grounds, and it evinced the multiple problems that gays or lesbians face in finding equity in treatment when it comes to services, housing, and life in general. The baker probably become aware of the couple's sexual preference through the marriage license, perhaps the names on the cake, or the couple's presence in the shop. The baker's opposition was claimed to be a matter of his personal, religious morals, but a stricture about being gay isn't even one of the ten commandments, the basic tenets of a moral Christian life. You have to dig around to find passages in the Bible that can be construed as anti-homosexual, and they are few and far between.*

*So, here are some individuals living their lives honestly, and they are refused service on religious grounds. But the funny thing to me about this, keeping the rudimentary ten commandments in mind, is: How many of the people that the baker has served have really kept the Sabbath as holy, or properly honored their father and mother? How many adulterers has he baked cakes for without even knowing or asking? How many murderers? And to extend the case to modern morals, how many liars, bullies, misogynists, or racists has he decorated his creations for? If a person is really basing his business on his personal morals, how many times has he hypocritically aided those who violate his personal standards? And who is he to judge in the first place? People walk invisibly among us who are secretly guilty of misconduct, and yet those seeking a civil union to express their love and commitment are the ones who receive persecution—in part because of their openness and honesty.*

*What are the chances that if the baker asked, 'Sure, I'll bake you a cake—bullied or lied to anyone lately? Slept with anyone other than your wife?' he would ever receive an honest reply? Is it his business to know in the first place? When it comes down to it, the eyes are neither the window nor the mirror to the soul. We are all living unrevealed existences, since life and past experiences are enigmas to anyone else but us. There is no knowing that someone is who he says he is, has done what he says he's done, or is as we take him to be. We just have to trust, as the baker should, that we are all only trying our best at this life and would like a cake to celebrate it.*

Galen was taken aback by this draft editorial. Closing his eyes, he thought, *He's made some good points, and he's absolutely right that, as a cop, I question the true background and intentions of everyone I pass on the street.* He sat back in his chair and stared again at the computer screen. *But on another level, and knowing what I know now, what if he's talking about himself?* He glanced at the last paragraph, finding *'or is as we take him to be,'* and for a moment a chill ran up his back. He had to have another conversation with Emma Armlin.

# Chapter 15.

THE EXTERIOR of the house on Myrtle Street was as immaculate as it had been on every one of his previous visits. The interior, however, was another story. Emma greeted him at the door, pleasantly, but without the openness and expectancy she'd manifested on his first visit. She appeared tired, drawn, and ten years older to his eyes.

"Hello, Emma," said Galen as he took her proffered hand, "I'm sorry to have to bother you again."

"Oh, quite alright, Detective," she said with little energy. "I'm getting used to your visits. Won't you come in?"

"Thanks," said Galen as he sat down in the chair that she'd suggested with a slight wave of her hand. The police had tried to be as neat as possible in the search of the house after they'd obtained the warrant, and Galen found the space exactly as he'd left it—not a single thing that they'd moved or stacked out of place had been put away, and now there were dirty dishes left on some of the living room furniture.

"I see nothing new or unexpected in the morning papers, so what brings you by this time?" asked Emma after she had perched herself on an antique straight-backed chair.

"Well," admitted Galen, "I wanted to talk to you a little bit about your husband to find out more about him."

"I think you already know..." she began, staring at him guardedly as he cut her off.

"To tell you the truth, I think I'm far from that—really knowing who he is," interjected Galen. "Let me just lay this on the table, but I have to warn you, some of it may be unpleasant."

"It already is awful, the things they've said about him," said Emma tightening her thin body and sliding slightly further back onto the chair.

"I realize that," said Galen, sympathetically. "But I need to try and understand him better. So here goes. To all outward appearances, your husband is a remarkable man. I've read some of his editorials—well, the non-political ones—and through them the picture I get of him is that he's thoughtful, kind, and extremely intelligent. In fact, I've come to respect his opinions and his unique way of looking at the world. And you, his friends that I've interviewed, and his co-workers all have nothing but good things to say about him." He paused, adjusted his position in the chair and gazed at her. "But we also have evidence, as unbelievable as it may be, that he appears to have kidnapped a young girl of four years. Given that information, I've read one of his draft editorials in a different light, and it appears that your husband also knew the darkness that can lurk inside each of us and he was very aware of our ability to hide it from others. I guess what I want to know from you, if it's possible, is this: If your husband should turn out to be guilty of this crime, is there anything you can think of where you'd look back and say, 'Ah, that's what he meant by that,' or 'Oh, that's why he acted that way.' Anything that has not synched with his external narrative? Do you see what I'm asking?"

Emma had been focused on a narrow high boy with a few framed pictures of the couple set off to the left side and partially obscured by some stacked dishes. She got up, moved the plates to another side-table, rearranged the pictures carefully, and then returned to her seat, pushing rigidly back onto the thin cushion.

"Yes, I know what you're asking," said Emma in a clipped and somewhat angry tone. "And these are the very same questions I've been asking myself since the news came out that he could have taken that poor girl." She looked up suddenly, obviously startled by her rough reply. "I'm sorry, Detective. I don't know why I'm so out of sorts lately, and I've completely forgotten my manners. Can I get you something to drink? Tea or coffee? Something stronger?"

Galen shook his head, "No, nothing for me."

"Well, I believe I'm in the need of some soothing tea," said Emma, and got up to make her way to the kitchen and set a pot to boil.

"The Girl Scouts came by the other day," she called out as he heard a drawer close. "Would you like a cookie?"

"No, thank you Emma, I'm good."

She soon walked back to her chair and took a moment to set the teacup and saucer on the side-table after placing a coaster underneath. Sitting again, she doffed her slip-on shoes and lightly curled her feet up under her. She took a small sip of the steaming brew and gazed at the hardwood floor before continuing. "Back in the old days, we never seemed to question anyone else's motives. Or at least I never did. But now we have all these psychological thrillers in the movies and books, and it seems like any one of us can be capable of any ghastly thing. It's always the nicest man who ends up being the stalker or the murderer. Look at John Gacy, or whoever he was—a party clown for kids, of all things." She stared more intently at the wooden flooring, as if trying to pick out something as yet unrevealed in its grain patterns. After a long moment she looked back up at him. "Anyway, yes, I've been trying to ferret out if the person I've lived with for more than fifty years has been someone I don't really know. If he lives some sort of double life. But I don't think so." She caught Galen's eyes and smiled. "I may be old, and I may be deluded, but Bob is and always has been the genuine article. What's that new saying, WOSIWOG? No, WYSIWYG. What you see, in his case, is really what you get."

"I appreciate that, Emma, and I can see that you've thought a lot about it, but I still have some unanswered questions."

Emma sighed and gave a slight smile as she reached for the tea. "I know," she said. "Go on."

Galen cleared his throat. "Has he ever been around or shown interest in young girls? Paid special attention to them? Have you ever, you know, caught his eyes following them or anything?"

"Goodness, no!" said Emma briskly, but then catching herself. "No," she said again, "but let me think." After a few minutes of staring at him and the floor again, she got up and went to a tall china hutch with some more pictures on the lower portion where she picked out two. "His brother Bruce and he took Bruce's two grand-daughters and Bruce's son on a fishing trip to Alaska three years ago. One of the girls is six and the other eight. Here, have a look."

Galen saw two delighted girls holding up a string of grayling in one picture and trying to grapple a big salmon in the other, with grandfather, father, and great uncle looking on. All appeared natural and relaxed. "He adores those two grand-nieces, and has spent hours with them, both with his brother and alone with me. There has never been a whisper of impropriety, and in fact, Bob is prone to seek time away from them just for the sake of his own sanity. I can't see how he could ever turn that kind of affection into the need to grab and control a complete stranger. Sure, Bob lives in his head a lot—but that's the intellectual world, not the world of fantasy. He dreams of how and why things work, not of odd urges—and certainly not of acting them out."

"That's good to hear," said Galen, "and they look like happy girls having the time of their lives, by the way." Emma nodded, set the pictures down on the coffee table in front of him, and returned to her chair. "I also have to ask, Emma, does he ever suddenly disappear? Spend hours away without you knowing where he is?"

"Well," replied Emma honestly, "I can say that he always lets me know where he's going, and I trust that he really goes there—but I've never felt the need to actually check in on his whereabouts. I don't think anyone does, unless they're a little touched upstairs themselves. Do they?"

Galen grinned. "Absolutely right, that would be paranoia, wouldn't it?"

Emma nodded back, "And neither Bob nor I are paranoid, or crazy."

"Thank you again for spending more time with me, Emma," said Galen as he rose to leave. "This has helped a lot."

Emma suddenly looked fearful and frail. "It's starting to drive me nuts, though, Detective. Too many thrillers. What if I'm wrong about him?"

"I don't think you are, ma'am," said Galen gently. "I agree with you that it just doesn't seem like him to do something like this. We'll find out the truth soon enough—I hope—and I don't know what the explanation will turn out to be, but it'll be shocking to me, too, if we find out that Bob is some kind of monster. He drafted an editorial that said we never really know anyone by outward appearances, but I don't think he was talking about himself. At least, I hope not." He let himself out with Emma remaining in her chair as dusk was beginning to descend with long shadows cast on the yard outside.

# Chapter 16.

GALEN'S FAMILY was enjoying a pot-roast that Jan had prepared, and the boys were excited that the last day of school was on the horizon in less than three weeks' time. "We need to get in touch with Uncle Mack and find out when we can drive out there and go camping," said Monty around a bite of boiled potato. Mack was the youngest of Galen's brothers and had stayed near the family home in Enterprise, Oregon. His place was a good stepping-off point for hikes and camping in the Wallowa Mountains and a favorite summer-time destination of them all. The boys also loved riding horses from the small stable Mack and his wife kept.

"First we need Grampa here to take some leave," said Ryan. Then turning in his chair and lazily pointing his fork, he asked, "So, Gramps, how much time can you get off? And when?"

"I don't know yet, Ryan," replied Galen noncommittally. "Things are busy right now, but that doesn't mean that they'll still be that way in a couple of weeks."

"Ri-i-i-i-ght," said Ryan and Monty simultaneously, and then both laughed.

"When are you gonna retire?" asked Monty. "We wanna do stuff!"

"Don't forget that piano lessons and soccer club are 'stuff' too," said Jan, offering up an assertion which was met with a roll of the eyes from both boys.

"I don't know, Monty," responded Galen, pointedly rubbing his sore shoulder. "But the way I feel lately, I think it should be sooner rather than later." He took a bite of pot roast, reflecting that his mandatory retirement age with the Bureau was now less than two years away.

"Great!" said Monty, beginning to launch into all of his ideas for a productive summer when Galen's phone rang. He peered at the screen and with a shake of his head said, "Sorry, I have to take this," while getting up from the table.

"Hey, Tom, what is it?" he asked as he moved into the adjoining family room. A muted Timbers' soccer game was playing on the big-screen TV mounted on the side wall. The Timbers were so far scoreless, and it was late in the game.

"Hey, Galen," replied Tom. "I don't think you need to come in tonight for this, but I wanted to let you know that we now have a confirmed eyewitness report of Melissa Davidson."

"Really? Where?"

"The Bureau here was just alerted that she was spotted at the Roosville, Montana border-crossing into Canada."

"Montana? Do they have her? Is she all right?" asked Galen hurriedly. "She's now in Canada?"

"Unfortunately, no, they don't have her. A silver sedan, similar to the one Lockhart reported as being sighted in Spokane, pulled up to the Canadian customs station at Roosville. The border guard noticed a girl in the back seat and brought up the

APB on his computer screen to see if his hunch that she was the Davidson girl was right. His hesitation spooked the driver who threw the car into reverse, did a 180, and sped down the border entrance-road the wrong way against traffic. There were few cars in the lane, so he made it through without hinderance. Canadian officials alerted the US border station and a patrol car there entered into a delayed pursuit from the border heading south, and at the same time the Montana Highway Patrol set up a roadblock in Eureka located a few miles further to the south. The car should have been trapped between the two, but as far as we know, it's disappeared. All this started at 8:30 Mountain time when it was heavily into dusk, and it's dark there now."

"How sure are they that it's Melissa?" asked Galen.

"Very sure. Facial recognition software is being run on the video images as we speak, but the border guard was positive it was her."

"What about Armlin? Where would an old guy like him learn to drive like that? He must be desperate."

"That's the other thing," said Tom. "Unless he dyed his hair and used heavy cosmetics, the driver wasn't Armlin."

"Well then, who the hell was it?"

"No idea, but they're trying facial ID on that image, too. We should have pictures to distribute by tomorrow morning at the briefing."

"If Armlin wasn't the driver, then where the hell is Armlin?" asked Galen.

"That's the question of the day, isn't it?" asked Tom Weston as he bid Galen goodnight.

Galen wasn't sure what time he drifted off to sleep that night, but it was certainly in the early morning hours. He couldn't stop going over possible scenarios for what was happening in the merged cases. *Robert Armlin has gone from being a missing person, to being a possible adulterer with Monica Stevens, to kidnapping a four-year-old girl, to...what? Where the hell is he? We know he was involved with Melissa somehow, because she was definitely in his car. Did he have a partner? Was he hiding in the back seat at the border? Was it him all along - driving in disguise? Did he hand Melissa over to a partner and arrange to meet in Canada? Was he himself carjacked?* These were among the myriad thoughts that tumbled through his head as he sought the sleep that only came much later that night.

# Chapter 17.

THE MORNING briefing was another melee of competing information and theories. The girl in the car was confirmed by authorities to be Melissa Davidson, so they knew that she was alive and had made it as far north as the Canadian border but was now somewhere far to the east of Portland in Montana. The car was identified as one that had been stolen from the front yard of a residence in The Dalles, a town upriver in the Columbia River Gorge, one day after Robert Armlin's disappearance.

That was all they knew. The facial recognition software had failed to find a match for the driver, but experts said that it would need to have been a professional make-up job if the man behind the wheel was really Armlin in disguise. The photos captured from the border video were being distributed after they'd all watched the footage on the big-screen console at the end of the room: the car pulling up to the booth, waiting for a few moments, and then roaring into reverse, sweeping around to head in the opposite direction, and then racing away to the south. The driver kept his face mostly averted from the camera, but a few good screen-capture shots were still possible. He looked nothing like Armlin—fuller and squarer of face, with short but thick black hair rather than the thin white halo of Armlin's. The silver sedan was now missing, but there was an on-going multi-state effort underway to locate it. That was all they knew, but there were plenty of theories to go around and they were all being tossed about at once.

"All right, all right," said Weston regaining control of the multiple discussions. "Let's see where we stand. Since Melissa has been confirmed to be in Montana, the FBI is being pulled in as this is now an inter-state case, and it will be up to them and the Montana authorities to locate her, so there isn't much we can do on that front, except provide them with as much information from here as we can. The local police in The Dalles and the Oregon State Police are both investigating the auto theft there, but so far, no abandoned car has been found that might have been used by the kidnapper to get to The Dalles in the first place. We can do our part by ferreting out how the kidnapper, whoever he is, and Melissa Davidson made the trip from here in Portland up to where the car was stolen." He started to make a list on a whiteboard next to the small lectern. "Jenkins, will you check the train and bus records and any available videos from those stations at both ends of the route on the day before and the day of the car theft in The Dalles?" Jenkins nodded. "Can I get a volunteer to drive up to The Dalles for the day and help scan plates for a car that might have been abandoned there?"

Galen raised his hand, "Sure, I can go—it's only an hour and a half drive."

"Thanks, Galen, but I was going to have you dig deeper into Armlin's case. We now know that we have no idea what's happened to the man. Pembrook, let's have either you or Cushing drive up there and try and liaise with folks in The Dalles. We want to interview anyone who might have noticed the pair in the vicinity of where the sedan was stolen. Take these photos of the driver we've printed and distribute them. Whichever one of you two doesn't head up The Gorge should stop by the Davidson's house and see if either parent—especially Joni, the mother—recognizes the driver of the car. A photo might jog her memory of seeing this guy in the mall. OK," he ended with a raised voice, sensing that the room was about to erupt into a clamor again, "let's get this done today, and save the theories for tomorrow. I want any reports as soon as they come in. Let's go." And the conference quickly broke up as police officers and detectives grabbed copies of the photos and headed for the door.

Galen made his way back to his office feeling a little discouraged. The main reason he'd wanted to make the trip to The Dalles wasn't to help in the search for a possibly non-existent car; it was to take advantage of the travel time to think. With the distractions in the office and the numerous tasks that needed his attention on the case, he rarely had time to mentally sift through what he already knew thoroughly enough for any intuition to spring out of it. He found that a long solo drive was one of the only times he could escape into much-needed contemplation in relative isolation. *Ah well*, he thought, *I guess I'll plow through a few more of Armlin's editorials and see if hints about him, or what might have happened to him, are hidden in them or the replies.*

§

Galen watched as various emotions played across Emma's face. "So, he's not the kidnapper after all?" she asked with an expression of immense relief. Then the frown developed as she asked, "But, what's happened to him then?" And even deeper furrows dug into her forehead as she pondered, "And the evidence that the girl had been in his car?" They were sitting in the shade on her front porch on a sunny Saturday afternoon, and Galen found himself curious about the state of her living room on this visit, but had no opportunity to view it. He'd noticed that the amount of disarray had a lot to say about Emma's frame of mind.

"Those are the exact same questions that we have at the moment," he replied, "and right now I don't think we're any closer to knowing the answers to any of them. I'm back to wondering why Mr. Armlin would decide to disappear, if he chose to do so on his own, or who would wish to harm him." Galen's cell phone rang, and he looked down at the screen to see it was Jan calling. He dismissed the call.

"And the connection with the girl?" asked Emma.

"Of course, I'm interested in that, too, but it seems like that's the most difficult detail of this whole case to explain at this time—if we ever do fit that little piece into the bigger puzzle."

"Well, to answer your first question, to me it would be just about impossible for Bob to have walked away from his life here. He loves his job, and he loves me. I know that. He wouldn't just... leave," and tears welled in her eyes from that adamant belief.

"I agree," said Galen, "so now I want you to think again about anyone in his personal or professional life who might want to harm him."

"I just can't..." Emma was saying when Galen's cell phone rang again, and he held up a finger to halt her for a moment. He shaded his phone screen with one hand and saw he had a voice message and that it was Jan trying to reach him again. *Must be important for her to call twice*, he thought.

"Sorry to interrupt," he said. "This will just be a second," and he turned a little away from Emma to converse with Jan.

"Hi, hon, look—I'm in the middle of something..." he began when he was cut off.

"What?" he asked in sudden alarm. "Is he hurt?" He listened patiently for a moment, then cut in himself. "Jan, is he alive?" After a pause and a deep intake of breath, Galen asked, "Where are they taking him?" He nodded as if Jan were before him. "I'll be right there," and he hung up the phone.

Galen stared for a long moment both at and through Emma, as if taking time to reorient himself, and then quickly rose from the patio chair. "Sorry Emma, I have a personal emergency."

"What is it?" asked Emma seeing the stress in Galen's face.

"My boy's been shot."

"Oh, my God!" exclaimed Emma. She was about to ask for details, but Galen was already half-way down the sidewalk and on his way to his car.

# Chapter 18.

THE OLD sedan rocked forward as Galen jammed the gears into 'park' the moment he'd squeezed into an available space near the emergency room entrance. He'd tried to call Jan back on his way to the hospital, but had dropped his phone onto the floorboards. Failing to reach it with much swearing at each of the far-too-many stoplights, he now wedged his door against the car next to him and just managed to feel and retrieve the phone that had worked its way under his front seat. He slammed the door and hit the lock button on his key fob, and was just about to sprint to the emergency entrance when he stopped at the rear end of his car. *I'm working myself up into a frenzy*, he thought. *Things will just spin out of control unless I'm in control myself, so I'd better make that happen.* He took a deep breath and looked around the parking lot for something to focus on. Spotting a bedraggled potentilla on a little island of landscaping near the entrance, he walked purposefully over to it and crouched down. He took his time and examined each branch and the few yellow flowers that the plant was offering the late-spring day until he was paying total attention to the plant. Feeling much calmer, he stood and took two deep breaths before he turned and walked with an even pace to the automatic doors of the emergency room and then inside.

Jan spied him approaching the waiting area and immediately burst into tears. He swept her up and held her tightly at first and then more comfortingly until she was able to find the words she sought. Ryan was on one of the hard-plastic benches with a tear-stained face and looking absolutely crushed. The thighs of his pants and front of his tee shirt were stained a dark red. As soon as Jan's breathing slowed, Galen held her at arm's length and said, "It's OK, Jan. No matter what, it'll be OK." He focused on her eyes until he had her attention. "Now, can you tell me what happened?" Jan began in a rush mixed with sobs for breath, and Galen held her again. "Just wait, hon. You don't have to tell me everything at once."

Finally, Jan drew back and said more determinedly, "Monty's been shot..."

"On accident!" squeaked Ryan, and then more gutturally, "I didn't mean to! It just went off!" The entire world had suddenly disappeared, including the waiting room that surrounded them. There were just him, Jan, and Ryan in the otherwise empty universe.

"All right, Ryan," said Galen in an even voice, "just calm down. I'm going to hear what your grandma has to say, and then you, too, OK?" And Ryan nodded, bending over and covering his head with his hands. "OK, hon," as he turned back to Jan.

She took a deep breath and then explained. "Monty's been shot and he's in the operating room. The medics said he has a wound in his hand and in his lower abdomen. They assured me that it doesn't appear to be life threatening, but they're unsure about the extent of the damage." Galen nodded, still processing what had happened. "I'd taken the morning for myself and gone to the Saturday bible study and then did some shopping on the way home. I turned into our street and saw the ambulance and police car with flashing lights. They were just trying to get the gurney out of the front door when I parked the car. The police were talking to Ryan, and they almost didn't let him come with me to the hospital." She paused and looked at the floor. "Monty and Ryan were playing with my gun, which I must have left on the nightstand, and it went off."

"We weren't playing!" said Ryan adamantly from the bench.

"Then, what happened, Ryan?" asked Galen.

"Aaaaaaarg!" the boy roared, startling an old couple in the otherwise empty ER waiting room. Galen could sympathize, because he'd been there before. The frustration at not being able to somehow grab ahold of time and wrench it backwards—wanting to feel it wriggling in your hands as you yanked it back. But this was impossible, and Ryan was just learning that sad fact: the plate as it slips out of your fingers as gravity takes over; the brake pedal pushed half-a-second too late.

Galen stepped over and put his hand momentarily on Ryan's shoulder. He didn't know if it helped, but he knew any kind of grounding would be a comfort. Ryan shuddered and couldn't meet either of his grandparents' eyes, but the words came pouring out.

"We were doing time trials. You know, like the police drills," and Galen pictured it immediately. He'd had guns in the house since before the boys had joined them. His gun safe held two shotguns, one 308 rifle he preferred for deer, a 30.06 for bigger game, and two handguns. And he always had a piece that he wore home from work, routinely locking it in a small bedroom safe soon after he entered the house. He'd taught the boys gun safety from the first moment they'd entered his household—how to clean, disassemble, reassemble, load, unload, check, and recheck each one. He'd taken them out to the firing range in Portland, or to his brother's property in Enterprise where they set up targets, and they knew to treat each weapon as if it was loaded, and to obey all of the rules of respect for a very dangerous piece of equipment. "Gram's pistol was out on the nightstand, and I noticed it when I set down the laundry," he choked but regained control. "We'd never taken a Ruger apart before, and so we made sure it was empty and then took it down as far as we dared and then put it back together again. Then I had the stupid idea to have a race—see who could break it down and put it back together again in the fastest time."

"So, then how did it go off?" asked Galen with a clenched stomach.

Ryan didn't answer, but only held his head in his shaking hands.

"Ryan? How did it fire?"

Ryan waited and then in a weak voice said, "We stopped the timer when the clip was snapped home." Galen gave an inner groan. "I'd just finished my trial and Monty was reaching out for it to take his turn when it just..." Ryan could barely get the next two words out, "went off," he whispered.

"Oh, Ryan," Galen couldn't help but mutter.

Suddenly Jan was lurching for a nearby wastebasket and vomiting violently, dropping to her knees with the spasms that wrenched her gut. She turned to him with eyes that Galen could easily interpret. Jan was wracked with guilt for having carelessly left her pistol on the nightstand. Guns were part of Galen's life—as a kid with a dad as a hunter, as a teen with his own shotgun and passion for shooting quail, as a brother who went on hunting trips with his siblings, and as a policeman and then detective who carried a firearm as protection at all times. Jan had been uncomfortable with having weapons around at first, but over the years, she'd begun to feel that the only way to keep herself safe was to own a handgun, too. She had friends who carried, and the news she and Galen watched nightly made them feel that the country was not the safe, homey place it had been when they were young. Galen had tried to dissuade her, solely because he'd seen what colleagues had gone through when they'd been required to use their weapons in the line of duty, and he questioned whether Jan would ever find herself in those dire circumstances when a gun would be necessary, in spite of how bleak the nightly news seemed to be. But Jan had insisted, and they occasionally went to a firing range together to practice, it becoming a sort of bond between them. "I... I took it out of the safe, and then forgot it in my rush to make the meeting," she managed before using the wastebasket again. *This is the same reaction I've seen in other folks who had to use their guns against another person,* Galen thought—as he bent over and helped her up. An orderly was at their side immediately with a damp cloth for Jan's face and forehead, and she gently removed the wastebasket from Jan's hands for cleaning.

Once Jan was settled on a couch and her shaking had subsided, Galen went to the admittance desk to see what else he could discover about Monty's condition, but the nurses were refusing to give him anything but platitudes until the surgery was completed, even with him flashing his badge about. He called Tom Weston and let him know the situation, receiving Tom's condolences and hopes for a positive outcome.

Two hours later, a doctor finally emerged and invited the family down a hallway and into a small conference room off the main nurse's station. "Monty is stable, and will survive this accident," he began as they were all seated. "The bullet went through his right hand where it shattered the third and fourth metacarpals, and then passed into the right side of his lower abdomen, fragmenting the back of the pelvis. We've repaired the intestines and have clipped together the major bone fractures on the hip. He's a very lucky boy. The bullet missed two major arteries that run through the hip to supply the leg, and the shockwave from the impact doesn't appear to have damaged any organs. All those abdominal wounds should heal well. We will need another minor surgery to remove some bone fragments pushed out into his gluteus maximus. The bullet deflected off the pelvis and traveled to his upper thigh, but we're considering leaving it where it is. It isn't lead, and it is in a more difficult spot to extract, however, it should do no further damage if left alone. The two longer-term problems are that the insertion points of several major muscles to the pelvis were severed or damaged, and that the hand will require extensive work in the future. We did our best to align what was left of the metacarpals, but there is bone, tendon, and nerve damage that will take several reconstructions and extensive physical therapy to heal properly."

They all three had the same reactions. Initial relief that Monty had survived the shooting, but a growing state of numbness as they thought of the journey he now faced. "Where is he?" asked Galen, and "When can we see him?" asked Jan at the same instant.

"He's unconscious right now from the anesthetics and pain meds and should stay that way for another four to six hours," said Dr. Axelrod. "We'll move Monty into intensive care, and you'll be able to visit him tomorrow morning. I'd say he's facing three days in the ICU, then maybe a week or two in general care," he paused and consulted a tablet he'd brought with him. "We have him scheduled for another hand surgery in two weeks, or sooner if the swelling goes down, and we're going to wait on the hip to see if things progress naturally, if that's alright with you." There were nods from both Galen and Jan as they tried to process the information.

"So, what are your expectations? Will he be able to use his hand? Be able to walk?" asked Galen.

"Oh, yes, certainly," said the doctor. "How well is the real question, and we'll have to wait and see before we can answer that."

When they left the conference room, there were two police officers standing a respectful distance from the entrance. Galen recognized one, and patrolman Black nodded back, stepping forward. "Hello, Detective Young," said Black. "As you can guess, we're here to get statements from those involved, especially Ryan, so I'll need to ask him to accompany us to a more private area."

Ryan had heard, but Galen said, "Ryan, these gentlemen will need to talk to you for a minute. Just be straight with them, alright?" Ryan nodded as the second officer led him back into the small meeting room.

Black touched Galen's shoulder and said, "I know this is going to be tough on you guys."

Galen nodded back and said, "It already is, John, it already is."

After the police were finished with Ryan, they needed to ask Jan some questions as well. She'd elected to stay with Monty in the recovery room, so the officers joined her there, and Galen drove Ryan home. "Why didn't you call your Gram when Monty was shot?" Galen asked out of curiosity as they left the parking lot.

"I could see it was bad, real bad, and so I called 911 right away. Then I was so busy grabbing towels and trying to wrap his..." Ryan was turning white and Galen pushed the button to lower the window on the passenger side, "oh, God... to wrap his stomach and put pressure on the wound to try and stop the bleeding." Galen pulled the car over along the entrance drive and it was Ryan's turn to be sick after he'd thrown open the door. Getting back in and buckling up, color was at least returning to his face.

They drove for a long spell lost in their own thoughts and then Galen asked, "Ryan, after all of the care we've taught you boys to take around guns, how could this happen? What were you thinking?" And Ryan lapsed into silence, sad and embarrassed, but giving this question serious consideration. As they neared home, he finally said, "It all seemed so under control. We were careful and made sure the first thing we did was take out the clip and check the chamber. Then we slowly took the Ruger apart and slowly put it back together. A fun time-trial just seemed like the next thing to do, and if it was a race, it seemed to make sense that the timer didn't stop until the clip was in and it was completely back together. It just seemed so natural."

Galen had nothing to say. He sensed that yelling at or disciplining Ryan would do absolutely no good—watching his brother try and recover was going to be punishment enough—along with the inevitable police involvement and interest by the media. He also knew at this point that even well-meaning words of encouragement would fall on deaf ears. It was best for him to just let his grandson be for now.

§

As much as he wanted to check in on Monty the next morning, Galen set off on a more important mission—telling the boy's mother, Beth, what had happened. It was a task he dreaded, but knew he was the only one in the family who would visit her, and a phone call simply wouldn't suffice for something of this magnitude. He was groggy from a fitful night of sleep and sipped at a travel-mug of coffee as he opened the front door to head to his car. Two news vans had already parked in front of the house, and he had to try and mutely walk past their television cameras just to get to the street.

"Detective Young," asked one reporter with a microphone just as he was passing the first unit, "what can you tell us about your son?" Galen shook his head and kept walking.

"Was it your gun, Detective?" asked a second reporter as he stepped onto the sidewalk.

"You know I have no comment, fellas," said Galen when members of several other news agencies started to converge. Cameras wielded by each paper's photographer clicked away as he reached his old beater, and he could just imagine the pictures that would be chosen for the next editions. *This is going to be worse than I thought*, came to him as he left the crowd behind and numbly drove down to Wilsonville, arriving at the Coffee Creek complex just at the beginning of visiting hours.

It took some time for Beth to enter the common meeting room since she wasn't accustomed to receiving visitors on the weekends and had been busy in the greenhouse at the far end of the facility. Her look of curiosity changed to one of worry as she approached Galen, knowing from his expression that something was amiss. "What is it, Galen?" she asked warily when she stood before him. "Has something happened?"

Galen again noted the lack of familiarity that she'd adopted toward him since her incarceration. He slowly nodded and then met her eyes with a level stare. "Beth, there's been an accident—Monty's been shot."

Beth sucked in her breath. "Is he alive?" she managed.

Galen nodded and said, "He's in the hospital, and they expect him to recover..." After the initial expression of total shock, her next reaction was totally unexpected. She attacked her father, launching herself at him, slamming her fists into his chest, rocking him back on his heels. "How could you let this happen?" she screamed. "I trusted you! I trusted you!" Galen tried to calm her and took several steps back from her flailing arms, but she kept coming forward and was in a fury. Two guards raced over and immediately restrained the frantic inmate. Within moments, she was being led away with her wrists strapped together behind her back. Galen followed as closely as they'd allow, trying to tell the guards that it was nothing—she'd received bad news and they needed desperately to talk. As a third guard stepped in front of him and blocked his path, Beth disappeared through steel security doors.

He spent the next hour trying to convince the prison authorities that her reaction was perfectly normal, and that he needed to speak to her. "I'm sorry, Mr. Young, but we can't allow this kind of behavior, no matter what the circumstances. Our rules are very clear—no contact other than a brief hug is to be allowed between the inmates and visitors, and we have a zero-tolerance policy for assault or any aggressive behavior," said the person of highest authority that Galen could summon.

"Yes, but these are extraordinary circumstances—her son's been shot, and I was relaying the upsetting news to her."

"I'm sorry, but rules are rules, and Ms. Young is going to have to face the consequences of her actions. We cannot allow you to see her now. You'll have to relay your information in some other manner."

He hated to try it, but in desperation he pulled out his badge, "Look, I needn't remind you that I'm one of you, Superintendent Mallory. Just a quick word is all I ask, please."

"And I hate to remind you that you're just another citizen in here, Detective Young."

Nothing could dissuade Mallory, so Galen spent another half-hour in barely contained anger and frustration writing out some scribbled pages that they would deliver to Beth when it was allowed.

# Chapter 19.

ASIDE FROM the hoses, tubes, bandages, and beeping machines, Monty at first looked surprisingly well to Galen. *I must have expected much worse*, he thought as he slowly became aware of the sallowness in Monty's skin tone and his labored breathing. Jan had been exhausted from the little sleep she got in the hospital the night before and had returned home while Galen was delivering the news to Beth at the Coffee Creek Correctional Facility, so he was alone when he took the bedside seat and watched over Monty for the next few hours. The boy would seem to come out of the sedatives and look blankly around, but then his eyes would roll up to the top of his head and he'd be out again.

Jan joined them in the late afternoon. "How's he doing?" she whispered as she pushed aside the thin blue curtain that served as a door and stepped inside the room. She herself looked much better to Galen and had gained a sort of resolve that said that she was now ready for the long haul—at least he hoped he was reading her correctly.

"Not any change that I can see—they still have him pretty doped up. How's Ryan?"

"He's coping in his own way. He says he finally crashed heavily sometime late last night and was just waking when I got home. I had to wade through a crowd on our doorstep when I got there. Ryan says that there were several knocks on the door and phone calls for the first couple of hours after that, but I slept through it all. The press finally cleared out after lunchtime when they saw that we weren't going to be offering them much in the way of interviews. No hangers-on when I left home, but I did notice some reporter-types at the reception desk downstairs just now. Thank God, they're not allowed into this section of the hospital." Jan looked from Monty, to the bed, to the instruments beside him, and then to her husband. "This is it, isn't it Galen? This is the real deal?" Galen nodded gravely. She dropped her head for a moment and continued, "Anyway, Ryan spent some time peeping out of the windows at the reporters and then after lunch he texted and talked to friends. When I left him at home, he was lost in a video game."

"Well, it'll take a few days for all of this to sink in," said Galen. "For all of us."

"I know," Jan replied in a deflated tone, studying the IV in Monty's arm. Then after a few moments her head popped up. "Say, do you happen to know who Liz is?"

"Nope... Liz who?"

"I don't know. I overheard Ryan..."

"Wait—yes. Monty was claiming that Ryan has a girlfriend the last time we went out to Coffee Creek, and he mentioned a Liz."

"Ahh, that explains it," said Jan now with a slight smile. "Most of his time on the phone was with Liz." She took the chair on the opposite side of the bed and held Monty's free hand gently in her own. There was no reaction from the boy. "So how did Beth take the news?"

"Not well. In fact, not well at all," Galen stared at her across the bed. "I started to tell her about the shooting, and she completely lost it. She whaled on me and screamed that it was my fault—until the guards dragged her away. I tried to get them to let me see her, but they refused. I'll try again tomorrow, but I think that outburst might have cost Beth some more of her freedom. I left a long note explaining what'd happened, but I'm not sure when they'll let her read it."

"Oh, great," said Jan in resignation. "She's always been the one to shut us out, and to top it off, it wasn't even your fault."

"Oh, yes, it was," lamented Galen. "I'm currently responsible for everything bad that's happened in her life."

They were silent for several minutes just sitting and watching Monty breathe. "So, what are we going to do about Ryan?" asked Jan in an anxious tone.

"Jeez, honey, I don't know," replied Galen. "I'm actually glad that he can try and lose himself in a video game at this point. I decided last night that lecturing him would do no good. He knows that he fucked up." Jan started, her mouth turning sour at his word choice. "Pardon my French," he added quickly, getting up and pacing a little. "I think the best thing we can do is to try and get him as involved as possible in his brother's rehabilitation. I think that'll be the most effective cure for the both of them." He walked over to the doorway as if he wanted to leave, but then returned to his seat. "How we're going to resolve things between him and his mother, however, I have absolutely no clue."

"Maybe that's the purpose for Beth's being there and away from all of this—to atone for her sins in confinement," said Jan with some intensity, "and now in solitude."

Galen realized that at times like this he hardly knew his wife at all. And yet he was getting used to Jan's increasingly judgmental attitude. "Yes, but her son—both sons are suffering right now and..." he began without a real means to finish his sentence. Silence filled the room except for a constant beeping in the background.

# Chapter 20.

GALEN FOUND a parking spot in the garage beneath the Police Bureau that Monday and, based on a few encounters on the way to the elevators, it was becoming obvious to him that word about Monty had spread throughout both the Bureau and the city. *Detective's Son Critically Injured by Gunshot,* said one column heading that morning, and *Brother Shoots Brother in Firearm Accident,* said another. He was greeted with several words of encouragement and pats on the back as he made his way, first to his office, and then to the conference room for the 8:00 AM briefing. "Galen, so sorry about Monty," said Jenkins, and "Hang in there, buddy," said Pembrook among the many condolences he received as he took his seat.

"OK everyone," said Tom Weston as he stepped up to the podium. "I'm sure you've all heard, but for those few hermit Scorpio's who haven't, we've had a personal tragedy this weekend. Galen's grandson was shot in an accident at home and is currently recovering in the hospital. I'm happy that you've joined us this morning, Galen, but I want you to know that you should take any time you require to see to Monty's needs. And let us know of anything we can do to help." Galen nodded his thanks, and there were some uttered affirmations and an awkward smattering of applause.

Tom glanced down at his notes. "First off, we have more information this morning on the Melissa Davidson case. The silver Nissan Sentra sedan that was stolen in The Dalles and showed up at the Canadian border has been found abandoned in Billings, Montana. A patrol car discovered it around 3:00 AM near the Billings Clinic Hospital. Montana State Patrol and the Billings Police Department are scouring the city for either the suspect or any cars that may have been stolen last night because, knowing this guy's M.O., he might have jacked another car. The Patrol is trying to set up surveillance stations on the highways along the state borders, especially at the North Dakota and Wyoming crossing points since he seems to be heading in that direction, but those stations will only work to spot him if he's taking a major route out of the state. So, as of now, we're awaiting any further word from Montana. Jenkins, Pembrook, anything new over the weekend on your end?"

Jenkins spoke first. "There's absolutely no trace of Davidson or her abductor on the security cam footages taken at the train and bus stations serving Portland and The Dalles. No one in the videos resembled either the perp or Melissa even remotely. Unless they were heavily disguised at the stations, I'd say he definitely took a car and headed out of Portland up The Gorge to The Dalles after he kidnapped the girl."

Pembrook was next. "I checked with the Davidsons, and Mrs. Davidson had absolutely no recollection of ever seeing the suspect's face before. She said she had spoken with Galen earlier and had easily recognized Armlin in his picture associated with his newspaper column. She has a memory for faces, so I don't think she ever saw the perp." And then Cushing spoke, "I joined the search for an abandoned vehicle in The Dalles and so far, they haven't discovered a single car reported missing from the Portland area. They're still running plates for registrations on nearly every car in town, but so far nothing."

"What if this wasn't the only car switch?" asked Jenkins suddenly. "What if he traded cars in Hood River, or, hell, even in Vancouver, Washington and then left that one in The Dalles when he jacked the silver sedan?" Tom thought for a moment. "Good point, Stan. We've probably got the Oregon registrations covered, but I don't know if they're keeping track of Washington plates." Turning to Cushing he said, "Follow up on this, Deb. See if any cars are missing from Vancouver that might have shown up there." Cushing nodded and entered this into her tablet.

Tom shuffled his papers. "We've had a huge lead on the murder of Cordoba, and so I want Pembrook to help out Daley on that one. Gang violence is expected, so our SERT will be involved, as well. Are you up to date on this, Michael?" Pembrook shook his head and so Tom said, "Daley, bring him up to speed. I can't think of anyone not up to their neck in other cases, but do we have any volunteers to help with this?" Two hands shot up. "OK, you two join Pembrook for the briefing and thanks."

"Now, the only thing left is the Armlin case, and it's losing steam since we've exhausted nearly all of our leads. Galen, I want this to be your prime focus now with any time you can devote away from your family." Galen nodded. "I think we should forget about the hairs from Melissa Davidson that were discovered in his car for the time being. Maybe that link will come to light later, but we need to focus on anyone at all who might have wished Mr. Armlin harm. Look at friends, friends of friends, jealousy at work, irate readers, anyone that sticks out. I think it has to be one of them—I don't think he just walked into the Columbia River."

"I don't think so either, Captain. I'll let you know what I find."

"OK, people, that's it," said Tom, stuffing papers into a folder. "Make us proud!"

Galen stepped into his office after the meeting to find a voice-mailbox filled with requests by the media for interviews. Unable to put off the inevitable, he dialed the first number in the list and talked to a reporter from The Portland Mail. He'd just hung up when he received a call from the County Prosecutor wanting to discuss the options they were pursuing in forming a potential case against Ryan. This call took the better part of an hour and, at the end, it left Galen feeling unsure of the path the Prosecutor would follow in charges against his grandson.

# Chapter 21.

WORD CAME later that morning that a car stolen in Vancouver, Washington was discovered behind a crumbling garage in Lyle, a small town up the Columbia River from Vancouver on the Washington side. Across the river and only about ten miles upstream from Lyle lay The Dalles. Tom called with the news of the discovery as Galen was driving back down to Wilsonville to visit Beth. "It looks like Jenkin's hunch was right. A car's been found in Lyle, Washington and is being dusted for prints, but some blond hairs and a doll were found in the back seat, so it looks like Melissa could have been transported in it," said Tom. "How the hell he got her to Vancouver, stole a car there and abandoned it in Lyle, and then got her the ten miles from Lyle and across the bridge into The Dalles with nobody noticing remains a total mystery. The guy's smart and as slippery as an eel."

"Well, at least the pieces are being filled in. Thanks for the update, Captain, and sorry I wasn't in the office..." began Galen.

"That's OK, Galen," there was a long pause, "and good luck with Beth."

Galen had talked to three administrators up the command chain at Coffee Creek before he was finally given permission to see his daughter. Separate calls from Tom and Chief Osborne had helped convince the authorities that there were extenuating circumstances which should be considered for her outburst. Still, when Galen arrived at the facility, he could only speak to her through thick glass.

"Hi, Beth," said Galen. "I'm sorry I didn't break the news to you more gently."

Beth had obviously been waiting for him for some time and glared back without saying a word.

"How are you holding up?" asked Galen. "Did they let you read the note I left you?" No reply from her. "Monty's still sedated but looking better." This was also met with stony silence and what he took as an unrelenting hatred from her eyes.

"Beth, they made special concessions to let me see you..." Galen began as his daughter rose, turned, and headed to the guard and door behind her. "You know, I'm not coming back unless you ask for me to," he said, unsure whether she heard him as she was let out of the small room.

Galen sat for several moments, surprisingly unsure what to do next. Pushing himself slowly out of his chair, he stood up straight, thanked the guard with him in the room on his side of the glass, and headed towards his car.

*What did I expect?* thought Galen as he chose I-205 to head north to Providence Medical Center. *She's just had terrible news about her 12-year-old son because of actions by her 8th grader; she's trapped where she is and has just made matters worse for herself with her outburst; and she's absolutely powerless to do anything about any of it. And then I strut in repre-*

*senting everything that's holding her back.* Muttering to himself, *Still, she acted like a little bitch*, he couldn't help but add.

# Chapter 22.

MONTY WAS awake when Galen entered the room in the general care wing just at lunchtime. He was being fed jiggly red Jell-O by a young orderly and was able to take sips from a cup of ice-water by himself. "How's it going, big guy?" asked Galen with a hopeful grin.

Monty flashed a weak smile. He had obviously prepared for this moment. "Guess I've taken worse hits than you, huh, Gramps?" he asked in a John Wayne-ish voice.

Galen's grin broadened. "I'd say so, bud," he drawled. "I'd have you for backup any day!"

Monty beamed at this, but then paid attention to the Jell-O, obviously craving more substantial food. The orderly could see it, too. "They said you should be able to start more solid food soon," she said. "Gelatin now, but milkshakes and hamburgers in a few days."

"Can't wait!" the boy exclaimed.

"So, how are you feeling, Monty?" asked Galen. "Any pain?"

"My hand sure hurt this morning, but they gave me something for it, and they're pumping ice-water over it to keep it cool for a while," he said, pointing to the blue tubes that ran up under his bandages from an ice-water container below his bed. He'd finished eating and took another sip of water. "How are Gramma and Ryan?" he asked, but was soon asleep in the middle of Galen telling him how they were.

Galen had come prepared to put in some casework while visiting his grandson and took out a bundle of folders from his briefcase as he took a seat at the bedside. These editorial articles now seemed to be the only link he had to Armlin, and he held out hope for either insight into the man himself, or clues about how others saw him. He flipped through the top editorials until he found one he hadn't read.

*Old and cranky*

*Is the end result of aging to become grouchy, opinionated, and cautious—the time-honored stereotypes? Three recent events brought this question to my mind, since they are pertinent to me at my stage of life. In the first instance, someone 'totally paused' instead of stopping at the red stop sign near our house and then roared up the narrow street past me. I yelled for him to slow (the hell) down and was rewarded with a single-digit salute as he disappeared up the street. In the second event, I was on a short bicycle trip with a friend and stopped near a young woman who was also out for a ride and I suggested that she really should wear a helmet to protect her head. I was met with an unkind glare as she pedaled off in a huff. And in the third, on that same mountain-bike outing, my cycling partner remarked that I should let loose more—that I was riding far too cautiously to have any fun. He said that I was riding like an old man.*

David Ackley

*Why did I yell at the speeder on our street to the point that he considered me an old grouch? I've been driving a car now for fifty-four years, and still thrill at the joy of a road trip and the sense of freedom a car can provide. However, I also now know the damage and destruction that such powerful machines can engender. When I was young, I rear-ended the car in front of me because of inattention and following too closely. I've been rear-ended myself three times and counting, by people following too close behind. I've taken off a door that was flung open by another car as I pulled into the parking space next to them in a parking lot. I've lost control numerous times on the ice and ended up in the ditch on several of those occasions. I've also been the first on the scene of three accidents that required ambulances, and I've witnessed five pedestrians and three bicyclists hit by cars, in all cases helping out the best that I could amidst the blood, pain, and suffering. Based on these experiences, I think we should all slow down and pay attention so that I don't have to behave like an old grump and feel the need to warn other drivers of awaiting calamity.*

*Why am I so cautious on the bicycle? In my youth, I had multiple bicycle accidents that resulted in scrapes to knees and hands. But this isn't the only reason that I exercise caution lately. I think experiences add up. I've been stung by swarms of wasps, hiked for miles with blisters, both cut and caught myself while fishing, cut myself cooking, slammed my thumb in a car door, tripped on pavement and cracked my head, slipped on black ice and broken my tailbone, broken two bones and dislocated a shoulder skiing, burned my fingers to blisters, cut my foot on glass at a beach, been beaten up and limped home, and endured other events too numerous to count. Everyone has their own list of injuries, so how has this affected me person-ally? If I see an older gentleman trip and go down, I hate to offend anyone, but my scrotum tightens up. I can't help it—my body reacts. It seems to re-live any pain it's suffered on seeing any similar misfortune happen to another person. I hate the so-called 'funny' videos where people are injured, and the event is caught on tape for others to laugh at. All I see is the pain.*

*So, is the end result of getting old to become grouchy, opin-ionated (as in this column), and cautious? Perhaps. But I also think a measured vigilance is a badge we start to wear that pays respect to the life we've lived so far, and the experiences we've survived. I'm not sure about my friend who is near my age, but the young simply haven't lived long enough to accumulate the scars. I wish I could pass this on to the driver, the cyclist, and my friend, but they'll need to feel their own bumps and bruises to earn that badge. I just hope they live to receive it.*

*Oh, my God, why should I be reading this now?* thought Galen as he looked over at Monty while reliving the sharp knife that had once tried repeatedly to penetrate his own ribcage, his broken nose, and the one gunshot he'd endured while on duty in Pendleton. *Here I am feeling my old scars, and this little guy's just starting out, already with a shattered hand and hip.* He sat back in his chair and took a deep breath. *I hardly remember my fall out of that tree when I was young though, so maybe Monty won't remember much of this either when he gets to be my age...* Galen reflected that he wasn't sure that he understood what Armlin meant about being grouchy about his experiences though. *Well, he is ten years older, so maybe I'll cotton to what he's saying in a few years.*

His thoughts meandered and then he ended up thinking about Jan, Ryan and Beth—none of them physically harmed. *I'm sure Armlin would have something to say about psychological bumps and scrapes, too....* He broke from his thoughts and picked up the next article which he found to be much more esoteric.

*Fact vs. Opinion*

*We don't know everything about ourselves, our planet, or our universe, but thanks to science and critical thinking, we've enhanced the level of detail that we as a species do understand. Rarely are the revelations cut and dried: 'Hey, that's not a solid; it's a liquid!'; rather, it's 'The solid state of this substance also shows some liquid properties,'—like glass. Science is a continual process of hypothesis, testing, and verification, building on what we've confirmed to create new hypotheses and so on.*

*I've been to several public meetings about roads, infrastructure, wildlife, and climate, and have noticed a common phenomenon. The person whose job it is to study the issue spends months or years collecting data, analyzing it, developing and running models, doing statistical analyses, having his work peer reviewed, and finally distilling the results for presentation to the public. I'm reassured when occasionally these results are confronted with an alternate study in disagreement with the* findings presented, verified data that does not jibe with that in the study, or different interpretations from another statistical method or model. That's how it's supposed to work—all the information is at the same level, meets that same standards—all based on fact. All subsequent arguments are based on the same footing.

What bothers me is when an opinion or a subjective observation is treated with the same weight as the scientific information. A previous meeting of the Pacific Fisheries Management Council had engendered numerous letters to the editor about sea lions and salmon, so out of curiosity, I attended a recent gathering of the Council since it was held here in Portland. What I heard at this session wasn't that controversial - they were being presented with rockfish population estimates and making recommendations on catch levels—but it provided an excellent example of my pet peeve. The population dynamics scientist had just concluded his presentation, and there were many questions about the model and assumptions that went into it. There had been some new studies that shed further light on the age structure of the population, and these had been incorporated into the model. The Council was just about to vote to put further limits on catch levels when an industry representative gave testimony that ran along the lines of, 'We've been fishing these seamounts for years, and know the fish patterns. The reason the age looks different is because you took your samples during the day. Everyone knows the bigger fish come up at night to feed, so your data is skewed. You should verify your results and come back next year.' This was enough to change the Council's votes for the year's quota.

The man could have been correct, and his argument sounded logical. The thing is, we don't know. The scientist was never given the chance to respond or state what he knew about the diurnal migration of rockfish. It could be this was included in the study or reflected in the model. What the man said might not even be true. What bugged me, and I have seen it time and time again, is that this one statement was given the same weight as the peer-reviewed, multi-year study by multiple professionals from an agency whose job it is to know about these fish. The anecdotal information didn't meet the same standards as the scientist's data.

The line between fact and opinion becomes blurred the more political the issue. On the local front, I've seen studies cherry-picked for the sometimes-rare statements that further the arguer's case regardless of the overall findings in the document. The data becomes twisted, ignored, or turned into its own opposite as each side struggles to make their points. I guess I'm sensitive lately about what truth is and become disheartened when in even the most science-based discussions, unverified information is allowed to enter the equation and is given credence. We get opinion letters to the editor daily, and that is what these pages are for. It's when opinions are presented as facts, or the arguments are based on falsehoods that bothers me, and here I am, the Opinion Page Editor. Now, in our modern political world it appears that promulgating falsehoods as facts has been elevated to the level of an art. Well, I say it's the art of persua-

*sion, manipulation, and obfuscation. It's the art of bullpucky, and we're losing our ability to see it as such.*

There was an attached reply, which he read as a follow-up.

*Dear Editor,*

*Why should I be surprised that another one of your articles should rub me the wrong way? I feel like I must stand up for the everyman and try to keep the record straight, because someone has to answer for your drivel. Did you ever think that science is just another cloak that the privileged throw about themselves so they can do as they want, and try and keep the rest of us in line? Of course, not—you're one of them.*

*I know exactly what that fisherman testifying in front of a panel of 'experts' was talking about, and yet you'd put down what he actually saw with his own eyes for the sake of some made up mathematical mumbo jumbo. Those 'models' and 'analyses' are the real make-believe and falsity—not the experience of someone actually on the fishing grounds who sees what's going on every day. At the same time, you're slandering centuries of knowledge by the Native Americans who've been fishing and hunting here far longer than us, and know the ways of nature, but they continually get put down by modern science.*

*And, of course, there was the obvious dig you made at our current President and legislatures—the ones, by the way, who are willing to call bullshit on all the pseudo-science, propaganda, and fake news. You, sir, are the fake news.*

# David Ackley

*James Madison*
*Portland, Oregon*

Galen gave an inner groan at the reply letter but had read it all before, the arguments and counterarguments, truths and half-truths, everything, he thought, blending its way into politics. *I could relate to the first article about what life throws at you, but is going through all of these just a big waste of time?* he wondered as he sighed, put away the folders, and just watched Monty's eyes flit beneath his lids as the boy dreamed.

# Chapter 23.

HE STARTED awake and immediately felt guilty. He'd come to the hospital to be with Monty and get some work done at the same time, but had fallen asleep in his chair, accomplishing neither task. Not one prone to napping, he found that his bedtime was becoming earlier and earlier with each passing year, while his time to rise never changed—5:30 every morning. *They say it comes to everyone eventually,* he thought regretfully, *the need to take an afternoon nap. Hopefully, I haven't quite reached that stage.* And yet he felt oddly refreshed. Monty was still sleeping, and he thought of reading another editorial article at his bedside, but decided to head back to the station instead.

On the way to the office, and stuck momentarily in traffic, he reflected on the articles he'd read so far. Armlin was smart, witty, and had obviously thought through his arguments with great care, yet he was also very biased, and Galen noticed that the response letters in the paper sometimes verged on strident. *I'll have to read more of the replies,* he thought, and then remembered. *I got sidelined thinking that Armlin was no longer a missing person—I wonder what happened to my request for the responses to his columns that never got printed?*

Headquarters was fairly deserted for a workday, and Galen was going to ask the receptionist about the reason for this when he remembered the Cordoba case which had probably pulled multiple officers into the field. There was a stack of newspapers from the last few days on his desk, and, with Monty's accident in the news, the articles in them had turned to gun safety, gun rights, and the fate of Ryan in the legal system. Following Galen's earlier telephone conversation with the County Prosecutor, he'd had several discussions with colleagues and attorneys, and they all ended up being depressingly vague and inconclusive. Each conversation underscored the uncertainty of whether or not his grandson would be charged with anything. The shooting was clearly an accident, but since an unsecured handgun was involved, and Ryan was under the guardianship of a police officer, the issue was receiving a high level of scrutiny.

Galen spoke to another reporter from his desk, caught up on some other paperwork, and then gave Monica Stevens a call. "Hello, Ms. Stevens, this is Detective Young again. How are you?" he asked.

"I'm doing all right, Detective," she answered. "I've heard on the news that your family has suffered an accident—I'm sorry about that."

"Thanks, Ms. Stevens," he replied.

"Your grandson is recovering?"

"Yes, he's out of Intensive Care and is doing well."

"Good. And I've also read that Bob is no longer a kidnapping suspect." There was a hint of derision in her tone.

"No, he isn't; you're correct," said Galen. "Mr. Armlin is once again a missing person, and I'm still trying to locate him."

There was a pause on the other end of the line. "Well, good," she said finally.

"And to that end, I was wondering if you were able to put together the replies to Mr. Armlin's columns that weren't published in the paper? We requested them awhile back, but things have been so busy, I dropped the ball on following up."

Monica thought for a moment, "Yes, I remember the request, and I'm fairly sure we compiled them. It was taking some time because the older articles had to be scanned in by hand, but I think they're done."

"Are they organized in any way?" he asked.

"Yes, they're cross-referenced and filed by date, respondent, title, and associated article."

"That will really help me," said Galen. "Is there any chance you could check on their status and let me know if they're ready?"

"Will do, Detective," said Monica, "and I'm glad you're still taking Bob's disappearance seriously," as she hung up.

There was a return call within half-an-hour by a staffer letting Galen know that he could pick up the files at his convenience.

§

Galen was at the office of The Oregon Sentinel the next morning, and Monica had the files already loaded onto a USB drive. To Galen's mild surprise, Ed Comstock was also waiting in Monica's cubicle when he was shown in. They shook hands and then Ed said, "I'm glad that you're still following up on

Bob's case, Detective Young, but I'm also worried that this is just going to fade into the woodwork. Bob was a friend and one of the most thoughtful guys I know, and hell, we can't even print an obituary for the poor bastard if we don't know what's become of him." This brought Monica to near tears again, despite her outward attempts to harness her emotions. Ed walked over and patted her shoulder. "And Monica has something she'd like to say to you, with me present."

Galen prepared himself for a possibly unpleasant confrontation as Monica dabbed at her eyes, cleared her throat, and began. "I'm sorry, Detective, but I feel I just have to say this. In my opinion, you've maligned both me and Bob in your investigation, and I feel that we're both owed an apology. Of course, I care for Bob, but your insinuations were way out of line as to our personal relationship. And then you wasted valuable time and energy suspecting him of being a kidnapper—a kidnapper of all things!" The last phrase was breathy as Monica struggled to maintain a professional response.

"I'm sorry you feel that way, Ms. Stevens," said Galen. "Sometimes the questions we ask are tough and personal, and they can appear to be out of line when the case turns in an unexpected direction, as it did this time. I didn't mean to disparage your character, and I hope you understand our need for diligence in trying to uncover what's happened to your friend and colleague." His phrasing wasn't natural, as Galen had uttered versions of this same speech many times under similar circumstances, but he tried his best to sound as sincere as possible.

Apparently, it was sufficient because Monica thanked him for his candor.

"You know, we live in a crazy world," said Ed after the exchange between Galen and Monica had reached an ebb, "with a lot of wacked-out people in it. I, myself, have received personal threats, just by running this newspaper, and I know that Monica and Bob have both been the brunt of abusive letters and phone calls. I hope that digging through these will help," indicating the USB drive in Galen's hand. "Maybe one of our nuts finally snapped off the tree, if you know what I mean."

"Maybe so," replied Galen, "and if you don't mind, I'd like to see a list of the people who've sent in the personal threats to you, too. We still don't know if Mr. Armlin's disappearance was intentional, like him simply walking away, accidental, or because someone was angry with him or the newspaper and took some kind of action against him. Have there been any recent threats?"

"Not since Bob's disappeared," said Ed, and Monica nodded in agreement.

"Well, let me know if you two or anyone else on the staff is threatened in any way. There may be no connection with a disaffected reader, but if there is, we don't want what might have happened to Mr. Armlin to become a trend," said Galen as he began his goodbyes.

"Detective?" asked Monica, interrupting him. "I thought you might also be interested that Andy down in archives who put the USB together mentioned that he had an odd request from Bob several days before he disappeared."

"What was that?" asked Galen.

"He said that Bob asked him to start going through every editorial by any of us that had anything to do with the government, politics outside of the election, guns, taxes, that sort of thing and start to compile a list of the responses and who made them. Andy said that he asked Bob if there was anything special he was supposed to be on the lookout for, and Bob simply said that he wasn't sure yet."

"I wonder why?" asked Galen. "Does he have the list?"

"Andy wondered why, too. No, he hadn't had time to start the list yet."

"OK, thanks, Ms. Stevens. That gives me more to think about."

# Chapter 24.

GALEN HAD checked back into headquarters and read through some reports before a planned visit with Monty in the hospital after the end of his shift. As he was finishing up some filing, Tom unexpectedly poked his head in the door. "Say, Galen, could you drop by my office before you head home?"

"Sure, Captain," he replied. "What's up?"

"Nothing urgent, I just wanted a quick chat with you when you're done here."

Galen looked at the stacks of folders and open drawers and said, "It might be, say, fifteen minutes?"

"Anytime, but like I say, it's nothing urgent."

Curiosity got the better of Galen, and so he wrapped up what he could in the next ten minutes and then left a small unfiled stack behind his desk.

"Hi, Tom," said Galen as he entered the Captain's office, "is now a good time?"

"Oh, hi, Galen," said Tom nervously. "Sure, now is as good a time as any. Could you close the door?" Galen did as he was asked and found himself oddly suspicious of his Captain's behavior. Tom rearranged some paperwork and then gestured, "Have a seat."

Galen had only seen him act like this once before. "Am I being taken off the case?" he asked.

"What?" asked Tom. "No! No, nothing like that," he said. He finished straightening the items on his desk, spread out his hands, and visibly calmed himself. "Ah, I get it," he nodded to himself and continued, "I'm acting like it's some big personnel issue, like when I have to discipline someone." Galen nodded at this and waited expectantly. Tom then almost laughed out loud. "Nope. It's my wife. And this is completely off the record—all right?"

"Yeah," said Galen, "but what is it with Carol?"

"OK, she'd kill me if I neglected to pass this on, but this is definitely not police business."

"What is it then?" asked Galen, "Is everything OK with you guys?"

Tom gave him an odd smile. "We're good. And this doesn't leave this office." Galen nodded and was about to reply when Tom continued. "Carol wanted me to give you this... information, and she wrote it down so I'd get it right." He picked up a lime-green notecard and began. "She said that she'd been thinking about your missing person, and quickly worked out that it was Mr. Armlin. She said that she held a tarot session with his picture from the newspaper and agrees with his co-worker who had a bad feeling about what might have happened to him. She's even underlined where she says she absolutely agrees. She said that in the tarot reading, the card in the most significant position came up as an inverted knight of swords. She says that this means someone has acted rashly, someone thinking it was for the best has rushed into a situation without thinking it through. She says that she's now worried that the bad feeling his coworker had is because someone has acted in an impulsive manner against Mr. Armlin."

Galen didn't know how seriously to take this and studied Tom for a cue, but couldn't find one. "Wow, well that doesn't sound good," he said. "How often is she right about this sort of thing?"

"You'd be surprised," Tom said, and handed the card over to Galen. "Well, I wouldn't read too much into this, but she was insistent that I tell you about it," seemingly contradicting himself. Galen left the office feeling confused, but realized that their marriage must be exactly like this on a daily basis, a strange blending of intuition and facts. However, Carol's note only increased the bad feeling he already had about the fate of Robert Armlin.

# Chapter 25.

RYAN WAS busy trying to play a game with Monty on his smartphone while Monty's ability for sustained concentration came and went unpredictably, much to the frustration of his brother. More importantly though, the younger sibling seemed to be happy with the attention that Ryan was paying him. Galen and Jan had moved over to some more comfortable chairs by the door. "The doctor says that Monty can begin therapy on his hip soon," said Jan.

"Fantastic," said Galen, "the boy's a trooper."

"The doctor also said that his intestines appear to be healing and that they'll start him on more solid foods tomorrow." Her voice dropped to a conspiratorial whisper. "Let's surprise him with a banana split—what do you think?"

"That sounds great," Galen replied. "Are bananas and ice cream allowed?"

"Absolutely!" whispered Jan excitedly. "I already checked!"

"When do you want to do this?" asked Galen. "I'll make sure I'm free so I can join you."

"I'm booked with clients from ten until four tomorrow," explained Jan, "and I don't see how I can get out of those appointments. How about five? Or, no—let's check when his dinner is scheduled and have it after that."

"Sounds good, hon," said Galen. He lowered his voice further so that even Ryan couldn't hear. "Hey Jan, is there any chance that you'd consider visiting Beth?" Her eyes shot up to meet her husband's. "I'm getting nowhere with her—in fact, I'm beginning to think that my visits are actually doing more harm than good. But she needs to talk to someone about what's happened to Monty."

There was a prolonged silence and then Jan whispered, "If I went, it would make matters even worse. She's so far out of God's grace now that I wouldn't even know what to say to her."

Galen listened stoically. Jan had become more rigid with every passing year, and he thought it ironic that she could spend hours in her day counselling others, and yet not be able to speak to her own daughter. "She needs to talk to one of us, Jan. I wrote her a letter explaining the details of the accident, but she stonewalled me on my last visit. She needs to know how Monty's doing. I mean, he's her son, for Christ's sake." He knew immediately that he'd chosen the wrong words.

"There's no need to use such language with me!" she expelled in a harsh whisper that raised Ryan's eyebrows. "If Beth wanted to know more about Monty, she should have been a better mother!" In his mind, Galen saw the wall between her and her daughter grow a foot higher. And he reckoned that the wall between him and his wife had raised a few inches more as well. He decided then to chance it going higher.

"And maybe you should have been a better mother, too," he said keeping his voice quiet and steady. "What were you thinking leaving your weapon out for the boys to find? What was all of that training for?" He was amazed at how calm he sounded since he found that he was absolutely furious with her. They'd been trading off shifts to sit with Monty and had had few moments since the shooting when they were alone together, so there had been no chance for Galen to speak his mind until now.

Jan was momentarily stunned, and he could see the fight to regain composure. "They had no business being in our bedroom," she began, but then checked herself. Galen was about to say, "But it was laundry day," however, he held his tongue, seeing that this was the next thought on her mind as well. "I was busy and forgot—but they knew the rules!" she hissed in frustration, turned her head to look at Monty, and then collapsed into a ball of grief.

# Chapter 26.

THE NEXT morning's briefing was uneventful, except for disappointing news about the Cordoba murder case—their prime suspect had suddenly vanished, and his apartment had been systematically ransacked. Galen grabbed another cup of coffee on the way back to his desk to perk himself up. *No word from Beth, no news on Melissa, no progress on Armlin, and the Cordoba suspect has disappeared,* he thought. *Wonderful!* Once settled and after checking his messages, he uploaded the information from the USB provided by Monica Stevens onto his computer, but decided to read another of Bob Armlin's editorials before he dove into the responses. He was looking for titles that might be controversial and provoke a heated response, but one with a scientific title caught his eye. He was curious where Armlin would go with the subject and read through it.

*Physics*

*I can still remember this vividly. Video footage of the 1994 earthquake in Los Angeles showed a car trapped on an elevated freeway just after the quake. Portions of the freeway had collapsed, and cars on the remaining sections had survived but were stuck on the upper level. With no apparent means to move forward, the idling car in the video had reversed, turned around, and then begun accelerating towards a large gap where* a portion of the freeway had disappeared, crushing the lanes below it. The moment the speeding car reached the gap, it immediately plummeted out of sight into the carnage below. There was no flying across empty space to escape unscathed; in fact, the speeding automobile didn't even come close to bridging the gap—the nose of the car disappeared from view in the milliseconds that it no longer had support from below. I hope the driver and passengers survived, because it was gut-wrenching to watch.

Contrary to what we might expect from what we view on television and in the movies, the car didn't even cover much distance before it disappeared from the camera's eye. What had possessed the driver to drive off into the abyss when he had escaped disaster and only needed to await rescue? It is possible, but unlikely, that he couldn't see the missing section of the freeway since he made no effort whatsoever to stop, continuing to accelerate over the entire distance to the gaping expanse. It's much more likely that he based his tragic decision on cinematic physics. In movies and on television, cars effortlessly jump other cars, clear obstacles, or, as in the movie, Speed, jump a non-existent section of highway—just as he had attempted—although this was a few months before the movie came out.

At 60 miles per hour, the doomed car and the bus in Speed under real circumstances, would have flown 22 feet, or less than two car lengths, in .25 seconds and would have already dropped 1 foot. After an entire second, the car, if still traveling forward at this point would have covered 88 feet and would have dropped 16 feet in the process. The bus in Speed inexplicably, except for movie magic, flew across the huge gap and survived. Some upward angle of exit is essential for any hope of a trajectory that will lift a moving object to briefly defy gravity, and there was no such aid shown in the movie. The videos of cars flying through the air of course don't show the ramps and gadgets necessary for the desired visual effect. The special-effects used on an actual bus in the movie Speed are very dated, and computer-generated imagery (CGI) is now the method of choice for the physics-defying images on the screen.

I'm not against special-effects and I love the movies. However, we all need to remember that we live in the real world: not all romances work out; not all heroes are handsome; no one can heal from a gunshot wound in half-an-hour—in fact, you just get worse in the short-term; very few people can plummet towards earth and grab a balcony railing and hold on; few can walk away from a serious car crash; few can dash through the flames in an inferno and not become seriously burned; and if Superman or Spiderman whisked by and grabbed you just before you hit the ground after a fall from a high place—you would literally become putty in their hands—your downward velocity is just too great to not turn you to mush. I'm sorry, that's just the way it is. In the real world we live very fragile lives. So, pay attention to your surroundings and remember that the actions and reactions in it behave much differently from the ones you see on the silver screen. Please, look before you leap.

*Whoa, Armlin should be the Science Editor*, thought Galen, but he wholly agreed with him. He'd seen the results of a snow machine trying to jump a barbed-wire fence ala Steve McQueen in *The Great Escape* only to end up with the near decapitation of the operator, and he'd witnessed the results of multiple drivers who thought that their cars were capable of much more than they actually were. But the most gut-wrenching examples were the best-intentioned poor souls who thought they could survive running back into a smoke-filled building, rescuing someone who was trapped on a crumbling embankment by themselves, saving someone by swimming a raging river, or stopping an out-of-control vehicle with their mere presence.

He shook his head at the memories as his thoughts turned back to Armlin. *What do I now know about the guy? He appears to love his wife and work, has friends that are devoted to him, and is obviously very well educated. Is he the kind of guy who would do a runner—just walk away from everything? I don't know. But he's obviously very aware of his own mortality and the consequences of not thinking straight. I'd label him a coward, no... cautious is more like it, from what he's written, but he sure isn't afraid to say what he thinks and doesn't seem to worry much about who might take offense. Did he provide hints of what might be askew in his life? Provoke someone in his editorials? Are Monica and Carol right in their feelings about him?*

With those thoughts in mind, he pulled out the next article, one with a title that now was of great interest to him personally and one that was sure to have many replies.

*Guns*

*As I mentioned in a previous column, the case for owning a gun in our social, urban-centric world of 7.6 billion humans needs careful reconsideration. If you own a gun for protection, that is, of course, your choice. We all want to feel safe, and in a country obsessed with guns, having a weapon to protect yourself against another gun makes sense to so many people. But in your normal life, how prepared are you for any sort of physical conflict? If, gunless, you suddenly found yourself in a fistfight with another physically fit person, how do you think you would fare, honestly? Especially if the attack was sudden? How about in an unexpected knife fight, even if you had a knife? Blades slashing, how do you think you'd stack up? Now, how about if you had a gun? Does that seem safer? If you were in a gun battle and there were loud booms and bullets coming at you, could you make an accurate appraisal of what was really happening, then shoot well enough to not hurt anyone else except your attacker? If you were surprised out of a dead sleep, could you correctly assess the situation, find and handle your weapon properly? If there was a hand on your shoulder, could you immediately tell the difference between a friendly pat or the start of an aggressive action?*

*If you own a gun, does every encounter suddenly seem to you like you're holding the only solution in your hand? Is this the way you want to interact with your fellow man? Think of the aftermath if you took another person's life, and you sur-*

*vived. Especially if you mis-judged the situation or your aim was bad. The denser the population becomes, does it really make sense to escalate our weaponry? Or, are there are too many of us armed to the teeth in an increasingly crowded society on a planet with finite resources? Have you thought about a home security system? A camera for hunting? Therapy?*

*Why is it we focus on the rare event of a home break-in and not on the not-so-rare events of gun thefts, mis-firings, accidental firings, accidental wounds, accidental homicides, and the frequent misreading of the situation at hand? I want you to be safe, but I want to feel safe, as well. Take a deep breath and think about all of the violence that does NOT happen in your life on a daily basis. Think about the people you know who have been the victims of gunshots—an ever-widening circle. I wish I could tell you to set down your weapon and back away, but I know what an enormous step this would mean to most of you. The news you watch may make it seem like a warzone out there, but that may be because you've amassed the arsenal to help make it so. Don't take this out on me, I'm only trying to help. What can you as a responsible citizen do to heal your community and make guns unnecessary? Isn't that the better long-term approach to take? Stop and chat with your neighbor, join a club, go to church or enroll in therapy if you think it would help, stop watching violent TV shows and read a good book, call your mother and tell her you love her.*

He let a huge breath empty his lungs. *But, goddamn it, why did Jan feel the need to carry a gun that she never needed to use, and likely never would?* There was no undoing the damage that had been done, both during the accident and in their conversation yesterday. Breakfast that morning had been frosty despite the late-spring weather, and Jan was in denial, attempting to start off her day as she would any other, except with a frozen veneer. Armlin's article made him wonder for the first time if the nation might be overreacting to the whole personal safety issue. *Maybe a home alarm would be just as effective?* he wondered. But then in his mind's eye, he saw someone break down their front door and assault his defenseless wife, and he shook his head. *What a fucking dilemma,* he thought. He glanced down at the accompanying response that had been published in the paper two days later.

*Dear Editor,*

*There you go again, blaming the solution instead of the problem. I hope you never have to stand by and watch your wife be raped, or your home destroyed all because you were not smart or brave enough to defend them and yourself. And it's been shown repeatedly that owning a gun for personal protection is the best and sometimes the only deterrent to physical violence against oneself, one's family, and one's possessions. While it might feel good to think about being able to turn the other cheek, if someone comes at me with a stick, I will want a bigger stick; if they come at me with a knife, I will want a bigger knife; and if they come at me with a gun, I will want a better gun, and I'll make damn sure I know how to use it. In fact, a good gun would solve all these problems in the first place.*

*Please stick to something you know about, like your paper's declining readership, rather than guns. They are the liberal's easy target, but if the second amendment was ever repealed that would be the end of the strong America that I know and love, and I won't stand by and watch people like you destroy it.*

*James Madison*
*Portland, Oregon*

*James Madison*, thought Galen, *sounds like someone using a pseudonym. Haven't I seen that name before? Is this why Armlin asked Andy in the newspaper archives to start putting together that list?* He checked back and found the same name on a response to the article about hunting that Ms. Stevens had read to him earlier, as well as the one about Fact vs. Opinion. He opened the files he'd downloaded from the USB drive that contained all the letters submitted to The Oregon Sentinel, published or not. After a search he found that several of the responses belonged to James Madison. He also noticed that Stevens had included letters that had been submitted independently to the paper for which Armlin had a reply. A letter from the previous year came to the top.

*Dear Editor,*
*This week most people will celebrate the 4th of July with a day off work, barbeques with hotdogs, and fireworks displays without a thought about what the day really means. I believe instead, we should be humbly honoring Independence Day. This is not a day to lie in a hammock and sip iced tea and*

watch the world parade by; it's the day that our founders stood up to a tyrannical ruler and risked everything to forge their own nation and be truly free. It's a day to ponder the rights and liberties for which those men long ago laid down their lives, freedoms so enduring that even today we're able to enjoy and maintain them.

We should set this day aside for reflection on what it means to be an American, because so many of our basic liberties are being threatened from within daily. Government has gotten to such a size that it has control of everything, all at the expense of our individual freedoms. Using terms like 'safety,' 'environmental protection,' 'security screenings,' 'consumer protection,' 'affirmative action,' and 'gun control,' the government is slowly restricting who can enter where, who can buy what, who can say what, and who can do what. Our choices are being taken away in the name of the 'common good' which is really a 'common bad.'

Liberty was the main concept in the establishment of this country. It means that we should be unimpeded in our personal, economic, and civil pursuits. We're not naïve infants who need to be protected from ourselves. We can make our own decisions about our health, safety, and welfare and live life however we decide to live it. We will never be free with Big Brother breathing down our necks at every step we take. My rights to that liberty were penned by the creators of our great nation and should not be taken away or diminished in any way.

The Declaration of Independence was created so that our individual liberties would not be trampled upon, and yet look *around you today. We're being wrapped, insulated, protected, coddled, and spoon-fed to the point that we can't talk or move without permission. Every new law or regulation is not set up to increase our liberties, but rather to diminish them, and I, for one, think that we shouldn't stand for it. So, on this 4*[th] *of July, enjoy your hammock because tomorrow it will be declared un-safe, or you'll have to register it after a 10-point inspection program.*

*James Madison*
*Portland, Oregon*

After a brief search, Galen found Armlin's expected reply a few documents later.

*Liberty*
*A recent letter to the editor addressed the meaning of Independence Day and the courage shown by our Founding Fathers who stood up to a tyrannical system of government. In the letter, the writer lamented the continual deterioration of our individual liberties caused by overreaching government regulation. Citing the Declaration of Independence, he correct-ly stated that liberty was one of the primary rights established by those Founding Fathers.*

*This has caused me to ponder the true nature of liberty, and how the author of that letter has missed the mark. You see, to me, the authors of the Declaration of Independence listed these three things: Life, Liberty, and the pursuit of Happiness, all together for a reason. All three are explicitly named because the Founding Fathers were wise enough to see that you can't have one of them to the exclusion of the others—they are a package deal, combined to form a larger concept, which I'll call Peaceful Coexistence.*

*A focus on liberty alone can lead to problems that become immediately apparent. Yes, you have the liberty to walk freely most places. No, you are not at liberty to walk into a stranger's house. Yes, I suppose you have the liberty to pee by yourself in the woods. No, you are not at liberty to pee in the middle of the Public Market. Yes, you have the liberty to drive. No, you are not at liberty to drive the wrong way on a one-way street. Yes, you have the liberty to own a gun and fire it in certain areas. No, you have absolutely no liberty to fire the gun in a crowded movie theater.*

*Why is this the case? There are several reasons, but the most obvious is that by stretching your individual liberties, you are impacting the Life, pursuit of Happiness, and/or Liberties of other individuals—and we all have exactly the same rights that you do. Having individual liberty does not mean that you are immune to the consequences of that liberty. Liberty does not guarantee impunity to your expressing that right without thoughtful consideration of its consequences.*

*The author of the letter also claimed that government regulations restricted his personal liberty. Now, I'm declaring right up front that I do not in any way condone the following, but if someone wants to advance the idea of liberty to the exclusion of all other considerations such as health, welfare, and safety, and extrapolate that idea into the right to some form of extreme freedom, then, by all means, add lead back into your furniture paint; add asbestos back into your insulation and ceiling stucco; put some pollutants into your drinking water; cut off your seatbelts and rip out your airbags; take off your helmet; buy meat and vegetables that haven't been screened for e coli or pathogens; don't wear sunscreen, for all I care. Just don't add lead, asbestos, or pollutants to anything you want to sell or give to others. Don't decrease our automobile, aircraft, motorcycle or any other safety standards. And don't do anything that will cause harm to another human being. You might not have thought things through, but the others of us are also guaranteed the rights of Life, Liberty and the pursuit of Happiness—I'm dubbing this Peaceful Coexistence. Don't blow it for the rest of us.*

Galen chuckled to himself. *Oooh, I bet that ruffled Madison's feathers. Was Armlin purposefully trying to egg him on?* He searched briefly for a reply to this from Madison, but found none. Included in the other letters written by Madison, however, were more ominous nuggets like *Maybe the world would be better off without you; ...send you back to wherever you came from; ...string you up just for being an idiot; I wish I could see you buried under the weight of your words;* and many more. Galen finally felt like he might be on to something.

# Chapter 27.

*IF JAMES Madison is a phony name, I'll never be able to track him down, but maybe there are really people out there with that name?* he wondered as he logged into the Bureau server and found, to his surprise, that there were actually four James Madisons listed in the greater Portland area. In addition to the basic information the computer report provided, Galen sent out a request for current street-level background about each of these four based on personal interviews by patrolmen, and by early afternoon he found that none were likely to be the authors of the letters to Armlin. One of them, James T. Madison, had said that he was a subscriber to The Oregon Sentinel and always wondered who the other James was who wrote into the newspaper so frequently, because he himself never had. Besides him, the other three were reported to be in their 70's or older, non-subscribers, and clueless about whoever their likely younger, engaged, and very opinionated namesake could be. Galen was provided with a list of the Madison's phone numbers and addresses along with summaries of the interviews, should he wish to follow up with more questions. None lived near Armlin's home address up in Goose Hollow—three lived across the river, and one lived further west towards Beaverton.

It was an hour before quitting time when Tom Weston summoned everyone into the conference room. "I have good news!" he announced as most were streaming in and still taking their seats. "They've caught Melissa's kidnapper, and the girl is now safe!" There was a clamor of voices for a moment and then Tom raised his hands for quiet. "The media is all over this, so you might have already heard that a Montana Highway Patrolman was cruising on Highway 212 which leads towards Wyoming and then over to South Dakota when he just happened to catch a glimpse of a girl with blond hair in the back of a red sedan. He pulled up the plates, and sure enough they were the same as those on a car jacked in Billings. He gave chase, but before he could stop them, the driver turned south onto Highway 112 that crosses the border into Wyoming. Luckily, Wyoming patrols had been alerted that the perp might be headed their way and they trapped him at a roadblock just inside the state line. Apparently, the kidnapper gave up without a struggle. He's in custody in Gillette, Wyoming, and Melissa Davidson is fine and being treated at the Campbell County Hospital there. They hope to have her reunited with her parents within the next 24 hours. This is going to be a real media event. The Wyoming police haven't found the guy's wallet or ID yet, so we still know nothing about the kidnapper, other than that his name is Gary Molitor. There are a number of Gary Molitors listed in our city, so we've started looking into them but we're awaiting more details before we can dig into his past here in Portland." There was a round of applause. "OK, we meet here at 8:00 AM sharp, hopefully with more information."

The dissipating crowd was focused on news of the arrest, but Galen found his mind on other things as he walked back to his office. The claims that none of the contacted James Madisons had written into the newspaper were bothering him to the point that he decided to check out at least one of the four before driving home to join Jan in bringing Monty some of his first solid food in a long time—a banana split.

He'd chosen the Madison living near Beaverton and drove until he found 5431 SW 49th Dr. just off the Beaverton-Hillsdale Highway. He pulled up in front of a faded-turquoise two-story duplex that was well maintained on the right side, but overgrown and ill-kept on the left. He got out and walked up the cracked walk to 5431 on the left and knocked on the door. After three tries, an elderly gentleman with long stringy white hair answered Galen's rapping. His mustache spread to cover his mouth and he hadn't shaved the remainder of his face for several days. "Yes, may I help you?" he asked in a mild British accent.

Galen showed his badge and asked, "I'm Galen Young with the Portland Police Bureau. Are you Mr. James Madison?"

"Why, yes, I am, what can I do for you officer? I was just visited earlier by one of your colleagues."

"And he asked you about whether you'd written letters to The Oregon Sentinel?"

"Yes, he did, and I said no, I hadn't. Would you like to step in?"

"Thank you," said Galen, and entered a somehow well-organized chaos. The tables were clean and the couch and chairs tidy, but they were surrounded by stacks of newspapers, magazines, and books—some of the piles on the verge of collapse.

"Do you happen to have any identification I can see?" asked Galen. "We just want to verify that we have the correct name."

"Yes, just a moment," said Madison and shuffled into the adjoining bedroom. When the light was switched on in that room, Galen could see that the situation was the same there— a made-up bed and sparse side-table, but the walls were lined with more teetering literature. Struggling to extract his ID from a worn billfold as he returned, Madison finally presented Galen with a recently-out-of-date driver's license containing a picture that matched the tall, thin man in front of him. He did a quick calculation and saw that James Madison was 78 years old.

"Thank you, Mr. Madison," said Galen. "How long have you lived at this address?"

"Oh, I'd say thirty years or so," replied Madison. "I moved to the States just after the war and lived with my daughter in Seattle 'til I came here. Seattle was just getting too crowded for me, so I needed to move. Portland was the right size at the time, but look at it now."

"And you live here alone?"

"Yes, my son lives in Beaverton, so he helps me with groceries and suchlike, but I prefer to be on my own."

"Can I ask if you have a computer?"

"I can't stand the things," said Madison, shaking his head. "As you can see," sweeping the room with his arm stretched out in a broad, dramatic fashion, "I prefer printed matter."

"I can see that," smiled Galen. "Do you subscribe to The Oregon Sentinel?"

"Definitely not, I'm a Mail man myself, along with The Guardian and The Independent from London, and the New York Times."

"So, no computer—how about a tablet or a cell phone?" asked Galen, being answered by a slow and deliberate shake of the head.

"Old school, huh? How do you manage, since so much is online now?"

"Oh, my son helps me out if there's something on the internet I need. He loves the modern things."

"And what is his name?"

"Thomas Redding," said Madison, and at a lifted eyebrow from Galen, he continued, "he kept my wife's last name. She wanted to make sure he remained an American citizen."

Galen nodded and took some notes, including Thomas's address and phone number. "OK, thank you very much, Mr. Madison."

"You're welcome, officer," said Madison. "Say, you never found my missing pickup, did you? I never drive that old yellow Chevy anymore, but I still wonder what happened to it."

"You say it's missing? Have you reported it?"

"Yes, about a week ago. At first, I thought my son had borrowed it, but later found out that he hadn't. He called it into the police for me, and we haven't heard anything back."

"I'll make sure to follow up on that, Mr. Madison," said Galen taking some more notes.

They shook hands as Galen bid him a good afternoon.

# Chapter 28.

GALEN WAS driving home from the west side and thought about his older grandson. Things were not going well for the boy. The school had made announcements in an assembly about the injuries to their 6th grade class member, Monty, without mentioning Ryan by name, but the entire school soon learned what had happened, both through the grapevine and from the local papers. Ryan had been pulled out of classes multiple times to meet with counselors and to speak with the police and prosecuting attorneys. It was not illegal in Oregon to leave a weapon unsecured and accessible to a minor, so Jan faced no charges on that account, but if Monty had died from his gunshot wounds, Ryan could have been facing charges for manslaughter. As it was, the boy was in limbo as to whether he might be charged with assault with a deadly weapon even though he was a minor, and the level of the crime if it came to that. Multiple conversations between the family, law enforcement, and lawyers made clear to him the very real possibility that he could still face criminal charges for shooting his brother, accidentally or not, and this was weighing heavily on him.

Luckily, the media outlets had abandoned their neighborhood stakeout, and Jan and Ryan were ready to head to the hospital the second Galen pulled into the empty driveway. They gave him a moment to change clothes and then hustled him out to the car. Galen hadn't seen Jan so hyped-up in quite some time. They chose the ice cream shop closest to the hospital, and Jan fussed over the ingredients that went into the banana split, finally deciding on traditional pineapple, chocolate, and butterscotch toppings for the three sections and covering it all with peanut and chocolate sprinkles. To Galen, the poor banana slices looked like pathetic afterthoughts. They let Ryan pick out a chocolate sundae as well, but Jan was too lost in the creation of Monty's extravagance to notice. "I think we should get some balloons to go with it," she said as they left the shop with her carefully cradling the insulated bag.

"Why?" was Galen's reaction. "Monty can eat some solid foods now, and we have a real treat for him—don't you think balloons would be a little bit over the top?"

"I just want to help cheer him up a bit," said Jan testily.

"Well, honey, I think a banana split will go a long way towards doing that, don't you?"

"I guess so," she said in resignation. "He's just been through so much. He needs to know that we care."

"I know," said Galen, "but it's going to be a long haul—this dessert seems just about right to me. It's going to take a whole bunch of these little steps until he really is healed."

Jan huffed as they maneuvered into the car with the frozen treats. The air-conditioning hopefully slowed the melting of Monty's ice-cream as well as Ryan's which was already half-way consumed.

They woke Monty with their entrance, but the boy was alert within seconds. "Hi, everybody!" he greeted them, and then, "Wow! For me?!" when Jan hauled the surprise out of the freezer-bag.

"How was dinner, bud?" asked Galen as Jan set the dish so that it was reachable by Monty's left hand and situated near his mouth.

"Great, Gramps," he said. "Mashed potatoes and gravy and a meat patty. I was soooo hungry, I ate the whole thing."

"Sounds like you have your appetite back."

"And how," managed Monty around a massive spoonful of ice cream. He had fewer tubes protruding from him than on the previous visit, and the bandaging on the hand was much reduced. Monty only made it part-way through his treat before he said, "Gram, can we save the rest for later? I honestly can't eat another bite."

Somewhat disappointed and fussing to help clean any drips off of the boy's face, Jan said, "Sure—I'll see if they can put this in a freezer for you—if you're sure you're done." Monty nodded, and she left the room to hunt down the nursing staff.

"What'd you do today, Monty?" asked Ryan. "Play video games?"

"Nah," said his brother with a yawn, "this morning, they already had me up and trying to walk down the hall, and then after a nap, they took off the old bandages on my hand and had me try and move my fingers. Man, it hurt like you wouldn't believe, but they made me do it—twice!"

"That's right, son," said Galen. "If you don't move it, you might lose it."

"That's exactly what they said," moaned Monty.

"Then it must be true."

Jan was soon back, and Monty was beginning to fade. He managed to stay awake another twenty minutes until the duty nurse let them know that visiting hours were over. They were about to say goodbye when their youngest grandson asked, "When can I go and see Mom?"

"I don't think that will happen anytime soon, honey," began Jan, "she has absolutely refused to see..."

"It might take a while for you to heal, Monty," interrupted Galen. "There'll be plenty of time to see Beth when you're up and about."

"Don't interrupt me like that!" ordered Jan in a staccato tone. Turning to her grandson she said, "Your mother is refusing to see your grandfather and she even hit him. I don't think she'll be seeing anyone anytime soon."

"Jan," began Galen, but then halted. "Don't worry, Monty, we'll see you tomorrow. Get some sleep now," he said, and ushered Jan out the door with a confused Ryan trailing behind. She yanked her elbow away from Galen's grasp the moment they were clear of the curtain, but didn't utter another word. Based on the experience of an entire marriage, Galen knew that there was rarely an argument like this that he could win, so it was best to join her in silence. Jan was headstrong with deep religious convictions and had been a good wife and mother. But she also had the personality traits that would brook no criticism and would rarely admit to a mistake. 'I'm sorry,' wasn't in her vocabulary. There had been occasions when Galen had objected to something or put his foot down when necessary and the marriage had survived, but this time he also had a clue as to the root cause of her behavior and so didn't press matters. He knew that Jan was feeling a deep guilt for what had happened to Monty, and possibly for her parenting skills with Beth, too—only she had yet to fully realize those two things.

The ride home was awkwardly quiet, and Ryan coped by diving into a video game in the back seat. Galen pulled into the carport, turned off the engine, and slowly opened his car door. The thought, *Jan, there's such a thing as Post Traumatic Stress Syndrome. I think you have it, and there are people who can help us deal...* was forming itself into speech with "Jan, there's...", but by this time Jan was already in the house. He suspected they would have little contact for the remainder of the evening.

# Chapter 29.

THE MORNING conference had been moved to the small auditorium which was already near-capacity when Galen arrived at 7:50. At precisely 8:00 AM, Chief Osborne began with a statement. "You'll be happy to hear that the high-profile kidnapping case of four-year-old Melissa Davidson came to a successful result at 4:45 PM Mountain Time yesterday. She received minor treatment at the Campbell County Hospital in Wyoming and is being flown home today by a private carrier to keep things discrete, but don't be surprised if the media figures this out. We've had discussions with the family, and they prefer to keep Melissa's whereabouts as private as possible. They've even arranged for all of them to stay with family friends in the near-term, expecting their own house to be surrounded by the press. We'll do our best to help them maintain their privacy for as long as we can. With that in mind, we won't be announcing where we'll be posting additional officers until just before Melissa arrives. I'll just say that we'll be counting on some extra staffing for the Northeast quarter over the next couple of days. We expect the news coverage of this to be heavy, and our public relations staff and I will be handling most interactions. Tom, I'd like you to assign a competent speaker, knowledgeable of the kidnapping, to join us at all of the upcoming briefings." He nodded back at her as she gathered her papers. "Captain, I'll turn it over to you now to update us about the perpetrator."

"Thanks, Chief Osborne," said Tom as he took his turn at the podium. "Gary Molitor is in the custody of the Wyoming Highway Patrol, and since he's guilty of crossing multiple state lines with a kidnapped minor, I'm not sure that we'll see him in Portland any time soon. The Patrol finally found his wallet and ID hidden in the automobile underneath the rubber floor mats. We've just received a warrant to search his house at 5433 SW 49$^{th}$ and will commence there directly after this meeting." *5433 SW 49$^{th}$,* thought Galen, *I know that number,* as Tom continued. "Pembrook and Cushing, I'd like you to lead the search in conjunction with Brenda Rigby and Forensics. I want the house taped off immediately and an extra cordon set up on the street to stop any of the public from approaching. Jenkins, I'd like you to stay in touch with these operations and join Chief Osborne in the media presentations." A faint 'ooooh' went up from some of the other officers, leaving Jenkins looking uncomfortable. "Let's find out everything we can about Molitor as soon as possible," said Tom, wrapping up the meeting.

Galen's hand shot up before any of the others, and he winced again at the pain in his shoulder that just wouldn't seem to go away. "Galen?" asked Tom. "Yes, Captain, that address—5433 SW 49$^{th}$—I know it. I was there just yesterday."

"You're kidding," said Tom. "Why was that?"

"I was interested in people who'd submitted nasty responses to Robert Armlin's editorials in the Oregon Sentinel, and a James Madison had written several letters that included veiled threats against Armlin. One of the four James Madisons listed in the Portland area lives in a duplex at 5431 SW 49th, and I interviewed him yesterday afternoon, although I found out he's not the author of the letters," and he paused, thinking a moment.

"That's an odd coincidence..." Tom began when Galen cut in.

"And he reported a pickup stolen from his yard about the time that Molitor stole the car in Vancouver. We should," pulling out his notebook and flipping to a page, "have the Vancouver police look for an old yellow '78 Chevy pickup with cream panels. I'd bet it's in the vicinity of that carjacking."

"OK, we'll notify them," said Tom, "and you go with the team and speak to Mr. Madison again about his neighbor, would you? That's it, folks, let's go. Time's a wastin.'"

# Chapter 30.

GALEN WAS back on SW 49th Dr. and this time the short street was packed with Bureau vehicles, flashing lights, and swarms of dark blue and black uniforms. Confused and worried neighbors began to gather, and, sure enough, the first TV news van had parked just outside the newly established police cordon. Wending his way through the vehicles and approaching the duplex, Galen could make out Mr. Madison peering through his window drapes, but Galen decided to have a look inside the Molitor house before talking to him. He followed Jenkins into the already crowded living room, staying inside of the lines demarcated by the Forensics Unit. The room looked like what one would expect from a reasonably neat bachelor, except that there were some coloring books and dolls spread out along the sofa under a partially opened window. Galen went no further inside the house but could hear that they'd already uncovered a small weapons cache in an adjoining study.

Making his way back outside, he returned to the street fronting the unit and stood studying the duplex with fresh eyes. Based on the condition of the two yards, he guessed he'd find there was little contact between the two neighbors and, in fact, there may have been some animosity, given that Molitor appeared to maintain a very well-kept exterior, mowing neatly up against the property line whereas on the other side of the boundary lay tall grass thick with weeds. A white Ford Focus sedan parked up close beside the Molitor half was being examined by some of the team. Galen walked over to the opposite side of the duplex, which was owned by Madison, and could see the patch of pale vegetation where the yellow truck must have been parked. He skirted the tangled yard to reach the cracked entry-walk, and Mr. Madison had the front door open before he reached the small stoop.

"Hello again, officer," began the accented voice. "Do you know what's going on? Is Gary alright?"

"Yes, I believe he is," said Galen. "Do you mind if we step inside?"

"Why all of the cars and police?" asked Madison, backing into his living room.

"Do you know your neighbor, Gary Molitor, very well, Mr. Madison?"

"Not so well. We say hello, but hardly speak other than that. The only time we converse is if our mail gets mixed up. I'm always getting letters for Molitor and he's always getting mail for Madison."

"What would you talk about?" asked Galen.

"Nothing much... the weather. That's about it. We didn't really have much in common."

"Did you ever visit him in his house?"

"No, in fact, I used to bring his mail over to him, but he asked me kindly to stop. After that he would bring my mail here and drop by occasionally to check for any letters I had saved for him. I got the impression he didn't like to be disturbed."

"So, he was a quiet neighbor?"

"Most of the time," replied Madison. "Except during the last few weeks he's been playing the radio or the TV really loud. I was going to ask him to keep it down, but I know he doesn't like me knocking on his door."

"Have you seen any children at his house?"

"No, why would I?" asked Madison. "He's a bachelor. What's this all about?"

"You'll hear soon enough that your neighbor, Mr. Molitor, has been arrested for the kidnapping of that missing girl, Melissa Davidson. It's vital if you can tell us anything about her or her being kept next door."

"No, that can't be," said an alarmed James Madison. "The only thing I've seen or heard over the last few weeks is the loud music. Nothing else."

"Are you sure? No children's cries or sobbing? No conversations or yelling?"

Madison shook his head, thinking. "Nah... The only thing was some cars racing up the street in the middle of the night about a week ago. It could have been anybody, but it woke me up and I'm a heavy sleeper."

Galen took notes and then looked up. "Thank you, Mr. Madison. If you think of anything else, please give me a call," handing Madison a business card.

As he headed back to check on progress in the other side of the duplex, Jenkins waved him over to the far side of the Molitor home.

"Galen, look at this," said Jenkins as he approached the Focus being swept by Forensics. The car was situated with the passenger side pulled up close to the building. Jenkins was shining his flashlight into the space between the duplex and the car and along the passenger door panel. Galen peered into the gap and could see a long crease along the side of the car. "Is it my imagination, or is that black paint in that crease?" Galen leaned over to try and get a closer look, nodding as he saw it. "Remind you of anything?" asked Jenkins.

Galen straightened and stared at him. "Armlin's black Toyota," as Jenkins smiled back. "And Lee Street's not that far from here—what five blocks?"

# Chapter 31.

AN HOUR later, Galen was helping catalog some of the items being taken from the house after Forensics finished with them, when he received a call prefixed with a Vancouver, Washington area code.

"Hey, Galen, long time," said a voice he recognized as Mike Yellen, a lieutenant with the Vancouver Police Department. Though on unfriendly terms when the two had been at the academy together, they'd developed a workable relationship over the last few years. "Break any bones lately?" a common greeting from Yellen.

Galen winced at the memory of accidently snapping another cadet's collarbone on a gym mat. "Not lately, Mike, what's up?"

"Hey, we found that truck of yours. The yellow Chevy pickup. Do I understand that it could be involved in that interstate kidnapping case?"

"Yeah, there's a very good chance it was taken from a neighbor's yard by Gary Molitor, the kidnapping suspect. You'll need to process it with that in mind. Anything obvious? Any clothes, toys, baggage?"

"From what I hear it looks pretty clean, Galen, but I'm going to follow our Forensics Unit down there and I'll let you know if I see anything."

"Where was it?"

"Northeast thirty-third, just a few houses from where the other car was stolen."

"I know you guys are searching the area nearby, but you wouldn't mind if I came over and poked around a little, too, would you?"

There was a pause, and then a chuckle, "Not in an unofficial capacity, no."

"OK, Mike, thanks," said Galen as he hung up and walked over to the other detectives to let them know that the Vancouver police had located the truck. He followed that up with another short visit with Mr. Madison to let him know the good news.

In the early afternoon, he was near the Portland International Airport driving north on I-205 before crossing the Columbia River into Vancouver when his cell phone rang. He looked down and recognized Yellen's number.

"I know you, Galen," said Mike when he answered. "You were going to come over here and tromp around the area until you found something else connected with the case. Weren't you? So, I had my boys really beat the bushes in the vicinity of the truck, and sure enough just around the corner in an overgrown lot, they found a bag with some children's items and a locked briefcase nearby."

"Mike, did you intuit that I'm just about to cross the river?"

"No need, buddy," said Mike. "Like I said, I know you, and we've got you covered. Of course, we won't know if they're connected with the kidnapping until we process them, but if they are, we'll make sure we get them to you."

"Thanks, Mike," said Galen as he took the last exit near the Home Depot before crossing the river into Washington State. "You've saved me a trip."

"Yeah, of snooping around someone else's backyard!" laughed Mike as he hung up.

Galen headed back towards southwest Portland. They'd learned that Gary Molitor worked as a delivery person for Miracle Furnishings located near Greenway Park—less than a quarter of a mile from the Washington Square mall, and Galen wanted to interview the owner. The small parking lot was already baking in the sudden and unexpected late-Spring sunshine, and he stepped from the tarred heat into another world. The air-conditioned, immaculate space was perfectly lit and artfully arranged with some of the most beautiful furnishings that Galen had seen. *A long way from our Ikea stuff*, thought Galen as he was greeted by a tall thin man in a tasteful suit. "I'm looking for the owner—a Mr. Nerland, I believe?" asked Galen.

"Yes, sir, his office is right this way," said the man in a gentle manner and offering no additional small talk. He tapped on the doorframe of an open door. "Mr. Nerland, a gentleman is here to see you," he announced and faded into the designer background.

Mr. Nerland rose from his desk and came around the end of it with his arm outstretched. "Oliver Nerland," said the man, possibly dressed more impeccably than the floor manager had been, "what can I do for you?" as they shook hands.

"Mr. Nerland, my name is Galen Young and I'm a detective with the Portland Police Bureau. I'm here to ask you a couple of questions about an employee of yours—a Mr. Gary Molitor."

"Welcome, Detective Young," said Mr. Nerland resting easily against the front of his large teak desk. "Yes, Gary Molitor is employed with us. Is there a problem?"

"That remains to be seen," said Galen. "Mr. Molitor has become involved in an investigation we're pursuing, and I'd like to know more about the man. Has he worked for you for long?"

"I hope it's nothing serious," said Mr. Nerland. "Mr. Molitor has delivered furniture for us for three or four years now and has always performed his job admirably. Why are you interested in him?"

"I can't really say much at this point in our inquiries, as you can imagine," answered Galen. "So, he's always met the job expectations here? Anything unusual in his behavior, especially recently?"

"No, as I say, he's been a model employee, and I hope he gets better soon."

"Better soon?" asked Galen.

"Well, yes," replied Mr. Nerland. "He's asked for sick leave over this past week or so. He said he's come down with a nasty case of the flu."

"I see. Other than his sick leave, has he asked for any special time off or had access to your computers during his free time?" asked Galen.

"Not that I can say," responded Mr. Nerland. "The delivery people pretty much stick to themselves."

"Would it be possible for me to speak to one of his co-workers?" asked Galen, realizing that Molitor probably wasn't often occupying the rarified atmosphere that surrounded Mr. Nerland.

"Yes, back in the storage area and delivery bays. Here, let me show you." They walked out of the office, around a corner, and Mr. Nerland pointed to a large garage door, and an entry door to the side positioned at the far rear of the store. Galen thanked him and headed towards the delivery area.

Stepping through the back door was again like entering a different world. Everything was clean, but rap music blasted out of a small side room off of the loading dock, and when he entered the delivery office, he found a young man covered with tattoos and piercings and just taking a puff from an electronic cigarette. The man jumped up on seeing his approach and immediately asked, "Hello, sir, can I help you?"

Galen flashed his badge and introduced himself. The young man showed no unusual reaction to his being a police officer and held out a hand saying, "I'm Emmanuel Soto, pleased to meet you," in a fairly thick Hispanic accent.

"I understand you work with Mr. Molitor, Emmanuel?" The man nodded while reaching over to turn down the volume on the radio. "Can you tell me a little about him?"

"I don't know what you wanna know, but Gary's just a normal dude," Emmanuel replied. When Galen waited without responding, he clarified, "The dude's been sick this week but otherwise he's always on time and he's never stole nothin' if that's what you're wondering."

"No, I'm just trying to learn more about him," said Galen. "How did he get on here at work?"

"Fine," said Emmanuel after a slight pause.

"Emmanuel, did he ever show any interest in children or very young women?"

"Gary? No—no way, man," Emmanuel was emphatic. "Sure, he's a little macho," with a slight grin, "I mean who ain't? But kids? No way. He does like the ladies though. Just ask his amiga."

"He has a girlfriend?" asked Galen, pulling out his notebook. "Do you know her name, Emmanuel?"

Emmanuel hesitated, obviously wondering if he was revealing too much about his co-worker, but then shrugged his shoulders. "Yeah, she's Sissy something... Sissy Ortiz, I think."

"Any phone number or contact information?"

"Nah man, he was always like talkin' to her on the phone, but he never really said much about her. I gather she was hot though, from what he did say."

Galen nodded and then thought back to the slight pause Emmanuel had shown when the detective had asked how Molitor was doing in his job. "But I gather everything wasn't perfect for him here at work?"

"Everything's fine. He's chill."

"Not everything, though. What is it?"

Emmanuel was reluctant. "Look, I don't wanna get nobody in trouble." Galen stared at him until he continued. "Gary likes it here, it's just that the dude gets so worked up about shit. He thinks too much."

"Like about what?" asked Galen.

"Hey, he's good at the job and don't disrespect nobody." Emmanuel stared off into space. "But the main thing that bugs him is we deliver to all these rich people who got like, mansions. And we're try'n to scrape by on barely nothin'. He always says the liberals got it all and the true American's got nothin'."

"Did he ever mention doing anything about it?"

"Nah, man, like I say, it's all in his head. He talks, but just because that's what he does—talk."

"OK, thanks, Emmanuel," said Galen as a tattooed arm reached out to turn the volume back up when he walked back onto the loading dock.

# Chapter 32.

RATHER THAN getting into his car, Galen walked the short distance down Stratus St. and entered Greenway Park before phoning headquarters. He was crossing a murky stream near the entrance when he noticed a sign announcing that it was Fanno Creek. *How weird. I had no idea the little creek was this long,* thought Galen as he sat down on a nearby park bench situated in the shade.

"Deb, this is Galen," he said when Cushing answered his call. "I just interviewed some folks at the furniture store where Molitor works, and one of them mentioned a girlfriend. A Sissy Ortiz. Could you run an address on her for me?"

Cushing was back on the line a few minutes later. "Hi, Galen," said Cushing. "There's a Sara Ortiz whose phone number matches that of one frequently called by Molitor, so that must be the same person. She lives on southeast Reedway—I'll text you the address."

Twenty minutes later, Galen pulled up in front of a small pink house in reasonably good shape with a neat gravel yard, but with a pile of old boxes and plywood piled up along one side. The doorbell was answered immediately by a thin tattooed woman boasting a thick pile of black hair held in place on the top of her head by a chopstick.

"Look, if your selling religion—or anything else, I ain't interested," she said in a tired voice and beginning to close the door.

Galen had his badge ready, and after flashing it, the door swung back open. "Galen Young, Portland Police Bureau," he said in his more official-sounding voice.

"Hey, we've kept the music down since the last complaint," said Ortiz.

"It's not about the music," said Galen. "Am I addressing Sara or Sissy Ortiz?"

"That's me," she replied with her already wiry jaw clenching tighter. She looked Galen up and down and then in resignation said, "All right, come on in."

Two card tables in the middle of the living room were piled with graphic images for tattoos in individual plastic sleeves. "You're a tattoo artist?" asked Galen, thumbing through some of them.

"Yup," said Ortiz, obviously not in a conversational mood.

"Ms. Ortiz, I wanted to ask you about your boyfriend, Gary Molitor."

"Gary?" asked Ortiz, suddenly concerned. "Why? Has something happened to him?"

"He hasn't been in an accident or anything," said Galen. "But he is a person of interest in a case we're working on." Ortiz relaxed somewhat, but her jaw was still working. "Can you tell me how you came to know Mr. Molitor?"

"Gary an' me been together for a coupla years," said Ortiz. "He came into my shop interested in a tattoo, but never ended up gettin' one." Ortiz had opened a packet of gum and popped two chiclets into her mouth. "Got me instead," she managed a smile.

"Are you two close?"

"Yeah, close," said Ortiz. "Not married, but close."

"What's he like?"

"Whaddya mean?" asked Ortiz.

"You know, a nice guy, political, thoughtful—you know, like that."

"He's nice, kinda straight, and not very happy with where this country is headed," replied Ortiz. "I guess that's about it. Oh, and a hard worker."

"Have you seen him lately?" asked Galen.

"Not in the past week or so," she said a little sadly. "He's got this niece he's gotta take care of, and she don't like strangers."

"He didn't mention being ill?"

"No, why?" asked Ortiz. "Is he?"

"Not that I know of—he did call in sick to work though."

"Probably didn't want them to know that he was babysittin', if I know Gary."

"So, you two talked on the phone?"

"Yeah, every day until a coupla days ago—can't seem to reach him now. Gary called lately 'cause he don't know much about what little girls like or need."

"What do you mean?"

"You know, Barbies, charms, play-cookin' stuff, that sorta thing."

"What do you know about his niece?"

"Not so much. He said his brother was havin' real marriage problems, and that he hadda take care of their daughter till things blew over. I said I could help out, but he said that she was like really needy and weirded out and would flip if she was with a strange person."

"So, you never saw the niece?" asked Galen.

"We were gonna meet this week, but like I say, I haven't heard from Gary for a coupla days now. Makes me kinda worried about him. Last I heard he said he might need to take her to her grandparent's house where it might be calmer for her."

"And where was that?"

"Dunno," said Ortiz.

"Do you know the niece's name or her parent's names?"

"Nope," said Ortiz.

"Well, thank you Ms. Ortiz," said Galen. "I may be in touch with more questions."

"Right," said Ortiz.

# Chapter 33.

"OK, WHERE are we?" asked Captain Tom Weston of his detectives, Jenkins, Pembrook, Cushing, and Young.

Pembrook took the lead and said, "Molitor had a small cache of weapons—a shotgun, two hunting rifles, and three handguns. Why he didn't take any of them with him when he fled with Melissa is beyond me, or if he had any more, we haven't heard about them. We're lucky he wasn't carrying because there might have been a shootout when he was stopped if he had. He'd collected a stack of paramilitary and survivalist magazines in his house and bought one of those emergency food kits to make it through a disaster for 90 days, but otherwise things looked pretty normal. We went through his mail, and there were no outstanding bills or anomalies there. I was surprised that there was no porn or kiddie-porn stashed anywhere, but we haven't been able to crack his computers yet—we have some IT guys working on them."

"So, no clues as to why he kidnapped the girl?" asked Tom.

"None that we've found, Captain," said Cushing. "He had appropriate food for her in the refrigerator, a stash of new toys, presumably to give to her when she tired of the ones that were laying about, the TV was tuned to a PBS kids' channel, and we found a camera in one of the kitchen drawers. All of the pictures in it were of Melissa, but none were inappropriate—

just her playing or smiling for the camera. Based on the date stamps, the pictures began on the second day after she was kidnapped. From what we've seen, it was almost as if he was adopting her, rather than caging her. Plus, the medical exam in Wyoming reported no abuse of any kind."

"You think she tolerated her captivity?"

"Hard to say, sir, but there was a window that was partially open, and no special locks were on any of the others, so either he had his eye on her the whole time, or restrained her somehow, or—he wasn't afraid that she'd try and escape. No obvious restraints were found."

"And what about the car?" asked Tom.

Galen's phone buzzed and he dismissed it. Jan was calling.

"We're having it analyzed as we speak," said Jenkins. "There were children's toys in it, and he'd rigged a little DVD viewing screen for the back seat with a few kids' movies in the glove compartment. The trunk was completely empty. We thought we could see a crease on the passenger-side door when the car was parked up against the house, and when we pulled it away from the building—sure enough it looks like it had had a run-in with a black car. There were large specks of black paint in a long scrape, and Galen and I immediately thought of Armlin's car that had traces of white paint from a Ford model car. Molitor's is a white Ford Focus."

Tom thought for a moment. "So, it looks like we have two links between Molitor and Armlin? Melissa's hair in Armlin's car and possible matching paint from a collision between the two cars? What does this mean?"

Galen spoke up. "It's possible that Molitor initially kidnapped Melissa, but that doesn't explain her hair in Armlin's car. It's more likely that Armlin abducted Melissa from the mall—for God knows what reason. But that leaves many questions. Were they possibly working together? Did Armlin do his part of the job and then split? Was Melissa taken from Armlin by force, especially given a collision between the two cars? Why would Armlin take her in the first place? Why would Molitor take her? Did Molitor get rid of Armlin?"

"Yes, yes, OK," said Tom. "There's obviously a lot we have to learn before we can piece this together. We need to crack Molitor's computers, we need to look for motives by either Armlin or Molitor, and we need to talk to Molitor. He's been moved to a cell in Cheyenne awaiting arraignment, but the various states and the FBI are still putting together the charges. He's been questioned several times and has admitted to the theft of several cars, but that's about it. He won't say a word about Melissa. I've asked if we can send someone over to question him when we have more information on our end, and they are amenable to that." He looked around the table. "Anything else?"

"I talked to his employer at Miracle Furnishings," said Galen, "and Molitor's held a steady job there for three or so years. He was said to have made some grumblings about wealth inequality and politics, but that's about it. I also spoke to his girlfriend, Sissy Ortiz. She didn't provide much information but said she hadn't seen Molitor lately because he was busy babysitting his 'niece'," Galen said making quotation marks in the air with his fingers. "So not much to go on there, but neither his co-worker nor his girlfriend seemed to be aware of his kidnapping the girl yet. We can dig further, but it's my reading that neither of those two were involved. The furniture store is about a quarter of a mile from the Washington Square mall, so we can guess that he wasn't a stranger to the area." He tapped the table with his fingers. "But going back to a previous issue, I've been wondering about the duct tape. We found the mostly-used roll near Fanno Creek and the small bit that had some of Armlin's hair on it. How does that fit? Did Armlin use it, or did Molitor? We haven't found it anywhere else—in the car, or in the house. Lockhart in Spokane said one of his officers thought he saw it on Melissa's arms, if that was her, but we haven't heard of her having marks from the medical check. Have bits of it turned up in any of the other stolen cars?"

"Not that I've heard," said Jenkins. "And using it on Melissa doesn't seem to fit with the almost domestic scene we encountered in Molitor's house, does it?"

"Unless Molitor's been very careful or tidy," responded Galen. "Was any tape found in his trash?"

"I'll ask," said Pembrook and made a call to Forensics.

"Well, that's another thing to add to the list of unanswered questions, if they haven't found any," said Tom.

After a short wait Pembrook shook his head, "Nope, no duct tape."

"OK, folks, let's keep digging and let me know of anything you find," the captain said as he stood, bringing the meeting to an end.

# Chapter 34.

GALEN NOTICED that he'd missed a message from Mike Yellen, and he read it after the meeting. *Galen, that briefcase was more interesting than we thought—phone me back. Yellen.* In a few moments, he had Yellen on the line. "Hey, Mike, I got your message, and what did you mean that the briefcase was more interesting than you thought?"

"Forensics here got it open and examined the contents. It belongs to your missing person, Robert Armlin, the newspaper editor."

*What?? How?* thought Galen. *Another connection between those two...* and he said, "Wow, Mike, that's a shock! What was in it?"

"Looks like some papers and a laptop," said Yellen.

"Excellent!" said Galen. "I think this will really help us along, Mike. How about the bag of toys? Anything interesting?"

"No, nothing other than that they appeared to be almost brand new," replied Yellen.

"When can I have the briefcase?" asked Galen.

"As soon as you get your butt over here," chuckled Yellen. "They're ready to turn it over to you, and I'll make sure it's waiting at the front desk if I'm not still here when you arrive."

"Thanks, Mike," said Galen. "Say hello to Sherry."

"Will do, Galen, the same to Jan—see you," and they both hung up.

The mention of Jan reminded him that his wife had tried to call during the meeting. He rang her back, but there was no answer and work took over his thoughts for the rest of the afternoon.

Galen went home after work to check in with his family instead of heading straight to Vancouver, and found them in tatters. Ryan had told Jan he didn't want to go "back to that stupid hospital," and had said he was going to see some friends instead. Jan had insisted he accompany her to visit Monty, but upon encountering a wall of resistance, she'd eventually relented, demanding instead that he be home by 9:00 PM. This had apparently precipitated another shouting match before he'd stormed out of the house.

During an early dinner of left-overs with his wife who had finally simmered down, Galen said, "I have to run up to Vancouver to pick up some evidence for my missing-person case, but I'll meet you at the hospital by 7:30 or so."

This was met with a glare from Jan who said, "When are you ever going to put your family first? Your grandson is hanging on by a thread, and you act like it doesn't matter."

"Jan," said Galen, "you know that it matters to me, and I'm going to be there, just a little later."

"Always later," muttered Jan. "Monty's going to feel abandoned—neither you nor Ryan are going to show up. And just wait, in a week or so, it'll be only me there—every single day!" as she inexplicably burst into tears.

"Jan," said Galen in a reasoning manner, "it's going to take Monty months to heal, and he's doing remarkably well. He's out of danger, and we'll all be there for him over the long haul."

"Right!" gasped Jan. "You're never here for anyone!"

*What?* thought Galen, "Jan, I..." And then, unbidden, came the thought, *and you've been there for Beth?* But he saw where this was all headed and didn't want to spend the next hour fighting. "I'll be there later, Jan. You'd better get over to the hospital, I'm sure Monty's waiting for you. And I'll try and have a talk with Ryan."

"You should!" exclaimed Jan. "He shot his brother and now won't even see him? He has some dues to pay!"

*I think he is paying them,* thought Galen, *and I think that you are, too.*

They both silently scraped their plates into the trash, and Galen left to pick up the briefcase.

His thoughts turned to his marriage while he headed north through the remains of rush-hour traffic. Jan had been open to adventure and new ideas when they'd first met, but he felt like now he was watching someone slowly calcify before his eyes. There was no denying that they were both getting older and slowing down—he could see and feel it happening in himself almost daily. He'd hoped for graceful ageing, but Jan was becoming more hunched, stiffer, shorter of temper, more judgmental, and less tolerant with every passing year. He felt like he had to bend over backwards more and more just to keep her happy but, unfortunately, he was becoming stiffer too, and just didn't bend as well as he used to. They'd managed an equilibrium so far, each filling in for the other's weaknesses, and adjusting to compensate. *What if Monty's shooting tips us over the edge?* he thought. *What if we don't bend anymore, but just break?* He tried to keep the rest of his thoughts on more positive things, but soon felt like he was driving downhill into a dark pit. The approaching lights of Vancouver brought him back up to the surface.

Yellen had left for the day, but the duty sergeant had the briefcase at the front desk, and Galen presented his ID and signed the custody form for its release. There was a small desk to the side of the counter, and he set the briefcase on it, popped the latches, and opened it. Inside were thin work-related folders, a daily planner, and Armlin's laptop computer. There was no cell phone. *Armlin must have held on to it,* thought Galen. He pulled out the laptop, opened it, and booted it up. He remembered the password that Emma had given him for Armlin's home computer, since it was easy to memorize. *Emma4life*—he was in immediately. Galen clicked through the folders of Armlin's published and draft editorials, documents with random notes and ideas, and a folder holding some family pictures. After a quick pass through the material, he'd found no hint of child pornography, interest in children, or any mention of the Davidsons. He shut down the computer and called Tom Weston. "Hi Tom, Galen here. Mike Yellen with the Vancouver Police Department searched the vicinity where Gary Molitor abandoned James Madison's truck and found a bag of children's toys and Robert Armlin's briefcase, both were apparently dumped in a nearby lot."

"Armlin's briefcase?" asked Tom. "Why would he have that? And why toss it in Vancouver?"

"I don't know why he had it, but I'm guessing he tossed it because he was travelling light, and because he couldn't easily get it open. It was locked, but Yellen's forensic crew picked the latches."

"And the contents?" asked Tom.

"I just went through them, and there are a computer and work-related files. No cell phone anywhere. I did a quick search of the computer and I can find no obvious child porn, nor connections to the Davidsons."

"OK, Galen," said Tom. "Make sure you log everything in so we follow chain of custody, and then go through it all with a fine-toothed comb. By the way, how did you get into his computer?"

"His wife Emma gave me the password that he used for just about everything."

"Figures," said Tom. "Don't tell anyone, but I use the same one for everything too. Good night, Galen."

# Chapter 35.

IT WAS 9:30 in the evening and Galen decided to skip the hospital—he wanted to check in with Ryan. The moment Galen pulled into the driveway, it was glaringly apparent that Ryan had made it home. A thunderous bass was vibrating the immediate neighborhood, and as he opened the front door, the music was deafening. He set down the briefcase he'd just retrieved, his keys, and coat, and then walked calmly down the hallway and knocked on the door, not expecting an answer given the noise. Sure enough there was no response. He knocked a little louder with no answer and then kicked on the door with the toe of his shoe. This time the music jumped in volume even more, only to be turned off immediately—the boy had heard him but turned the dial in the wrong direction.

"Sorry, Gramp," said Ryan as Galen opened the door. "I flipped it the wrong way." His face was puffy and his eyes red, but he looked like he'd worked through a spate of emotions to reach a more peaceful place.

"How are you doing, Ryan?" asked Galen as he sat beside his grandson on his bed.

"OK," was his reflexive response, but after a moment he glanced at his grandfather and added, "No. Not so OK, I guess."

"It's going to be tough for a while, son," said Galen speaking slowly and making sure that Ryan had his space and that the conversation went at his pace. "You've made the jump into adult problems about five years too early is all," going for a bit of humor.

"But everything's wrong now," said Ryan obviously determined not to cry again. "Absolutely everything."

"I know, bud. You've just got to be as strong as you can, every day."

"But it's not that easy," Ryan whispered, staring at the floor. "Everyone's acting all weird and ghosting me—even Liz is sorta freaked out. And now some of the gangbanger-types in school think I'm like this badass and want to be my friend—probably because I shot my own brother!" He shook his head. "One of my teachers today asked why I even bothered to come to school..."

"Oh? Which one?" asked Galen seriously.

Ryan looked over at him. "Mr. Richter—but no one else could hear and he said it was because it's so close to the end of school, and that I'd be preoccupied with all that's going on. He didn't mean I shouldn't be in his class." Galen nodded at the explanation. "And he's right. All of a sudden, I'm adulting and don't have my own life. I have to see the school counselor before and after school, the newspapers and TV people all want interviews, we have those visits with the lawyers and the police, and they still say I might end up being charged..." Ryan lost his battle with his tears.

Galen put his hand on the boy's back. "It's going to be all right, buddy. Right now, everything seems like it has to happen all at once, but these things have a way of stretching out and changing. Your friends are reacting to this news and trying to absorb it, but if they know you, they'll be back soon enough. The whole media thing will fade away and be completely forgotten by next year. And the police know it was an accident—they just have to make sure they follow all the procedures in such a visible case." Ryan had stopped his silent sobs and was nodding his head. "And the most important thing is that your brother loves you and he'll improve quickly, especially knowing that you love him. All the other stuff will pass, and you'll still have your brother."

Ryan let out a huge yawn, and Galen could now see that the boy was overwhelmed with exhaustion. "Go ahead and turn the music back on—I don't mind," said Galen as he rose and headed for the door. "Maybe not quite so loud though," which brought a brief smile to Ryan's face. Ryan must have decided on either no music or headphones, however, because the house was silent for the remainder of the night.

# Chapter 36.

GALEN LOGGED both Robert Armlin's laptop and his brief-case into the Bureau's repository as possible evidence in an as-yet-to-be-determined crime, and the staff in 'The Vault' were more comfortable providing him with the xeroxes and digital files he needed rather than let the detective maintain possession of the contents of the briefcase. An hour later, Galen stopped by the cafeteria for another cup of coffee and walked back to his office with a folder of paper copies in hand and the USB drive the repository had given him in his pocket. He turned on his computer and then simultaneously brought up the files that were provided by Monica Stevens from Armlin's work computer and the files that were copied off Armlin's laptop to compare them. The laptop held several editorials that were obviously works-in-progress as well as numerous notes, out-lines, and personal logs not included in the files obtained from his office. He read a draft with a title that caught his eye—one that he expected might generate some interesting replies once it was published.

*Patriotism    Note: for July 4, 2019?*

*I know that I'll receive many protests to this piece, but hey, it's my opinion spot—go get your own! (said with a tongue planted firmly in my cheek).*

David Ackley

*I saw a truck drive by the other day with two American flags proudly waving from each side, and it brought up several questions. What country does the driver think he's in? Don't we all know that we're in America? Who's he flying them for—himself or everyone else? Is it disrespectful to fly our flag to tatters from a hopped-up truck at 60 mph? Is he trying to show that he's patriotic? More patriotic than the rest of us? How do you 'out-patriotic' someone? How do you 'out-American' them? Is it based upon who's been here the longest? In a country that's only been in existence for 240 years—which is 12 generations (based on 20 yrs. per generation) or roughly 10 generations (based on 24 years)? How many generations would it take to be more American than the next guy?*

*I believe, in his way, this flag-waving driver is trying to show that he cares about being an American. Being an American is easy for most of us—you just need to be born here, so the bar is set exceedingly low to begin with. Caring about your country is another matter, however. It's entirely possible to live your entire life here and not give a hoot about it. There are no standards you must meet before you get kicked out (in fact, unless you are a naturalized citizen, nothing you do can send you to another country). You don't have to vote, exercise your right of free speech, not even pay taxes—though you might face other consequences if you don't. We're pretty tolerant—even with a huge amount of effort on your part, like a treasonous act, you can't get kicked out of here.*

*But I also believe that if you care about your country, and you should, you can't just go part way. The words of the*

Constitution and the Bill of Rights apply to everyone. They don't specify which religion should be allowed to be followed freely, who should have the right of free speech and of assembly, who should be protected under the laws of our country. These laws and protections belong to everyone—*every last one of us.* These critical documents say nothing about the language you speak, the clothes you wear, the god you worship (or don't), your ancestry, the color of your skin, your sexual preference, your wealth or lack thereof, your social standing, your memberships or lack thereof, or whether or not you like rap. Everyone, *either born in, or obtaining citizenship in, our great country has* exactly *the same rights that you do. It doesn't even matter if you don't accept what I'm saying, it doesn't alter the fact that everyone is an equal member of these United States of America. The 14<sup>th</sup> Amendment was crafted for the sole purpose of making this abundantly clear.*

*This is such a great country that you have the personal right to disapprove, and say that you disapprove, of someone's religion, sexual orientation, dining habits, firearm ownership, memberships, or choice of presidential candidate—as long as you are civil and don't veer over into libel and slander. However, you have absolutely no right to infringe on another's choice of religion, sexual orientation, dining habits, firearm ownership, memberships, or choice of presidential candidate. Being able to say something does not give you the right to control something, and let's not forget that. You might not like the color of my skin, and you have the right to say that, but you have no right to control me because of my skin color. Too often lately the right of free expression is taken as the right to control another person, of which there is absolutely no right—it is a wrong. So, go ahead and label yourself as more patriotic than the next guy. All that gets you is bragging rights—a right that comes with absolutely no real extra privileges, standing, or status.*

*The Founding Fathers were big on tranquility and the pursuit of happiness, meaning maybe we should leave each other alone a little more and get along. Embrace our differences, because we have no right not to. Have a happy 4ᵗʰ of July, the day in 1776 when we adopted a declaration to the world that said, among so much else:* **We** hold these Truths to be self-evident, that all Men are created equal, that they are endowed by their Creator with certain unalienable Rights, that among these are Life, Liberty, and the Pursuit of Happiness.

Again, Galen was surprised at his reaction after reading one of Armlin's articles. Considering himself to be a flag-waving patriot, he had at first bristled at either the tone or the message of the essay—he wasn't sure which. But by the end, he found himself agreeing with the man, although he wasn't necessarily happy with the way he felt about it. Somehow Armlin was making him examine his own beliefs, but presenting his argument in such a way that it was like he was stabbing Galen in the chest with his forefinger while doing it. And Galen was someone who didn't like being lectured to.

*Still,* he thought as he recalled the other editorials he'd read, *I feel like I'm learning more about myself from my reactions than I am about this guy. He's made a career out of stating his opinion and opening himself up to the world, making it this far without getting fired. His boss, Ed, sure likes him and his work, and I get the feeling that Armlin's preaching to the choir for most of his readership. The ones who complain obviously get off on being able to reply to him, otherwise they'd just switch to a different paper and ignore him. They like the 'little soapbox' as much as he does, and maybe it's just a fun game to most of them. Or were they really upset by what he says? Had his finger jabs gotten to someone so that they'd want to jab back?*

Frustrated with how little he still knew about Armlin, he began to flip through the xeroxes of the diary/datebook that had been in the briefcase. One of the more recent entries scratched in by hand caught his eye.

*Freedom of the Press*

*James Madison. A Founding Father. Fourth President of the United States. Major essayist in The Federalist Papers.*

*James Madison. Apparent Libertarian. Rightwing wingnut. NRA supporter. Anti-government press-bashing bigot.*

*Oh, the irony. I receive multiple letters a year from someone who is the exact opposite of his namesake. The thoughtful contributor to the Constitution of the United States, the Bill of Rights, and the First Amendment to the Constitution among so many other writs and actions undertaken in the founding of these United States was a firm believer in freedom of the press, and was the main force for its enshrinement in the First*

*Amendment. And here is his shallow counterpart besieging the press about its duties, responsibilities, and my right to express myself as I see fit.*

*I could go on, and I will...*

*Are these just notes, or was he going to publish something like this?* wondered Galen. Below this on the page, Armlin had listed each of the four James Madisons in Portland along with their addresses and made the notation: *3 of them are 70 or older.* And another: *Who is the real James Madison?*

*How did he know their ages and addresses?* Galen wondered until he recalled that this information was readily available on the internet. Just below these entries was scratched: *Madison = Leavy??*

Galen searched back and found the reply Leavy had written to his essay on *Anonymity* and had to agree that the tone of this reply was very similar to those by Madison, but then again so were the replies by many of the others, at least they seemed that way to Galen.

*So, Robert Armlin was definitely interested in James Madison and who he really was.* He decided he needed to look into this Oliver Leavy and to make another visit to Gary Molitor's next-door neighbor.

# Chapter 37.

"HELLO AGAIN, Detective," said James Madison as he opened the door.

"Hello, Mr. Madison," said Galen. "I see you've mowed your lawn."

"Not me," said Madison, shaking his head. "My son saw the news coverage when they—you—raided my neighbor Gary's house and he was extremely embarrassed when the cameras panned the yards to take in both sides of the duplex. He mowed the grass the next day."

"Ah," said Galen, as Madison invited him inside. The interior looked much the same as when the detective had last visited. "I hate to trouble you any further, Mr. Madison, but I have just a few more questions."

Madison nodded and offered Galen a seat with a theatric gesture accompanied by a slight bow. "Ask away, words rarely hurt anyone," as before, making a sweeping movement with his arms as though to encompass the stacks of books surrounding them.

"I was just curious about whether you were recently visited by a Mr. Armlin?" At raised eyebrows from the old man, he clarified, "Mr. Robert Armlin, an editor at The Oregon Sentinel?"

"Ah, the one who went missing. Nae, I've never met the man," replied Madison shaking his head. "How or why on earth should I have?"

Galen realized that he'd left any pictures he had of Armlin in his car and, explaining the fact, said "I won't be a minute." When he returned, he pulled a recent picture of Armlin from a folder and handed it to Madison.

There was no hesitation, "Oh, Bob, the newspaper salesman!" said a surprised Madison. "No wonder he looked somehow familiar."

"Newspaper salesman?" asked Galen.

"Yeah, he said he was. He stopped by about a week ago or so to ask me if I was satisfied with the quality of the news printed in The Oregon Sentinel. I told him that I didn't know, since I was a Portland Mail man, and never read his paper. He offered to give me a free copy and a subscription form, but I said I wasn't interested."

"He did, did he?" asked Galen. "Was that the extent of the visit?"

"Oh no, we had a long chat about my accent, and I told him a bit about myself, then, of course, local and national politics came up, so we hashed that out, too."

"Was the conversation confrontational?"

"Confrontational? No, in fact, we found we were in total agreement on most things. Maybe because we're about the same age. I told him he could stop by anytime. In fact, I'd asked him over for a glass of sherry the next evening, but he never showed up."

"Ah!" Galen exclaimed softly. "The new friend he was going to have a drink with. Can you confirm which night that was?"

"Not exactly—like I said, about a week ago or so."

"Well, thank you again, Mr. Madison, you've been very helpful," and Galen left sharing a growing curiosity with Mr. Armlin about who the James Madison in the letters to the editor really was. He found out as soon as he returned to the station.

# Chapter 38.

**GALEN HAD** just turned on his computer when Doug Olson from IT rang his office. "Galen, I was told you'd be interested in this—could you come down to my section?"

"Sure, Doug, what's it about?"

"We cracked some of the files in Gary Molitor's computer."

"Some of them?"

"I'll show you when you get down here."

In five minutes, Olson was showing Galen what they'd discovered so far.

"It was tough to get in—Molitor password-protected individual folders and even had pass codes for many individual files within them. Why would he do that?"

"Paranoid?" asked Galen shrugging his shoulders and wondering how adding passwords to folders was even possible.

"Yeah, who knows?" asked Olson. "But we did get into some folders, and this is what we were told you should see."

Olson opened a folder and then clicked open a series of documents within it. Each one began *Dear Editor* and each one ended *James Madison, Portland Oregon.*

Galen sat up straight for a moment. *This sort of makes sense,* he thought. *Molitor is Madison—Molitor took Madison's name because they're neighbors, and the old guy doesn't subscribe to the paper, so he'd never see his own name in print. But why didn't Molitor use his real name?*

Fifteen minutes later, Galen was sitting on the other side of Tom Weston's desk, and going over the Armlin case with him, Jenkins, and Cushing.

Tom started the meeting. "Galen has some news to share, but first I wanted to let you all know that Wyoming provided Molitor's prints to our Forensics Unit, and Brenda reports that none of the fingerprints discovered on Armlin's Prius match those they sent her, although the partials lifted from the interior are still inconclusive."

"Neither Molitor's nor Melissa's prints were inside?" asked Cushing.

"Nope," replied Tom. "Melissa's hair was found, but neither of their prints—however, remember that there was an attempt to wipe the entire interior clean."

"So, maybe Molitor entered the car wearing gloves and with some of Melissa's hair clinging to his coat?" asked Cushing. They all nodded at the possibility.

"OK. That's all we know right now, but that means we still have several things that positively link Armlin and Molitor," summarized the Captain. "The lab tests show that the paint on the two vehicles—Armlin's Prius and Molitor's Focus—match in height and substance so that there was definitely a collision between the two cars at some point. Circumstantially, we have Armlin's recovered briefcase that was apparently tossed by Molitor in Vancouver, and, of course, hair from the abducted girl in Armlin's car. And based on what Galen's just learned, we now know that Molitor was writing into the newspaper under the name James Madison, and that the letters he submitted were often hostile toward Armlin and his views. Galen?"

"Yes, Captain," said Galen, a little formally. "And those links lead us to highly suspect that Molitor had something to do with Armlin's disappearance. Armlin was becoming suspicious about the true identity of the James Madison who was writing into The Oregon Sentinel. He interviewed the real James Madison living next door to Molitor and found he couldn't possibly be the author of the letters. I don't know if Armlin looked into the other three Madison's as thoroughly, but it's a huge coincidence that Molitor, the actual author of the letters, lived right next door to someone Armlin visited in person."

"What about the timing?" asked Jenkins.

"The ex-Brit James Madison is unsure about the dates, but within a few days, it looks like Armlin visits Madison, Armlin disappears, and Molitor takes off with Melissa Davidson."

"OK, Galen," said Tom. "I think we have enough reason and evidence to justify sending you and Jenkins to Cheyenne to interview Molitor. I want you to find out anything you can about the Armlin connection and tag team with Jenkins. Jenkins, I want you to concentrate on finding Molitor's motive for abducting Davidson and his activities between the time when he kidnapped her and when he fled the state with her some days later." He looked at the calendar. "Oh, but that will take three days, Galen, and if you leave tomorrow it'll include Wednesday, the day when you normally visit Beth. Will that still work?"

Galen shook his head, but answered in the affirmative, "Yeah, it'll work fine, Tom. Beth is refusing to see me, and I'm not going to try another visit until she asks me to."

"That's too bad," said Tom. "Is it because of the accident with Monty?"

"Yep. I'm somehow to blame for all of it."

# Chapter 39.

GALEN WAS just leaving the parking garage after work and heading to the hospital to visit Monty when he suddenly decided to turn at the next block and find a parking space near the Kells Irish Pub. As he thought he might, he spied John Doherty after he'd parked and entered the bar.

"Hello, Mr. Doherty," said Galen. "Do you mind if I join you?"

Doherty looked up and immediately recognized him, "Not at all, Detective Young. Have a seat," he said somewhat dejectedly. "No chance you've found Bob?"

"I'm sorry, no..." Galen ordered a Harp Lager when the waiter appeared from out of nowhere at his side, and then turned back to Doherty. "Are you doing all right?"

"Oh, yeah, I guess. I think the permanence of not having Bob around is starting to really sink in—that and it's making me face my own mortality on a beerly, um, daily basis," he said with a sad smile and tipped his glass of stout towards Galen. "Still no word on what's happened to him?"

"Nope. I assume you're all up to speed with the kidnapping arrest?"

"Yes, they found Melissa Davidson, and have the kidnapper, alleged kidnapper, in custody—thank God it wasn't Bob. Why?" asked Doherty.

"Well, believe it or not, Mr. Armlin is still wrapped up in this. We now suspect that there's some connection between the kidnapper and Mr. Armlin," said Galen, taking a drink of beer when it was set down beside him. "What that connection is, we're not quite sure, but I wanted to ask you again about your last conversation with Mr. Armlin. You said at the time that the discussion involved questions about identity and how a person could know who anyone really was?"

"Yeah, he seemed to be either excited, or agitated about it. I was waiting to read his editorial on the subject to find out which it was."

"Did he ever mention either of these two names—Gary Molitor or James Madison?"

Doherty thought for a moment and then said, "Nope, but I recognize the first name—the alleged kidnapper. Bob never spoke about him. Who's the other guy, James Madison? Not our Founding Father?"

"Nope. He's a person who was a frequent written respondent to Mr. Armlin's editorials, and what he wrote was almost always negative. In fact, he seemed to be downright hostile toward Mr. Armlin and his opinions. We've just discovered that Gary Molitor may have been using James Madison as a pseudonym—so that's the connection between the two that I'm looking into. And it ties in with your last conversation with your friend about identities and identity theft. Is there anything more you can remember about your discussion that might be of help?"

Doherty gazed into his glass of stout, recalling that evening. "He didn't mention any names, but he did spend some time contemplating how you could discover the identity of someone if you knew they were using a phony name and address. In fact, he even wondered if the police could get involved, if it was serious enough."

"I guess so, because we're involved now. So, he never said anything about James Madison or possibly his next-door neighbor?"

"No, why?"

"Well, there's a real-life James Madison living next door to Gary Molitor's residence, but Armlin, Mr. Armlin, met the real-life James Madison and found out that he wasn't writing into the newspaper. I don't believe Mr. Armlin knew that it was really Gary Molitor next door who was doing the writing, and that's what I'm trying to confirm."

"Wow," said Doherty. "Well, that explains why Bob was so worked up about identities, but I don't remember anything else he said that might help you. Sorry."

"I am, too," said Galen, and they drank their beers together, turning their attention momentarily to an Irish band that had begun setting up for a gig later that evening.

§

The mood in the hospital room wasn't lightened by Galen's announcement that he needed to be in Wyoming for the next three days. Monty was becoming aware of how long his recovery could be and boredom was setting in, Jan was concerned about being able to keep all her counseling appointments, especially if Galen was away, and Ryan was hiding behind a thin shell of cheerfulness. "Party time!" yelped Ryan giving his brother a playful high-five on his good hand, eliciting a smile from Monty and a frown from his grandmother.

"I hope you mean with your brother," she said in a serious tone.

"Of course!" said Ryan, again, a might too chirpily.

"Well, I suppose we could have a pizza party one of those nights," she relented.

"Yaaaaas!" said Monty.

"Hey, Jan, maybe you could..." Galen was about to say *call or visit Beth*, but he suddenly remembered the argument that had started the last time the subject came up, "save some of that pizza for me?" he asked randomly instead. Jan gave him an odd look and then asked, "Have you ever tried to save pizza from these two?" and they all chuckled.

On the drive home Jan said, "You know, when we were sitting around the hospital bed, I realized that we're exactly like the families I counsel every day. Why I didn't see it before, I just don't know. We're missing Christ in our lives, and it's showing. I think we need to spend a little more time being mindful of our Lord, and much more time in church. We've been getting lax in the only thing that really matters in our lives."

"OK, honey, maybe you're right," said Galen. "We can give it a try." He was surprised that rather than feeling like this was

the solution, he was thinking that Jan was subconsciously seeking a way to hide from all of the real issues that beset them.

# Chapter 40.

PART OF the reason that it took most of a day to travel to Cheyenne was that the airport with the best connections available from Portland at the time was located in nearby Laramie, still an hour's commute to the larger city. Jenkins elected to drive the rental car from the airport, and they headed east as the afternoon sun was lowering behind them. They'd talked over the case both on the plane and during the layover in Denver, so after saying "How about steak tonight after we check in?" with a reply of "Sure, sounds good," they lapsed into silence for most of the ride, except to talk about the herds of antelope they saw near the road.

"You ever hunt antelope, Galen?" asked Jenkins who'd grown up in Eugene, Oregon and never been around the animals.

"Yep, when I lived in Pendleton, I shot a few, but the herds aren't as big there as they are around these parts."

"How did it taste? Like beef?"

"No, it's more along the lines of venison," described Galen, "and you need to keep it cool, otherwise it can taste a little wild."

"I'd like to try it sometime," Jenkins nodded. "Maybe they'll have some at a restaurant in Cheyenne." As they drove on, Galen found himself thinking of Armlin's article on hunting. Somehow, the game population numbers he'd published made Galen aware that the herds weren't quite as limitless as he'd once imagined.

The next morning, Galen had some oatmeal and coffee while Jenkins devoured a huge skillet-style breakfast following the large dinner they'd eaten the night before. *Oh, to be young again,* thought Galen, *although Jenkins doesn't have many years before his metabolism slows down, too.*

They passed through the secure entrance at the Sheriff's Office situated in the Laramie County Detention Center building and met with two detectives who'd been working on the Molitor case. After initial greetings and small-talk, the Sheriff strode in. "Gentlemen, it's good to meet you," said Sheriff Bowers shaking their hands. "We feel a little like a carnival act here lately—everyone around the country is popping in to check out our main attraction."

"Thank you for fitting us in," said Jenkins.

"Fine, fine," said Bowers. "The funny thing is, I don't think Molitor, or whoever he is, is going to be able to get used to all of the inattention once this whole thing blows over and he's doing hard time with no visitors."

"Whoever he is?" Galen asked, picking up on the strange choice of words.

"Yep, whoever he is," restated Bowers. "That's why I wanted to sit in on the start of this meeting with you two. You see, we think that Molitor might not be Molitor after all." At the raised eyebrows of the two Portland detectives, he continued. "We can't find any record of this guy who claims to be Gary

Molitor before he appeared on the scene about ten or fifteen years ago. His fingerprints aren't on record, and they don't match the Gary Molitor he claims to be. We learned yesterday that the Gary Molitor we do have the fingerprints for died from injuries soon after returning from the first Iraq war. This guy—we don't know. His DNA doesn't show up anywhere, so the best we can do is look for matching dental records, or hope he has a bone fracture that was treated in a medical facility. We've taken x-rays and impressions of his teeth and hope that something shows up through them."

"Of course, he won't tell you anything," Jenkins guessed.

Bowers shook his head. "We've tried, the FBI has tried, and some detectives from Montana have tried. So far, nothing. We'll be interested in your interviews because we hope like hell he slips up somewhere along the line."

Outside the interview room, it was decided that Jenkins would go in first, and Galen and one of the Cheyenne detectives would observe through the one-way glass along one wall of the chamber. Molitor wasn't anything like Galen had expected. He wasn't lean and hard as might be imagined from someone working as a furniture mover, or from the survival gear and magazines stashed in his house—his body and face appeared soft, almost doughy, and unweathered, although he was by no means overweight. His hair was thinning and the smile lines around his eyes made one think of a pleasant receptionist or car salesman. His mannerisms, on the other hand, contrasted with his outward appearance. The Cheyenne detective, Abbott, had told them that Molitor had a quick intelligence and was prone to 'put on' slightly different styles of speech, almost as if adopting different characters at a whim. Of course, this was all for show, but he'd suspected that this was a strategy Molitor adopted to keep himself from becoming complacent and unintentionally giving away something he didn't want to reveal.

"There's no reason for you to deny it," Jenkins was saying. "She was with you in the car. In fact, we've found her fingerprints and DNA in every car you used to get from Portland to Wyoming. We've been going over your house in fine detail—the very place you held her unlawfully for days, I might add—and found her DNA there, too. It's glaringly obvious you've kept Melissa Davidson under your control for nearly two weeks."

"I'm not denying I had a girl in the car with me when I was stopped. Do you think I don't know that I did? Of course, I know that. Why would I deny it?" To Galen, his response looked and sounded exactly like a Martin Short skit from *Saturday Night Live*. *Maybe that's where he picked it up*, he thought.

Jenkins sighed for the umpteenth time. "So, we have absolutely no problem proving that you kept Melissa Davidson from the moment you abducted her at the Washington Square mall in Portland until you were captured here in Wyoming. My question is why?"

"Why what?" asked Molitor.

"Why take a little four-year-old girl from her mother? Did you know her, or was it just a random, spur-of-the-moment kind of thing?"

There was no answer, but the pause had made Jenkins suspicious.

"Did you know her before you took her?"

"How could I know her?" asked Molitor.

"Did you know the mother? Were you looking for some kind of revenge on the family?"

"What family?" asked Molitor.

Jenkins changed tactics. "You like little girls—it's obvious. We've cracked your computer and we know which folders have the kiddie porn. You wanted to have your way with her."

"Kiddie porn?" asked Molitor, "are you joking?"

"No," Jenkins lied. "And we saw how gently you were treating her. How lovingly. And you had her all to yourself, it was just a matter of time before you..."

"Are you out of your mind?" asked Molitor, suddenly out of character. "I'd never treat my..." and then he stopped cold.

"Treat your what?" asked Jenkins, trying to prod him just a bit further. "Your lover?" No reaction. "No? Your own daughter?" Then Jenkins stared intently at Molitor as he said, "You know Melissa is referring to you as her uncle."

An almost imperceptible smile swept across Molitor's face. "She did?" And after that Molitor refused to say another word.

The detectives met after the interview and had the feeling that they were close to something. "He reacted to that," said Abbott, "to the intimation of his abusing her and to the bit about her calling him her uncle. That's the most we've seen him respond to any questions yet, and I'm impressed," he looked over at Jenkins. "Why did you say that part about her thinking of him as an uncle?"

"Because it's true," responded Jenkins. "The family won't let us anywhere near her yet, but we've spoken to the parents and one thing they did say is that Melissa was led to believe, by Molitor, that he was her uncle."

Galen had been briefed about this on the plane trip, so it was no news to him, but it was to Abbott. Galen interjected, "He made her feel like she was family from the very beginning, and it's obvious she was, or represented, someone that he would place on a pedestal—although that's not the right word—give special status to. There were some things he would never do to her, thus the reaction to the comment about kiddie porn."

"Yeah," said Abbott, "but does he place all preschool girls in the same category, or was it just Melissa in particular for some reason?" The question was answered with shrugs from the two others.

"Well, at least we've found a spot where we have more digging to do," said Jenkins.

Molitor was much more guarded during the interview with Galen that afternoon. "Mr. Molitor," Galen began, "I'd first like to know why you assumed the name of your next-door neighbor in writing letters to The Oregon Sentinel."

"What letters?" asked Molitor, predictably.

"Why, the ones we found on your computer, addressed to Robert Armlin, the editor of the newspaper, and signed by you as James Madison, the name of your seventy-eight-year-old neighbor."

"I didn't write any letters," said Molitor, and Galen swore he could see gears turning in the man's head.

"Yes, you did, we have them on your computer."

"I didn't write them, detective. I liked the way James Madison expressed himself in response to that ass Armlin and copied his letters from the internet."

"We can prove you wrote them," said Galen, wishing he knew more about computers.

"Oh? And how will you do that?" asked Molitor obviously sensing Galen's insecurity about the subject.

"By the date stamp," said Galen, winging it and now positively cursing himself that he didn't know more about computers.

"Like I said," replied Molitor smugly, "How's that?"

Galen quickly changed tactics. "It's obvious from the tone of the letters that you felt some animosity towards the editor, Robert Armlin."

"Yeah, the guy's an elitist jerk," said Molitor adamantly.

"So, you admit that you felt antagonistic towards him?"

"Sure," said Molitor. "How do you feel about..." trying to gauge Galen's political leanings, "Joyce Klemper, from the New York Times? A little bit spiteful now and then?"

Galen had never read her columns, but knew that she was a liberal voice, and he rarely agreed with anything he'd heard that she'd written.

"OK," said Galen. "Fair enough—that's the public voice of the man. But how do you feel about him as a person?"

"How should I know? I never met the guy," replied Molitor.

"You never, say, crashed into his car?"

"What are you talking about?" asked Molitor.

"We have white paint from your car on Armlin's Toyota, and Armlin's black paint on yours," said Galen. "Sounds like a collision to me."

"What?" asked Molitor with an air of disbelief. "Someone stole my car and crashed it?"

And that was all that Galen could get out of Molitor.

"That's OK," said Jenkins sympathetically on the plane ride home the next afternoon. They'd both tried fresh interviews with Molitor that morning, but he'd stonewalled the both of them. "At least we know that he cared about Melissa for some special reason, and that's more than we knew before."

"Yeah," said Galen morosely. "Which isn't much, is it? That slimy bastard could drive me to drink if I had to be around him all of the time—poor Abbott," as he nursed the second of the two beers they were limited to on the flight.

They each had messages chime when they took their phones off airplane mode after landing in Portland. From Sheriff Bowers: *We now have Molitor's identity. He's Gary Rockney from Ames, Iowa. More info to follow.* Galen and Jenkins looked at each other. "So, Madison wasn't Madison, and Molitor wasn't Molitor," said Galen as they disembarked from the plane. He noticed that he had another message below that one as he walked towards the parking lot. It was from the Coffee Creek Correctional Facility: *Galen, please come by. I need to see you. Beth.* Galen sat in his car before turning the ignition and stared out across the fleet of automobiles in the gathering dusk. *What now?* he thought and wished that he didn't have to wait until visiting hours tomorrow to find out.

# Chapter 41.

"JUST TELL me what happened!" Galen had said, a little too forcefully, and then in a calmer voice, "Please, honey." Jan had hit him with a verbal assault the moment he'd walked in the door and set his bags down.

"I didn't want to bother you in your precious work," she'd started, "and I knew you couldn't do anything from Wyoming or wherever you were anyway."

"Do anything about what?" he'd asked.

"Everything!" she'd shouted, throwing up her clenched fists and dropping into the nearby couch.

He was now sitting beside her and took the chance to put his hand on her shoulder, which she either didn't notice or grudgingly accepted.

Jan took a deep breath and sagged visibly as she let it out. "Ryan disappeared from school today, and I had to cancel a ton of appointments to deal with it. It was a nightmare."

Galen glanced over towards Ryan's room and could see a light shining from under the sill, so he guessed that his grandson was home. "Is he in his room now?" he asked just to be sure.

"Yes," admitted Jan, "but it took the police to find him."

"Did it? Where was he?" asked Galen.

"They finally found him wandering around Mt. Tabor Park," said Jan.

*That's where I would've gone if I were him*, thought Galen, *a quiet park*. "How is he?"

"Who knows?" She sat up and nearly screamed, "He's like a different person! I gave him what-for, but it was like water off a duck's back!" Her neck muscles tensed even more. "He's destroying this family," she said adamantly.

"I'll talk to him, hon," said Galen, suddenly feeling the exhaustion from his trip. Or at least that's what he guessed it was.

He was once again rapping on the door, but the room was quiet this time. "Come in," came Ryan's defeated voice.

There were no tears, but Ryan looked hollow and somehow ten years older.

"What happened, Ryan?" asked Galen. "Why did you walk out of school?"

The boy paused before answering. "Have you ever felt alone, Gramp? I mean really, truly alone?" asked Ryan from a small space inside himself.

"I think I have," said Galen, "but maybe not like you're feeling it. Maybe not so much."

This might have buoyed Ryan somewhat, but he looked like he'd sunk even a little deeper.

"Liz left me," said Ryan after several moments. "She said that it was just too much for her to deal with."

"You mean the accident?" asked Galen.

"Yeah, and all of the stuff that's happened after."

Galen nodded. "Well, I hate to say it, but it probably is too much for her. Just think about it, son. She's really still just a girl even though she's fourteen years old," he took a guess.

"Almost fifteen," muttered Ryan.

"But most people don't have to deal with issues like this until they're in their twenties. And look at you—like I said, you've been kicked forward another five years by this. I hate to be brutally honest, but either she'll get over this and deal with it like most of your friends will, or by the time she doesn't, you'll have moved on."

"But I loved her," began Ryan, although without choking up.

"I know, I know, I know," said Galen. "Every one of the dozen more times in the years ahead will hurt just as much, but she's either the right person for you or she isn't. Only time will tell."

Ryan let out a huge breath and collapsed back on his bed, staring up at the ceiling. "I'm sorry I bailed on school, but I'm just sketched out."

"Only another week, Ryan. It's just another week before school's out. You can do this, and it'll be worth it to finish out this school year. Do you really want to do it all over again next year? Relive eighth grade and middle school?"

"Oh, damn!" said Ryan, realizing what that meant. "No! Definitely not. Never again."

"Get some sleep, kiddo," said Galen. "You look like you need it."

Ryan nodded as Galen gently shut the door behind him.

# Chapter 42.

GALEN AND Jenkins briefed the morning session on what had transpired during the Molitor interviews, and had just mentioned the text message about him being identified as Gary Rockney when Pembrook broke in.

"Yeah, the Captain put me on it, and we have more information about him now," he said, consulting a sheet of paper. "He was born Gary Rockney in Ames, Iowa. His father was a grocer, and his mother was a housewife. Not much to report there. But when he was eight years old, his family was in a terrible accident on a car trip when they were crossing the bridge from Dubuque into Illinois. The mother, father, and six-year-old sister were all killed, and Gary Rockney was severely injured. They did some dental reconstruction after the accident, and so that's how they were able to identify him through his front teeth. After he recovered, he was put into foster care in Des Moines where he graduated from high school and then he completely disappeared off the face of the earth. He reemerged as Gary Molitor, but how he chose that identity, we still don't know."

Later that morning, Galen requested some leave and drove down to Wilsonville to visit Beth and hear the reason for her change of heart, fearing the worst.

Come to find out, there was no burning issue. His daughter simply wanted to talk.

When she entered the room, he began, "Beth, I'm sorry I wasn't very gentle in the way I broke the news to you about Monty."

"That's OK, Dad," said Beth. "I've had lots of time to think about it, and I know it's not your fault."

Galen was stunned and he tried hard not to show it. His daughter hadn't called him 'Dad' since she was incarcerated, and he hadn't seen her so contrite in years. "Are you doing OK?" he asked.

Beth shrugged her shoulders and looked down at her hands. "Yeah, I am," she said. And in a moment of honesty continued, "That news about Monty being shot showed me more about myself than I thought possible. I've been seeing a therapist since then, and she's helped me to realize that I've been working myself further and further away from my kids with everything I've done, and I want that to end." She quickly brushed away a tear and flashed a rare smile. "They've told me that Monty made it through surgery and is in recovery. So, is he coping OK?"

"Well, I've only seen him in the hospital bed, but on the outside he's looking good."

"How long will it take him to recover the use of his hand? How long before I can see him?"

"They think he'll be out of the hospital in a week or two. About his hand, they're not sure. They say that it'll take several operations to make it fully functional, and they're going to see how the muscles and tendons on his hip heal and perform before they worry about it needing further work. We'll get him here as soon as possible."

"Thanks," she nodded. "I can't wait to see him. And how's Ryan holding up?"

"Not so good, Beth," said Galen. "He was in denial at first and has lashed out some while he works through it. The true consequences will sink in over time, but I can see he's already having trouble dealing with his guilt. I personally think that he's both too embarrassed and too ashamed to see you right now."

And in an unexpected moment of candor Beth said, "Tell him from someone who's screwed up—a lot—that I understand, and I forgive him. Tell him I want to see him."

"I will, Beth," as the guards announced that the visit was over.

"Thanks for coming down, Dad," said Beth.

*Thank God*, thought Galen as he drove out of the parking lot. He'd recently found himself worrying about how Beth would survive two more years in confinement if she cut off all contact with those who cared about her the most. He knew that she must have been experiencing some of the initial stages of grief when she lashed out at him and then refused to speak— maybe now she'd worked her way to one of the final stages. He knew not to get his hopes up too much about this being a real turn-around since he'd witnessed her several back-slides over the years, but he also knew that she was now more mature and might finally be dealing with some of her personal issues. And she was seeing a therapist now, something that she'd balked at her entire life, so he took that as an incredibly positive sign. He, for one, couldn't wait to watch the reunion between her and her sons.

# Chapter 43.

EMMA ARMLIN'S expression changed immediately from one of expectation to one of resignation the moment she saw Galen's face. "Still nothing?" she asked in a flat tone while inviting him inside. The house was neat and clean on this visit, which Galen noted with some relief.

"I'm sorry, Emma, we still haven't found your husband, but we do have more information that I wanted to ask you about."

"Anything I can do, Galen," said Emma. "You know that."

"I'm sure that you've read about the capture of Gary Molitor, or Gary Rockney as we've discovered his true name to be, in the kidnapping of Melissa Davidson," said Galen as he took a seat. "And there's a connection between your husband and Mr. Molitor-slash-Rockney that we're trying to understand."

"What kind of connection?" asked Emma. "The girl's hair found in Bob's car?"

"No. We're still wondering about that, too, but this has to do with letters he received as newspaper editor. You see, a person named James Madison was a frequent respondent to your husband's articles, and they weren't always the kindest or most agreeable in nature."

"Yes, I know the name," said Emma. "Bob often joked that his next editorial would really send someone like James

Madison off the deep end. He once said that Mr. Madison was like a caricature of an Oregon redneck."

"Oh, so he'd mentioned him before to you? That's very interesting because I'd found in his notes that he was very curious about Madison. Did he mention that he was going to visit James Madison right before he disappeared?"

"No, not Madison. He said that he'd made a new friend and was going to visit him without mentioning who he was," said Emma. "But if that was James Madison, I'd think it very strange indeed—the two were like oil and water from what I understood. They probably would have killed each other if they met."

"Well, as it happens, James Madison wasn't who Mr. Armlin thought he was," replied Galen, and at Emma's raised eyebrows, he continued. "In his briefcase, your husband had the names and addresses of the four James Madisons living in the Portland area, and he was obviously curious if the person writing into the paper was one of them, a real person in other words. He posed as a newspaper salesman and met the one he thought wrote the letters, but the man, an older English gentleman, was not even a reader of The Oregon Sentinel. Mr. Armlin found they had a lot in common and was scheduled to have a drink of sherry with him on the day he disappeared."

"So that was the new friend," said Emma. "He actually made friends with James Madison. Isn't that funny?" After shaking her head and thinking for a moment she asked, "So who wrote into the paper under that name then?"

"Well, that's the connection with Gary Molitor. Gary Molitor lived right next door to Mr. Madison and used the old man's name, and probably his address, to write the letters to the editor. I interviewed him in jail recently and found that he didn't much care for your husband as the author of editorials, but swears that he never met him in person."

"That's just bizarre, isn't it?" asked Emma. "Do you think he did something to Bob?"

"We think it's too much of a coincidence, too," said Galen, ignoring the question about her husband and slightly changing the subject. "Did Mr. Armlin ever mention a Gary Molitor or a Gary Rockney?"

Emma thought carefully and then replied, "Neither of those ring a bell."

"OK, thank you Emma," said Galen, rising. "As usual, I'll be in touch if we learn anything new." Emma showed him to the door and stood watching as Galen walked to his car and drove off.

# Chapter 44.

TOM CALLED Galen and Jenkins into his office a few days later—an interval that had been filled with routine business and with nothing substantial provided by either the various state agencies or the FBI concerning Rockney. The Captain was just about to brief them on something when his phone rang, and the two detectives chatted quietly in the background while he took the call. "Sorry about that, gentlemen," he said, hanging up. "As I was about to say, we've heard an interesting piece of news from Melissa Davidson's mother. She called earlier today and said that Melissa is opening up more and more about her experiences during the abduction and she mentioned the nice older man who reminded her of her grandfather at Molitor's, uhm, Rockney's house—but then she apparently broke down into tears at the recollection a few moments later." Jenkins and Galen exchanged looks.

"An older man?" asked Jenkins. "Could it be Armlin?" asked Galen.

"Who knows?" asked Tom. "The family's been keeping Melissa protected from the outside world and they've been working privately with therapists, but Mrs. Davidson said that she's willing to allow an interview with Melissa as long as she and a therapist are present and that we follow her guidelines. We've set up a meeting for this afternoon, and I'd like you to take the lead with the questions, Galen—a single interrogator so that we don't overwhelm her—and Jenkins, you can help watch for any indicators that your partner might miss. Make sure you bring a photo of Armlin for the girl to examine."

"Will do, Captain," said Galen. "Are the Davidsons back in their home now?"

"Yes, and they're expecting you."

"Has the arraignment of Rockney been processed?" asked Jenkins as they got up to leave.

"Not yet, it's scheduled for tomorrow. And the official guess is that he'll be housed in Cheyenne for the foreseeable future."

§

As requested by the family, Galen parked the car a block away from the Davidson's house and he and Jenkins walked the remainder of the way. The media blitz had died down, and the family wanted to minimize anything that might attract undue attention. Joni Davidson met them at the door, and Galen was surprised that he'd thought of her as mousey on his first encounter. Her hair was done up in a simple but more professional manner, and the woman herself appeared to be much more confident and self-assured.

As they walked into the living room, Joni announced, "Melissa, these are the two men I told you about who wanted to come for your lemonade party."

Melissa jumped up from the couch and formally shook each of their hands. "Would you like cookies as well?" she asked in her most adult manner.

Both men nodded and Galen said, "Yes, that would be nice."

"Would you go and get the cookies from the kitchen?" Joni asked of her daughter.

When she left the room, Galen asked, "Does she know that we're police officers?"

"I think she does," said Joni. "I haven't mentioned it to her, but I don't mind if you do. Oh, and this is Collette Rankin, her main therapist." There were more introductions and hand-shakes as Melissa came in burdened by a large plate of cookies which she handled admirably.

As they sat down around a small table, Melissa took up a carton her mother had set there and began pouring lemon-ade, holding the heavy container with both hands. Galen raised the glass she'd just filled and said, "This looks good, Melissa. Thank you for having us over. Did you make the lemonade?"

"No, silly, it came from the refrigerator," said Melissa with a smile.

"Ah, I see," said Galen, taking a cookie that was now of-fered. "Did you know that Stan and I are policemen?"

Melissa nodded quickly and said, "Yes, I guessed when Mama said you were coming and wanted to talk to me."

"Do you know why we want to talk to you?" asked Galen as he took a sip of his lemonade. "Mmmm. My favorite."

Melissa shook her head and Galen said, "It's because you mentioned a man who looked like your grandfather when you were staying with Mr. Molitor. Do you have any pictures of your grandfather?"

Melissa nodded and Joni said, "Why don't you go get the picture off the refrigerator, sweetie?" Melissa hopped up and ran into the kitchen only to reappear a moment later with a worn photo in her hand. She held it out to Galen, and he looked it over. "My, he's very handsome, isn't he?" Melissa nodded back. "But he's dead now," she added.

"I know, and I'm sorry," said Galen.

"It's OK," said Melissa. "He was old."

"I suppose he was," said Galen, pulling a photograph out of his jacket pocket. "Say, he looks just like the man in this picture, don't you think?"

Melissa studied the picture for a moment and exclaimed, pointing, "Yes, that's him! See, I told you Mama—he's the man who came to Uncle Gary's!"

Galen continued calmly, "Was he a friend of Uncle Gary?"

"Um," said Melissa slightly shaking her head. "I don't know. We played a whisper game."

"A whisper game?"

"Yes, he said that we could talk, but only if I whispered—he called it the whisper game."

"And this was at Uncle Gary's?"

Melissa nodded. "Yes, but he didn't come inside—we talk-ed through the window. We whispered through the window," and she continued to make some wuh, wuh, sounds to continue the alliteration.

"Could I have another cookie, please?" asked Galen, and Melissa happily got up from her chair and brought the plate over to him. He chose an Oreo and asked. "Should I eat the middle first?" Melissa grinned up at him. "With your teeth!" she laughed.

After downing the creamy filling, Galen asked, "So, what did you talk about? Whisper about?" asked Galen, "with the man who looked like your granddad?"

"Grandfather," corrected Melissa.

"Grandfather," said Galen.

"He wanted me to come with him," she said. "He said it was a surprise for Mama."

"A surprise?" asked Galen.

"Yes, he said my time was done staying with Uncle Gary, but he didn't say Uncle Gary, he said Mr. Manison. He said my time was done and it was going to be a big surprise—he was going to take me home to Mama."

"Did you go with him, Melissa?" asked Galen.

Melissa looked down and gave a small nod with a guilty look on her face. The detectives, Joni, and Colette all exchanged quick glances. It was evident they were heading into dangerous territory.

Joni patted her hand. "I know we've talked a lot about never going anywhere with strangers, honey, but I'm not going to be mad. This time, it's OK."

"He said he wasn't a stranger," said Melissa, still looking down. "He said he knew you. And he knew my name."

"I know, honey. That's why it's OK this time."

"So, you did go with him, Melissa?" Galen asked gently a second time.

Melissa nodded and said to the table, "He lifted me through the window and held my hand and we went to his car. He said Mama was going to be so happy. He said it was still a whisper game, but we had to whisper with our feet. I remember that. Whisper with our feet."

"And did he drive you?"

"Yes, but then Uncle Gary came running out when we started moving. He was yelling," Melissa began with a tear, but then was suddenly sobbing. "He told me later that I'd been... That I'd been bad!" she choked.

They all knew at once that the session was over. Collette and Joni took Melissa into the bedroom while Galen and Jenkins sat at the small table, toying with their lemonade glasses. "Now we know how Melissa's hair got in Armlin's car," said Galen. "The guy was trying to rescue her. But then what happened?"

"She said they were driving," said Jenkins. "Maybe Rockney followed or chased them in his car and they ended up on Lee Street?"

"That would explain the collision," nodded Galen. "Rockney forced him to a stop with his car?"

"That makes the most sense," said Jenkins as the two women and the girl emerged from the bedroom, Melissa with a freshly washed face.

"Thank you so much for the lemonade party, Melissa," said Galen reaching out his large hand to shake her small one. "I'm sorry that what we talked about made you cry."

Melissa nodded and then remembering her manners said, "Thank you so much for coming." Looking up at Galen she asked, "Do you know Uncle Gary, too?"

"Not really, Melissa. I've only met him one time, but we didn't get to talk too much."

"Oh," said Melissa, "he talked to me a lot," and at her mother's urging she offered them each one more cookie before they left.

Colette followed them outside. "You sure are good with children, Detective," she said. "I haven't seen her open up to anyone as much since I've been working with her."

"You can't imagine how many tea parties I had with my daughter when she was four," said Galen. "She reminds me a lot of Beth at that age."

"I could see that you wanted to ask more, but I'm not sure we'll get her to go much further than that," said Colette, "until she makes more progress in dealing with her abduction. You of course understand that that night was extremely traumatic for her."

Galen nodded. "Unfortunately, I do. And I realize that these questions weren't easy for Melissa, but at least we now know that the disappearance of Mr. Armlin happened on the exact same night that Rockney... Molitor bolted with her—probably because he'd been found out." Colette turned to go inside when he asked, "Ms. Rankin, if you think Melissa gets to the point where you believe she can take more questioning, or if she pops out with anything that you think might help us, could you please give us a call?" handing her his card.

"Yes, I'll do that, Detective." Joni and Melissa were both waving at them out the window as Galen and Jenkins waved and walked back up the street to their car.

They caught Tom at the office before he left for the day and briefed him on the interview.

"That sure changes what we know about Armlin now, doesn't it? What do you think was the sequence of events?" he asked.

"Well," said Galen, "it seems that Armlin got Melissa into his car, he tried to leave with her, but they were followed by Rockney. Rockney may have stopped them with his own car and retaken Melissa. Now I'm guessing that he somehow got Armlin down by Fanno Creek and they had a scuffle or fight and then he somehow tried to truss Armlin up with the duct tape that we discovered near the disturbed vegetation."

"But there are still a lot of questions, aren't there?" asked Jenkins. "How did Armlin find Melissa? Just notice her through the window?"

"Wait a minute, that makes sense," said Galen. "He was going to visit James Madison next door for a glass of sherry and happened to recognize the kidnapped girl who had her picture plastered all over the papers."

They all nodded as Jenkins continued, "Then, of course, there's the question of what happened to Armlin? Did Rockney do something with him? Truss him up with duct tape? Did

Armlin flee—maybe wounded somehow? And then Rockney takes off from his house on his flight to Wyoming—why didn't he use his own car? He happily jacked cars all along the way—why leave his with evidence on it next to his house? Why take Madison's truck instead?"

"Now that's a good question," said Tom. "Have we revisited the neighbors in the vicinity of Fanno Creek since the initial interviews?" Both Galen and Jenkins shook their heads. "Then let's try again with some of this new information in mind. Good work, guys. See you in the morning."

# Chapter 45.

JAN HAD an evening service and prayer meeting to attend, and Ryan had said that he wanted to go to the end-of-year party that the middle school was throwing outdoors on the intramural field given that the weather was so nice. His grandparents had both warned him that it might not be easy and that he might not be so welcome by many of his classmates, but he insisted on going almost in spite of those facts. Galen was happy to spend an evening at the hospital with Monty.

"Rummy!" cried Monty with a big smile. "That's four games to one now, Gramp!"

"For a one-handed player, you sure are a card shark," laughed Galen. "Have the nurses here been teaching you tricks?"

"Just lucky!" bragged Monty. "Wanna play one more?"

"I'm playing until I beat you, pipsqueak!"

"Go ahead and try, ya big lug!" laughed Monty while Galen dealt out another hand.

The doctors had decided to keep Monty in the hospital for at least another week. His hip was healing well, but there were still problems with a persistent infection in his abdomen. Nothing showed up with ultrasound, but there was some swelling and pain, so they were going to try another round of aggressive antibiotics and anti-inflammatories before opting for any exploratory surgery. The boy's hand was also healing well, and it was responding to the physical therapy regimen as expected.

Things were not going as well as Galen had hoped between the two brothers, however. Rather than wanting to spend time with Monty, Ryan had pulled away. Galen and Jan had mandated in-person facetime between the two, but so far, Ryan was keeping up a seemingly unassailable mental wall between himself and his brother. Galen guessed that it was a combination of guilt and not wanting to show his brother any signs of weakness—Ryan simply couldn't bring himself to act at ease around, nor comfort, Monty. Jan and Galen had agreed that if his attitude persisted much longer, counseling or therapy would be the best alternative for him. The only problem in Galen's eyes was that Jan was adamant that he needed spiritual counseling, either by her or a close friend of hers, whereas Galen thought he needed traditional psychological help, although he hadn't as yet expressed his feelings about this to Jan.

"So, Ryan went to the graduation bash?" asked Monty, gathering his cards with his good hand.

"Yep, he wanted to celebrate the end of middle school the right way," said Galen.

"I wish I could have gone," said Monty, though not dejectedly. "Just think—Ryan is now going to be a high-schooler while I'm still stuck in the seventh grade." Juggling the cards awkwardly in his hand, he set them down, picked up one card from the deck, tucked it into his set, and discarded another. "He'll probably think he's too cool for me next year."

*He's being too cool with you now*, thought Galen. "Well, that happens sometimes, Monty," he said instead. "You're luckier than me with my brothers—I got beat on for being too young and I got beat on for being too old."

"Wow, it sounds like you got pounded a lot," said Monty.

"You have no idea, son," said Galen, discarding one of his three-of-a-kind.

§

Galen was going over the Armlin files when Cushing popped into his office just before lunch. "Galen, several patrolmen and I recanvassed the neighborhood around Lee St. and Fanno Creek and we found out something you might find interesting." Galen set aside the folders as Cushing continued. "I spoke to an older guy who lives near the end of Lee St. where a path goes down to Fanno. He said he couldn't be sure of the exact evening, but when I asked if he'd seen anything unusual around that time period, like the white Focus or a yellow pickup truck, he immediately said yes, he'd seen the pickup. He said the reason he remembered it is that he'd gotten up to pee at his usual time of about 3 AM when he looked outside and saw a truck parked near the street light that was exactly like one he used to own in the 70's, only his was more of a burgundy color instead of the faded yellow that he saw out the window. I asked him if he saw anyone in or around the truck and he said no. He did say he'd been looking forward to checking out the truck in the morning since it brought back a lot of memories, but it was gone by the time he'd started making breakfast."

"Thanks, Deb," said Galen. "Do we know where the truck is now? Is it still in Vancouver or back with Madison?"

"I don't know, but I can check," she replied.

"No, that's all right. I'll give Mike Yellen with Vancouver PD a call. I want to doublecheck on how thorough they were with the truck," said Galen. "Hey, thanks, and good work."

"Sure thing. I'll let you know if anything else turns up."

Galen was on the phone as soon as Cushing was out of the office. "Hello, Mike, this is Galen."

"Galen, you missed me, didn't ya?" asked Yellen with a chuckle on the other end of the line, and not mentioning bone breaking for a change.

"Like a migraine, Mike," replied Galen. "I just wanted to see if you still had that yellow '78 Chevy pickup that was used by Gary Rockney?"

"Who?" asked Yellen, and after a pause, "oh, yeah—that Gary Molitor as he was known?"

"Yeah, him," said Galen.

"Just a sec, let me check," and after a minute Yellen came back on line. "Yep. We haven't released it yet, but the boys said that it's ready to go any time."

"Do you know how well it was gone over? A full forensic exam?" asked Galen.

"Wow, you want everything, don't you? Just a sec and I'll get the file sent up here. Shouldn't take a minute." He was quickly back on the phone. "They're bringing it up now," said Yellen. "So, how about them Mariners?" and the two chatted about baseball for a few minutes. "Here it is, and…" flipping through pages, "it looks like the pickup was given a quick once-over when we first found it, but due to the high profile of the kidnapping they went over it in detail when it came back to the shop."

"Even the bed?" asked Galen.

"Yep, the entire thing," replied Yellen. "And it looks like someone was tidy. There were traces of bleach, and the whole exterior had either been washed by hand or taken through a carwash."

"So, they found nothing on the exterior, no blood, duct tape, hair, fluids?"

"Clean as a whistle. The cab of course was filled with hair, DNA, and prints from the owner and some from both Molitor and the girl, but you knew that—nothing else was found."

Galen sighed. "OK, thanks, Mike. I guess it was too much to hope for. We're suspecting now that Molitor did something with a missing person we have here named Armlin—oh yeah, the owner of the briefcase you found for me—anyway, the bleach makes me even more suspicious."

"Too bad," sympathized Yellen. "I don't want to think about what the bleach was used for. We should have that truck back to its owner soon."

Galen set the phone gently back into its cradle with an even worse feeling about Armlin, if that was possible.

Galen's forebodings about Armlin hit rock bottom when Cushing slid quietly into his office an hour later and said softly, "Sorry to disturb you, Galen, but I thought you should know that they found a body in the river this morning."

Galen's stomach tightened, and he raised his eyebrows for her to continue.

"It was found by some fisherman near Kelly Point Park where the Columbia Slough feeds into the Willamette. Forensics is on it, but Brenda said specifics might take a while. No identification has been made yet, but the body has been in the water for some time and is in pretty bad shape. We know that it's male, around six-foot, and older, but that's about it so far. Also, there was a crude attempt to weight it down, but it was wrapped in plastic and duct tape and whoever did it did a poor job of it."

"Oh, no..." moaned Galen to himself, shaking his head at the news.

He found it difficult to concentrate on anything for the rest of the afternoon and made several calls down to the lab after Brenda returned with the body for a more detailed analysis.

Just as he was about to leave for home, Brenda called with news of the identity. *Thank God for red herrings,* thought Galen as he walked over to his car after the conversation. The corpse ended up being Manuel Estaban, the suspected murderer of Cordoba. With that call, things lightened up considerably for Galen while plunging the team searching for Cordoba's killer into utter darkness.

*Ah man,* thought Galen as he turned his beater out of the parking garage and into rush-hour traffic, *I must be getting old—why am I so emotionally invested in this case?* He eased back in the driver's seat and consciously relaxed his grip on the steering wheel. *For a moment there I thought we'd lost him.*

# Chapter 46.

As GALEN opened the front door, he heard Jan saying, "…
and that is no tone to take with me!" He set down his briefcase
and walked quietly into the kitchen where the conversation
was taking place. Jan was on the telephone, and he immediately assumed that she was having an argument with Ryan. "We
need to do what we see fit, since you're obviously not taking
care of him!" He then realized that she must be bickering with
Beth. "No, I will not!" spat Jan. "He needs a solid upbringing
and some spiritual guidance, that you…" There was a lengthy
pause and then Jan calmly said, "Well, you obviously aren't
listening to what I have to say, so I'm ending this conversation
now, Beth. Goodbye…" She was just about to hang up the
phone when Galen managed, "Just a sec! I want to talk to her,"
and grabbed the receiver from her before it hit the counter.
"She's in one of her moods," said Jan disgustedly, "so you're
wasting your time," and she walked out of the room.

"Beth? Are you still there?" asked Galen.

"Yeah, Dad, I'm here," said Beth, "and I'm not in one of
my moods—Mom is!"

Galen was reserving his judgement about this for the moment. "It's so rare for you to call," he said, "you probably
caught her by surprise."

"I just think she doesn't like to hear what I have to say because it goes against what she wants." Beth's words had been rushed at first, but she'd quickly calmed down.

"What were you telling her?" asked Galen.

"Well, I've been worrying about Ryan since your visit, and I talked to my therapist who said she couldn't believe that Ryan wasn't in therapy already. She said that he's been through one of the worst traumas anyone can face and he's at a crucial stage in his social and mental development, so that if he isn't helped through it, it could end up being a disaster for him."

"The school counselors were working with him nearly every day…" began Galen.

"Yes, she guessed that they had, but she doesn't think that's enough, and neither do I."

"So, you think we should get him some professional help?"

"Definitely! And that's what I tried to tell Mom. But she said that she's already started some spiritual counselling sessions with him at her office and is now making sure he goes to church every Sunday! That's insane, and I tried to tell her that!"

Galen peeked around the corner to see if Jan was within earshot, but she appeared to be in another room. Still, he kept his voice low when he said, "She means well, Beth, but I think this whole thing has gotten to her more than any of us. She's become a changed woman and believes that her faith is the only thing to see her through. Unfortunately, she's also convinced that this as the sole path for Ryan, too."

"I hate to put my foot down here, but I'm making some changes, as well," said Beth. "Those are my kids, and they're still my responsibility." She paused for several seconds. "I know I haven't been there for them since I've been in here, but I can see now that my only way forward is to grow up and own up to my mistakes. I talked with my therapist and a legal counsel here and know that I still have rights to say how my kids are raised. I must insist that Ryan gets professional help. I absolutely don't want him to end up like me. The facility here offers family counselling, and my therapist says that she'd love to provide sessions for both Ryan and me. Maybe when Monty is better, we can all three meet."

"That sounds great, Beth," said Galen. "What do we have to do to make that happen?" As she described the details, he found himself thinking that the best outcome of this was that Beth was coming back. She was taking an interest in her family again. He, himself, had never seen the need for therapy, and so he had only just recently realized that Ryan could be a true candidate. However, he also found himself thinking that by the time he did recognize the signs of things going downhill, it would already have been too late, and he hoped it wasn't so already.

"OK," said Galen as they wrapped up the conversation. "Now the only thing I have to do is talk to your mom about this."

"Good luck, Dad, and thanks for being there for me—I'm counting on you being my advocate in this," said Beth. And then just before she hung up, she said again, "Good luck."

Galen set down the phone, steeled himself, and went to find Jan.

# Chapter 47.

**A FEW** days later, Galen received a phone call from Joni Davidson. "Good Morning, Ms. Davidson, oh, um, Joni—what can I do for you?"

"Hello, Detective," said Joni. "I'm calling for another reason, but first I wanted to let you know that Melissa keeps talking about the lemonade party we had and wonders if you want to come over for a tea party sometime."

Galen chuckled, "Sure, tell her that would be fun to do. What can I help you with?"

"Colette, Melissa's therapist, said that you'd be interested in anything Melissa said about the kidnapping, especially as regards that older gentleman—Mr. Armlin?"

"Yes, anything she can recall will help. Has she remembered something?"

"A few things," said Joni. "First off, she claims that 'Uncle Gary' talked to me on the phone nearly every day, but never let Melissa speak to me. I never received a single phone call from that," lowering her voice to a whisper, "monster." Galen guessed that Melissa was probably within earshot in the room.

"Ah, I think I know who that was," Galen replied. "From phone records and interviews we know that Rockney spoke to his girlfriend on a daily basis and must have used your name to make Melissa think that you and he were in daily contact."

"Oh, ... I guess that would explain it. I'm not sure how important these other things are, but," and she began to read from a list, "he made her egg salad sandwiches every day for lunch in his house, and now I can't get her to eat any eggs at all. He was apparently a fan of 'Jeopardy' and spent a lot of time on the computer. I don't understand it, but she still asks about him, still somehow thinking that he's her uncle. And the last thing is that he kept telling her that he was going to take her home to Iowa, and that I was going to meet her there." She again lowered her voice to a whisper, "He was a nutcase."

"Yes, he was... is," said Galen. "All of this information will help us get a better picture of what happened when she was with him, so I really appreciate your calling this in, Joni."

"You're welcome, Detective," said Joni. "I'll let you know if she mentions anything else." Galen was just about to hang up the phone when she suddenly yelled, "Oh, Detective? You still there?"

"Yes," said Galen, returning the phone to his ear.

"This is also probably nothing, but the other day we were driving by a carwash, and Melissa said that she'd been through one with 'Uncle Gary', and it was fun. She said that the only thing that wasn't fun was keeping her eyes closed until they got inside it."

"Did she say why she had to keep her eyes closed?"

"No, just that 'Uncle Gary' got mad at her when she tried to peek."

"OK, thanks again, Joni—bye."

That nasty feeling returned, lodging in the pit of his stomach, and he wondered this time whether it would ever go away.

# Chapter 48.

GALEN STARED glumly out of the window on another flight to Laramie. "That would be just like a reward," Jan had said in disgust. "A reward?" Galen had erupted, and continued, "The poor guy's been ostracized by his friends and is living in guilt. Give him a break, Jan!" That was how the fight had started. Since Galen had lost, Ryan wasn't with him on this trip to Wyoming. His idea had been to let his grandson come along, just to get out of Portland, but Jan had been adamant in her refusal. For the first time in years, Galen found himself pondering where their marriage was heading. *What's a single example of when we've seen eye to eye lately?* he asked himself as the plane descended for the long layover in Denver. Jan had eventually relented on the counselling issue, and Ryan was now scheduled to attend two sessions each week with Beth and her therapist, some as a trio and some with Ryan meeting one-on-one with the therapist. Jan had still insisted on her own approach though, and so with some cajoling by Galen, Ryan and Beth had both agreed that as a concession, he go to church on Sundays and attend one spiritual counselling group session run by Jan each Tuesday night.

Even though Ryan wasn't with him, it felt good to get away from home, which was saying something in itself. The escape from Portland was refreshing, but he wasn't looking forward to another interaction with Rockney. *The guy is a viper*, he thought as he walked into the nearest waiting-area lounge and ordered a beer. Despite repeated offers by the waitress, this was the only beer he bought and yet he nearly missed his connecting flight, becoming lost in thought for the duration of the time spent nursing it.

He met with Detective Abbott the next morning in the Cheyenne detention center, and Abbott agreed to accompany him into the interview room. The Cheyenne detective had observed or attended so many exchanges with Rockney that Galen was hoping for some insight or, possibly, helpful intimidation if he needed it. While Abbott went to get coffees and he awaited Rockney's arrival, Galen flipped through the thin files the federal investigation had gathered on Rockney's early life, with most of the information consisting of newspaper clippings about the tragic accident that had claimed the other members of his family. He'd just read two articles and flipped to the next cutting when the picture caught his eye. There, staring up from the page, was the spitting image of Melissa Davidson. The girl in the photograph was Rockney's little sister Emily Rockney. *So that's why he took Melissa,* thought Galen, *he was reclaiming his sister.* He thought for a moment. *But am I the first to make this connection?*

Rockney was being escorted to his seat across from Galen as Abbott came in with the coffee cups. "Gene, can I see you outside for a minute?" he asked, scooping up the folders and leaving Rockney in the interview room with a guard. "Why,

Detective," said Rockney as they were closing the door, "leaving so soon?"

"Gene," said Galen when they were in the hallway, "look at this picture and tell me what you see."

Abbott examined the somewhat grainy newspaper photograph and said, "A young Rockney and his family."

"And the girl?" asked Galen.

Abbott peered closer. "A six-year-old girl with... Ahh, she looks a little like the abducted girl, Melissa Davidson, doesn't she?"

"Right," said Galen. "And Melissa's mother mentioned that Rockney wanted to take Melissa back to Iowa with him. To me, this explains both his motive and the purpose of the path he took heading east. He noticed Melissa and thought she was his dead sister Emily—or at least considered her a good substitute for her. He made her feel like family, and I think he wanted to start a new life with her in Iowa."

"That sounds creepy, but plausible," said Abbott. "Our psychiatrist was stressing the impact that the tragedy of losing his family would have had on his life, and he guessed that Melissa was somehow being used to fill that void, but I don't know that he noticed the physical similarity between the two girls. This should give him more to work with."

They reentered the interview room to a relaxed-looking Gary Rockney.

"Gary, I need you to tell me what happened to Robert Armlin," began Galen immediately. "That's why I'm here, and I'll leave you alone as soon I have what I need."

"You might be here for a long time then, Detective," answered Rockney. "I have absolutely no idea what you're talking about."

"We know all of the events leading up to his disappearance. We just need to know what happened to him in the end."

Rockney lifted both his arms off the table, palms up. "Search me," he said.

"Look, we'll find him sooner or later," said Galen, "so it'll be better for you if you just tell us where you put him."

"Put him?" asked Rockney. "It's a free country and he's a free man—he can go wherever the hell he damn-well likes."

Galen showed a slight sign of frustration, immediately hoping that Rockney didn't catch it. "We know there was a collision between your two cars, and then a physical altercation down by Fanno Creek. We know you fetched Madison's truck when you fled with Melissa, and it was seen by a witness down near the creek. We also know that you washed out the bed of the truck before you'd let Melissa open her eyes, and then you abandoned the truck. We just need to know where you dumped him."

"Like I said, I don't know what you're talking about. I don't know this Armlin."

"Of course, you do," said Galen. "You admitted that you hated the guy the last time we spoke."

"No, I believe I said that I hated his editorials," retorted Rockney.

"But you threatened him in letters and then when you encountered him in person, you saw your chance for revenge.

You attacked him and trussed him up in the bed of the truck," said Galen. "That must have felt very gratifying—the same person who stole Melissa from you turning out to be the man you already despised."

"But I didn't know that was…" began Rockney, immediately realizing that he'd slipped up. Galen could see him withdraw into himself and away from the interview in that instant.

"Ah, so you did attack someone?" asked Galen, not expecting an answer and not receiving one either.

In an effort to draw the man out again, Galen tried a different tack.

"You'll never be able to bring her back—you know that, Rockney."

Rockney looked up with raised eyebrows, but kept silent. "Emily—your little sister. She's gone forever and will never return. You'll have to face up to that sometime."

Rockney couldn't help himself. "You try and lose your family and see if that doesn't stick with you just a little bit," he said bitterly.

"You went with a substitute, though, and I'll bet she didn't even come close to the real Emily, did she? Did you really expect her to?"

Everything was calm on Rockney's exterior except for the eyes which drilled into Galen.

"It doesn't matter," said Galen, trying once more to get a rise out of him, "you'll spend the rest of your days in a cell and never get another chance to try." And that ended up being the conclusion of the interview. Once again Rockney had completely shut down.

Galen and Abbott rose to leave and were heading for the door when Rockney suddenly spat, "And you can spend the rest of your life searching for a substitute for that bastard Armlin, Detective. You'll never find the real article."

Galen turned, but this time it was him who remained silent. "And I hope you die trying, you asshole," Rockney growled.

"Wow," said Abbott when they were again in the hall. "I guess we finally found a way to get to that fucker."

Galen nodded, "Yeah, but it didn't do me a lick of good."

# Chapter 49.

GALEN HAD a beer on each of the legs back home and two in Denver. Not normally one to turn to alcohol other than for relaxation, it was the only thing he could think of to dull his anger at Rockney. He was now sure that Robert Armlin had met his end at Rockney's hands, but was left with no way to prove it and no chance of finding the victim. And, since there were no clues and no body, it was likely that the kidnapper would never end up paying for his far worse crime.

Galen took the next day off as personal leave. Monty was being released from the hospital, so the preparations and joy at having him back home pushed any thoughts of Rockney far underground for the entire day. Monty was ecstatic to be able to sleep in his own room and to be eating Jan's home cooking, but he barely made it through dinner before Galen carried the sleepy boy from the dining room to his bed.

His frustration over the interview with Rockney had abated a few days later, and Galen decided to not give up on the case, dedicating the morning and most of an afternoon to reading or rereading all of Armlin's more significant editorials and recent rough drafts as well as the replies that accompanied them. He was wrapping up when he received an email from Doug down in IT. Doug had discovered an editorial in a draft folder that IT hadn't noticed on the initial sweep of Armlin's computer files, and Galen read it with interest.

*Draft: Courage*

*I hate it when a perfectly good, noble word becomes over-used or subverted so that it loses its true meaning. Like the word 'hero.' I recently saw an ad that exclaimed,* Here's to our heroes in the military. *Now, before you rush to your computer and start firing off a burning reply, please realize that I'm talk-ing about the word, not the people, and I'm using the military only as an example. Some of those in the military might become heroes, but otherwise our brave and committed service mem-bers are paid federal employees who know that their job will entail training, hard work, and travel. In my opinion, it's only extreme circumstances that will make any one of them into a hero. There are many other branches of government work, but few provide the crucible necessary for the true heroics that the armed services can provide.*

*This led me to another question: What is bravery? What makes a hero? And I believe the answer has to do with some-one being willing to risk death or serious consequences for the benefit of others. There's an element of bravery embedded in the definition of heroism, but not all brave people are heroes. It took bravery to march for civil rights in the '50's and '60's. It took heroes to sit in segregated seats and face arrest or beat-ings. It takes bravery to march into battle. It takes heroes to stand in harm's way and protect their fellow soldiers. It takes bravery to recognize your true identity and come out of the* closet. It takes a hero to take a stand against homophobia on the national stage.

You might think from this that I am denigrating bravery. No, not in the slightest, I'm just demarcating the rarified atmosphere that should be reserved for heroes. One of the greatest, most laudable human accomplishments is bravery, and sometimes I wish I had the opportunity to achieve it. It is something easy to imagine and nearly impossible to accomplish. And then there is heroism. What does it take to leap onto tracks in front of an oncoming train to pull aside someone who's fallen there? What does it take to run into gunfire to drag another to safety? What does it take to wiggle out onto ice that you know is too thin, to jump into water that you know is too cold or too swift, to run into a room that you know is too hot, to stand up to an attacker that you know is too strong? I really have no idea what that is or where it comes from. The real human condition is based on survival—survival of the self and survival of the species. When the flight or fight conditions hit, I'm guessing that flight wins out 90% of the time. We're conditioned to self-preservation, and necessarily so.

I have absolutely no idea of when or where that remarkable switch flips, or how I would react if it did. I'm the same as the vast number of you. I can sit and imagine all kinds of scenarios where I would at least try to act in a heroic manner. I can see myself bowing to an appreciative crowd afterwards. But I've run from a wasp. I've crossed the street when approaching a heated argument. I've ignored a beggar. I've avoided chances to make a new friend. I haven't volunteered to help at a local *charity. I skipped the chance to vote in a local election. Am I really going to leap onto the tracks in front of an oncoming train? I don't know what that special something is that those few brave people have, but I hope that I rise to the occasion if I should chance to recognize it. But then again, I'm over 70. Chances aren't good"I hope they are for you. The world could use more heroes.*

Galen looked up from the screen and slowly exhaled. *What was he, some kind of seer?* he wondered. *It looks like you saw your chance and took it, Bob. Thank you for trying.*

# Chapter 50.

THAT FRIDAY afternoon, Galen knocked on the now-familiar Myrtle St. front door, and an unexpected face, though very similar to Emma's, was on the other side when it opened. "Hello, may I help you?" the woman asked.

"Um, yes," said Galen momentarily taken aback, "is Emma Armlin at home?"

"Yes, may I ask who's interested?"

"I'm Galen Young with the Portland Police Bureau, and I wanted to update Emma on some information about her husband. And you are?"

"Maureen Summers, Emma's sister. Emma's mentioned you, Detective. Won't you come in? I'll go and fetch her."

While Maureen was walking towards the kitchen and Galen entered the foyer, the smell of something being fried with garlic as a main ingredient hit his nose. He stood in the vestibule and thought about what he might say to Emma. They'd had a staff meeting that morning and, at Chief Osborne's urging, Tom had decided that it was time to make a public statement about the developments in the Armlin case. And that was always difficult at this inconclusive stage of an investigation. No trace of Armlin had yet been discovered, but they had enough information that they could paint a fairly accurate picture of what had taken place at the time of his disappearance. His involvement in the kidnapping case was apparent—they had the indications of physical contact between Rockney and Armlin, and they had a verbal description of what had occurred on that fateful evening, albeit from a four-year-old girl.

Tom had said that although no substantive progress had been made, the press was still clamoring for information, and they needed to emphasize the Bureau's continuing efforts towards resolution. However, he was adamant that they not release anything that might jeopardize possible future proceedings against Rockney, especially regarding his likely role in the disappearance of Armlin. So, they were going to issue a press release on Monday that would run vaguely along the lines of: *The Portland Police Bureau now has evidence that Robert Armlin, the missing editor for The Oregon Sentinel, may have had a hand in the recovery of the kidnapped girl, Melissa Davidson. It appears that Mr. Armlin became aware of the whereabouts of Melissa and undertook efforts to expose her location and end her captivity. Mr. Armlin's whereabouts are currently unknown, but he is believed to be the cause of Gary Rockney fleeing his hideaway, an event that led to his ultimate capture. Specifics, of course, cannot be revealed at this time, but it is in the public interest to make his contributions known and hopefully this insight will help prompt those with any useful information to contact the Bureau at their earliest convenience.*

"Hi, Emma," said Galen as Emma entered the living room wiping her hands on her apron. "It's good to see you again."

"It's good to see you, too, Galen. Any word?" she studied his face. "At least it doesn't look like it's bad news if there is any."

"We've had some recent developments, but I'm sorry to say that we still have no idea what has become of your husband."

Emma sighed and met Galen's gaze. "But there are developments?"

Galen nodded. "Yeah. How about if we take a seat, and I'll tell you about them?"

Emma was just indicating a seat for Galen when she stopped mid gesture. "How rude of me! I'm sorry, I forgot to make introductions. Maureen, this is Detective Galen Young, and Galen, this is my sister Maureen Summers."

"Yes, Emma—we introduced each other at the door," said Maureen.

"Ah, well good!" said Emma, turning towards Galen. "My sister has come from Maple Grove in New Jersey to spend some time with me and help me through this."

"It's good of you to help out your sister, Maureen. I know that these have been stressful times for her." Maureen nodded in reply, and Galen looked around the immaculate living room, noticing her immediate contribution to her sister's well-being.

Galen relayed the sequence of events as the Bureau knew them, and then told the sisters about Armlin's last editorial draft. The sisters were seated side-by-side on the couch and hugged each other as he concluded. Emma was about to speak and suddenly burst into tears, and Galen walked into the kitchen to give her time to compose herself. It looked to him like shrimp scampi and linguini was in the offing for dinner. He suddenly felt a hand on his shoulder. Expecting Emma, Maureen was there when he turned around.

"Thank you, Detective," she said. "You can't know what a relief it is for Emma to finally know something about her husband's disappearance. She says she's ready to see you again."

Emma was in a familiar pose—shoes off and feet tucked under her in her favorite chair. But Galen noted that all signs of tension and using the chair as a refuge had evaporated.

"Thanks, Galen," said a red-eyed Emma as Galen took his seat across from her. "You can't know the relief of learning more about Bob. And the connection with his last article! I always told him that he was such a good editor because he seemed to intuit the near future—and then people would read about it the next day and it would be current news." She took a final wipe at her nose and then continued. "What I don't understand is why? You're saying that Bob might have tried to rescue that girl? Risked his life? Why?"

"I don't think he knew how perilous his choice was at the time, but—and as I said, this is still off the official record—it looks like he managed to get Melissa into his car and begin to drive away with her before they were discovered—and Rockney took action. Yeah. He risked his life, but I still hold out hope that he either escaped or is being held himself somewhere. Rockney is absolutely silent on the matter so far."

Emma shook her head and looked down at her lap for a long moment. "He should have just sat in his car and called the police," she eventually managed in a low voice.

"Yes, he probably should have," responded Galen as he rose to leave.

# Chapter 51.

THAT WEEKEND, Galen decided to wander through the Portland Saturday Market, and he strolled along the Willamette River walkway to the Burnside Bridge where the event was held. It was becoming more common for him to find an excuse to avoid being at home lately, but this time a reason had been readily supplied—Jan was hosting a tea and planning an event for an upcoming church function and had asked if Galen minded finding something else to do for the afternoon. Ryan and Monty had said that they'd be happy to immerse themselves playing video games in the back bedroom during the gathering. Galen had run Ryan to the Coffee Creek Correctional Facility for his therapy session and taken Monty to his physical therapy appointment in the morning, so he felt like he'd at least accomplished his parental duties for the day.

The crowds were thick and gathered around musicians or magic acts and spread out among what seemed to be acres of vendors selling everything from honey to metal lawn ornaments. His attention was momentarily drawn to a man who was offering rainbow baths by holding up a transparent sheet with a spiral of color between the sun and the bather. Based on the serene expressions on the faces of those who tried it, Galen found himself wondering if this might actually have some effect. He roamed the booths, and then neared a spot along the perimeter where the surrounding green was more apparent when he noticed a small tent that read 'Psychic Readings and Tarot.' There was no line at the moment, so he popped his head in to say hello. Carol Weston was busy with a client, but she raised a finger to indicate that it would be for just a minute more. When the young woman dressed all in black stepped out, blinking into the sun, Galen parted the curtain and took her place inside.

"Hi, Carol," said Galen. "I noticed your tent, and thought I'd say hello."

"Hi Galen, it's good to see you," said Carol, studying him with a smile.

"How's business been?" asked Galen.

"I think you know I don't really do this for the money," replied Carol, "but there has been a steady stream of curious souls through here these last few weeks." Galen had expected this type of answer and nodded back with a grin. Carol looked at him again more intently and then asked, "What is it, Galen? Something's eating at you, and I don't think it has to do with Monty's accident. Is it still that case with the newspaper editor?"

This wasn't a question he'd expected. "There's nothing eating at me, Carol," he responded. "Sure, that case has been dragging on, but so many of them do—I'm used to it. Work's been busy as usual, and I'm thinking more and more about how I can manage retirement with every passing month, but other than that things are fine." "Here," said Carol across the small table from him, "take a seat and let me see your right hand."

She examined his palm and traced some of the major lines on it. "OK now hold out your left arm, palm up." He did as she bid, and she placed three fingers of her right hand along the thumb side of his left wrist, as though taking his pulse. After a minute, she leaned forward and ran both of her hands along Galen's head, shoulders, and torso without actually touching him. Carol sat back when she'd finished. "You're physically healthy, you know, except maybe your kidneys are starting to act up, and your arthritis is getting bad. But psychically you're boring a dark hole somewhere. You're focusing so much one single point that it's become an unhealthy obsession. You need to let go of that, or it will only get worse and start to do you some real harm. Oh, and I'm not talking about your troubles with Jan."

Galen was taken aback. He'd never been on the receiving end of a consultation with her before and didn't know what to think. *How does she know about my arthritis?* he wondered, *I thought she was all about the mental stuff. And how does she know that Jan and I are having problems?* He was about to say something light and make a joke out of the little séance, but instead said, "OK, I have to admit that the Armlin case has been driving me nuts. Maybe that's what you're noticing. Armlin's never been found and, in addition to the insight you gave at the picnic, I now have all kinds of information that says he's met a bad end. It's impossible to get anything out of the person we think was responsible, and no new leads have developed. The thing is, Armlin was an admirable person, and the thought that he may have been murdered and then made to disappear is the height of injustice to me."

"I can see where that would cause you worry and frustration," said Carol, "but you'll need to let go of it for your own good."

"How can I?" asked Galen. "I think the guy was a true hero, and he ends up vanishing with no acknowledgement of what he tried to do?"

"What did he try to do?" asked Carol. "Tom hasn't been able to talk much about it."

"He tried to rescue Melissa Davidson when she was being held by the kidnapper, Gary Rockney," said Galen. "He saw an opportunity and went for it—with a very unsuccessful outcome as it turns out," he continued in a deflated tone, "but at least he tried."

"Galen," said Carol and stared at him until he met her gaze and held it. "Then I'm afraid the reading of the tarot cards I had Tom give you at the office was wrong. The inverted knight of swords obviously didn't mean that someone would act rashly against Mr. Armlin—it meant that he would do something impetuous himself. He acted without thinking it through and that might have been fatal for him. But you know what? You might never be able to do anything about the injustice against him or his failure to right that wrong of the kidnapping. And there's something very important you have to realize before you can move on and not allow this to affect you so deeply."

"What's that?" asked Galen.

"Mr. Armlin is all right," said Carol.

"All right?" asked Galen, raising his voice slightly. "We think the man is dead. Maybe murdered!"

"Yes, he may even be dead, but he's all right." She paused a moment. "You can worry about the details all you like—his murderer, finding evidence, or even locating his body, but you need to stop worrying about him. If I walked out of this tent right now, you'd never know if you'd see me again tomorrow or possibly never. Anything can happen to either one of us when we go our separate ways, so it's impossible to know. But you're on your own path, and I'm on mine. Ultimately, it's only what happens to you, yourself, that's important—we can't live each other's lives. And if Mr. Armlin was killed, he's gone on to other things, other planes, other existences. Or even if he's just blinked out, as some people mistakenly believe, he's where he's supposed to be. He's on his own trip. He's all right."

Galen envisioned nothing of the kind. After death lay heaven or hell, and he ended up turning what Carol had said into a vision of those two—Armlin was probably now in either one of them, most likely the former. Seeing her read his reaction and judging from her resultant facial expression that the conversation was finished, Galen rose and offered his hand. "Thanks, Carol. This is something I'll need to think about." As he said goodbye and emerged from the tent, the thought, *I suspect Carol had a little bit too much fun in the Sixties,* came to him. But as he walked along the river and considered their encounter, Galen was surprised to find himself agreeing with her in a way. *I can keep looking for evidence, and grilling the hell out of Rockney, but I have to let Mr. Armlin go.*

Galen glanced down at his watch and, noticing it was nearing 5:00, turned suddenly on his heel and headed through the Market, across the MAX line, and along the few blocks to the Kells Irish Pub. *There is something I can do for Armlin though,* he thought. In the cool, darkened interior, he approached a familiar figure sitting alone in one of the short booths.

"Hi, Mr. Doherty... John," said Galen taking the empty seat across from him. "Do you mind some company?"

"Not at all, Galen," said Doherty with a smile. "I hope you're starting to make these afternoon visits a regular thing?"

"I just might," replied Galen, raising his eyebrows as the waiter set a Harp down next to him without him needing to ask.

"I know there's no news about Bob, but it's good to have the company," said Doherty.

Galen nodded. "Well, as a matter of fact, there is going to be an update issued to the press on Monday," and he told Doherty what they had learned and what was going to be released to the public. "So, in light of that, I have a favor to ask."

"Oh, what's that?"

"You mentioned that you're an editor or writer for that weekly, The Messenger, isn't that right? Do you write columns like Mr. Armlin did?" He noticed that he was now using the past tense to refer to Armlin.

"Have you read The Messenger, Galen? I can write damned near anything I want, as long as it doesn't land us in jail."

"So, you can write an opinion piece?"

"Well, I try," replied Doherty, "but I'm not nearly so well-spoken or as eloquent as Bob is."

Galen took a sip of beer and found he was enjoying the pub and John Doherty as he imagined Armlin might have. "So, I was wondering if you'd consider an idea I had for an editorial about your friend—he was, after all, a true hero."

# Acknowledgements

I want to thank Lynn Ate and Brianna Ackley for their time and skills in editing, and Jessica Hatch of Hatch Editorial Services for another insightful editorial assessment. The beta readers at Entrada Publishing also provided most welcome comments about the first draft.

I also want to thank Helen Jung, an Opinion Editor with The Oregonian, for providing helpful background information.

## ABOUT THE AUTHOR

David Ackley grew up in Fairbanks, Alaska and raised a family in Juneau. His professional career in Alaska included both fisheries biometrics and management positions with the state and federal governments. David is now retired and living in northern Idaho, where he began a small business in lutherie—building guitars, Irish bouzoukis, and ukuleles (www.dastringedinstruments.com). While his wife was conducting research during a recent stint in India, he devoted time to trying to improve his Tamil and writing fiction to escape the heat of mid-day. Finding himself unable to multi-task easily, the lutherie business has flagged somewhat while he gets some stories onto paper. Please visit the Rain and Breeze Books website, www.rainandbreeze.com, for more information about David and his books.

CPSIA information can be obtained
at www.ICGtesting.com
Printed in the USA
JSHW020452050720
6480JS00001B/7